ALSO BY SUSIE BRIGHT:

Susie Bright's Sexual Reality

Susie Sexpert's Lesbian Sex World

Editor, *Best American Erotica 1993*

Editor, *Herotica, Herotica 2*, **and** *Herotica 3*

The Best American Erotica 1994

Edited by

Susie Bright

A TOUCHSTONE BOOK
PUBLISHED BY SIMON & SCHUSTER
New York   London   Toronto   Sydney   Tokyo   Singapore

TOUCHSTONE
Rockefeller Center
1230 Avenue of the Americas
New York, New York 10020

TOUCHSTONE and colophon are registered trademarks
of Simon & Schuster Inc.

Designed by Hyun Joo Kim
Manufactured in the United States of America

10   9   8   7   6   5   4   3

ISBN 0-671-89942-2

This 1994 volume of *Best American Erotica* is dedicated to the memory of John Preston and John Rowberry.

Contents

Contents

❧❧

Contents

Acknowledgments

All my deepest thanks to my assistant Georgia Kolias, and my editors at Colliers, Mark Chimsky, and Carlo DeVito. This edition of *Best American Erotica* owes special appreciation to Jo-Lynne Worley and Joanie Shoemaker, William Bright, *Fact Sheet Five*, Jon Bailiff, Good Vibrations, Honey Lee Cottrell, Lisa Palac, and Donald Paul.

Introduction: How to Write a Best Erotic Story

Susie Bright

There aren't too many birthdays after sweet sixteen that you get deluged with cards and letters. As I turned thirty-six this year, I was prepared to face the occasion without a lot of childish expectations, but when my mail service called to say I had ten packages waiting, I lost my cool. I'd finally hit the birthday jackpot!

It was a jackpot all right. Every single one of those packages, be they Federal Express, Priority Mail, or Blue Label special, contained the same item—a thick stack of erotic manuscript. Ten wanna-be erotic authors, passionate lovers all. Something about the spring equinox next to my birthdate seemed to bring a particularly heavy blast of pornographic post.

I've been receiving and scrutinizing erotic fiction for twelve years now. Most of the stories and poems I look at I won't be publishing, since my ratio of hits to misses is currently about one in twenty. My criterion for choosing the best erotica is simple enough—it must sweep me away. If it doesn't pass what author Dorothy Allison calls the "wet test" at first read, then it must haunt me later, at all kinds of strange hours.

What makes a great erotic story, one that makes the most tired libido twitch with anticipation? I would like to propose a series of erotica guidelines, written in cream, faithful as sweat. Maybe I can improve the odds on the unsolicited stories I get in the mail and clear the air for some straight talk about what's genuinely sexy and what's not.

The Sexual-Fantasy Bill of Rights

First, a caveat: every human being has the inalienable right to compose his or her own sex story, love poem, or erotic fantasy. Writing one's expression of desire is one of the few times that ordinary people (i.e., nonwriters) spontaneously put pen to paper and go for it. I often get a copy of such an erotic flame burst, perhaps with the line "To Sylvia" scrawled at the top. And even if I think the prose is the tackiest, most unreadable crap I've ever laid eyes on, there's always the part of me that knows that this meant more to Sylvia (and her lover) than any publishing contract could deliver.

People don't routinely write sonnets to their cars, vulnerable confessions about their jobs, or fantasies about ever-lasting friendships. The novice pen comes out for birth, death, and lust, and it's almost immaterial whether anyone else appreciates it. Therefore, even though every piece of erotica that gets rejected may be turned down for craft reasons or commercial reasons, it cannot be rejected as that particular lover's moment of truth.

Having said that, let's get to what sells: what other people like to read, what turns the masses on.

A good sex story is something that arouses the author.

That seems obvious enough in other genres—who ever heard of a chef who wrote a pickle-relish recipe when her true love was pastry?

Yet there is so much nonsense circulated about what is "sexy" that often writers will hide their preferences behind superficial sex hype. The worst offender is fake romance, followed by winkaholic tits and ass.

Don't invent fairy princesses and magnificent sailing ships to cover up your real-life fantasy of being serviced on the D train. It's not impossible to write a successful erotic story that is science fiction or gothic fantasy, but the characters' erotic motives must match up with contemporary hooks that readers can relate to.

In "None of the Above," Bernadette Lynn Bosky writes about a future world where the heroine has group sex with a life-form that is neither male or female. However, her story sinks its teeth in with the timeless hook of sex with a stranger, a stranger you don't understand and are a little afraid of. I wouldn't give a damn about the texture of the alien's interplanetary skin if I didn't have a very human erotic point to connect to.

Faux romance as an erotic error is closely followed by literary lechery—the leering expectation that, by simply repeating a woman's measurements over and over, some orgasmic effect will be achieved. The fact is, most tits-and-ass storytellers (aside from a few true lingerie fetishists) are a bunch of prudes. They love to scream "Fuck!" in a crowded theater, but you'll never find them actually *doing* it in a dark matinee. Good porn writers will always display the naked truth.

Teasing, Timing, and When to Let Out the Clutch

I once got a good short lesson from a veteran stripper on how to undress for an audience: "Look 'em straight in the eyes and start unbuttoning like you've got all day."

The finest erotic authors are the greatest of all prick and cunt teases. They get the readers hanging by their short hairs, then spin them around and make them forget what they came for, only to pull them in like so much taffy. It helps to tell a story and make a context that's bigger than "boy/girl meets girl/boy."

Every reader approaches an erotic story with a pat, and quite realistic, prediction of what will occur. They know the protagonist has to get satisifed, and it's easy enough to skim for the "good parts." But if your characters are compelling, and your plot diabolical, we won't be tempted to cruise for the dirty words. A great erotic story will create uncertainty in readers, no matter how smug they were when they opened the first page.

The Big Blowout

Everyone knows how brief the orgasmic moment is. But writing a good orgasm scene can take hours, weeks, forever. Don't you dare cop out of it—it's the nineties now. The days are gone when you could cut to "I woke up and had no idea where I was." You know damn well where you were, and if your character had a blackout, you'd better get someone else in the story to re-create the action.

Reading about an orgasm is always brief, perhaps ever quicker than the real thing. Writers who insist on drawing it out for paragraphs, with detailed ocean metaphors and inner bursts of karmic sunlight, only bore us to tears. The orgasm scene is the final shoe dropping from the prosy foreplay you've been tango-stepping all along. When that relief comes, it better be exquisite, sweet—and brief. Multiple orgasms are exceptions, of course.

Use the Entire (Fucking) English Language

Everyone complains that English doesn't have the variety of vocabulary to creatively hone the sexual experience, but this complaint is based more on laziness and prudishness than anything else. English, like every language, has wonderful innuendos and descriptions for the most intimate parts of our lives and bodies. Four-letter words are like a spice you want to use choicely. *Fuck* is a word used all over the world by other-language speakers who realize that nothing compares to it in, say, French. Also, the most unliterary expressions, such as "38C," can pack a wallop when used at the right moment.

Look how Marianna Beck, in "C Is for Closet, Crevice, and Colossus" manages to refer to a woman's pussy eight times in succession without ever making us weary, as we always learn a bit more:

"She stepped right over me, naked except for her brassiere, and provided me with a direct shot of her *furry cleft*. Up until then, I'd only heard about *these things*. My mother had once referred to a woman's *Schmuckkästchen—little jewel box*—in relation to some neighbor who was pregnant. So I naturally thought that females possessed *something with a lid which they regularly flipped open to have children*. What I saw was decidedly much different, something considerably more *alive, forbidden, mysterious—something I wanted to touch*. I wanted to know what those *puffy banks of hair* felt like and where that *thin, dark crevice* disappeared to between her legs."

Pornographic language is also often a spike to an erotic volley. Look at Anne Tourney finish off her sex scene in "Full Metal Corset":

" 'This time I'll reward you,' he says. He seizes her knees, spreads them, and leans down to cleave her lips with his tongue. Removing his tongue from her steaming hole, he spears her clit with it. She comes in seconds."

Bring in the Killer Clichés

It's easy to produce plain brown wrappers. Every woman over the age of fourteen can rattle off a bodice ripper scenario, and all *Playboy* readers can tell you what any typical centerfold model's "turn-ons" and "turn-offs" amount to. It's easy to be cheesy about sex, and the population shares a collective cynicism about sexual stereotypes.

Ironically, the object of erotic foreplay is to get your reader in such a tizzy that, when the moment of truth arrives, your heroine can yell, "Take me now, Brad!" or "Hard-uh, deep-uh, fast-uh!" while said reader loves every second of it. Certain expressions, such as those above, or the classic "I love you," can never be replaced, yet they must never be obvious or expected if they are to be successful.

Some writers pump up the clichés by unabashedly using them in a satiric or pop-culture onslaught. In Mark Butler's "Cool and Clean and Crisp," our man doesn't mince clichés in his climactic scene:

"We got into the Land Rover just as the storm hit, and she caught just enough rain to make her hair so sexy wet that we just had to do it one more time, so I strapped her down roughly in the backseat with safety belts as she pouted.

"I mounted her as she squirmed rain-wet slippery silly under the bondage of state law, moaned, 'Oh, what a feeling!' and balanced our beer cans on her breasts. Then, as I drove her perfect willing ass into the soft Corinthian leather . . ."

—well, I don't want to spoil the end for you.

Satire aside, the best way to roar up to a killer cliché is with expert detail and imaginative description. In

"Unsafe Sex," Pat Califia has her two male players talking the kind of trash you could hear in any kind of $2 porn movie, but observe how she leads into it:

"I make one more attempt to get what I really want, and he slaps my butt. Hard. So hard it takes my breath away. I hate that. Of course, it also makes my asshole open up like an umbrella. He's a marvelous fuck. It takes a lot of skill to drive something that big. Too many well-hung men think all they have to do is the old in-out. But this man is teasing me, stroking all points of the compass, doing everything inside me except turn cartwheels. I wish it were enough, I really do. But I know he isn't going to lose his stinking, filthy load in me, really use me, soil and despoil me. And without the fillip of that violation and defilement, I can't let go."

(And here it comes . . .)

" 'You like come so much, I wanna see yours,' he pants. "Get it out and jack it off, boy. Show your master how much you love taking his hard dick.' "

After/Grow

It seems all erotic writers have one place where they choke. Either they know how to talk dirty but can't leisurely play out the seduction, or they have a beauty of a plot but start feeling embarrassed and stiff when the sex gets explicit. In either case, they may not have a plan for "life after climax"—and there certainly is one.

A lot of writers conclude a fabulous sex scene by metaphorically jumping out of the bed. They go off into some bathroom the rest of us can't see and do God knows what.

Once you've written your erotic climax, it's true you can't stay on that precipice. But coming down has its fine moments, and a good erotic writer won't ignore them. Erotic hindsight is always popular—how the characters look back on their bodies, and their desire. If you have a strong story that's been supporting the sex the whole time, you won't end with only a come stain on the sheets. I've rarely seen "and they lived happily ever after" work as a conclusion, but some authors have made a sick *noir* twist on the old chestnuts. Danielle Willis concludes her saga of teenage-idol lust, "Elegy for Andy Gibb," by memorializing her biggest crush:

"Anyway, the day he died I was sitting in a torture chamber in Berkeley crossing and uncrossing my legs in agony because my golden-shower client was almost twenty minutes late. I reached for the newspaper to distract me from my by now almost uncontrollable urge to run to the bathroom, and there on the front page of the entertainment section was the headline 'Andy Gibb Dead of Natural Causes at Age 30,' along with an airbrushed photo of Andy in his heyday. He really was cute."

No Excuses

I once attended a social workers' seminar where a trial specialist asked the audience to break up into pairs for a little exercise. She told us to agree to confidence with our partner of the moment, then to tell them our last erotic experience. (Later, she told us she was just testing our shyness, but I took her instructions dead seriously.)

I happened to be sitting next to a pasty-faced mill-town girl who looked frightened out of her wits. I decided to act cool and go first. "Well, I have a woman lover," I ventured, to see if that made her turn on her heel. She didn't flinch. "Lots of times I get ideas from books we read, and lately we've been reading all this stuff about whether S/M . . . sadomasochism"—I spelled it out, searching her face for how this was going over—"is good for you or not."

She was being so still, I had to interrupt my story. "Do you want to hear this or should I just shut up?"

"No, go ahead," she said, as if I were asking for a second helping.

I took my biggest breath yet. "So, I said to my girlfriend, 'Why don't we try this and find out whether it's totally evil or totally hot.' "

I further explained my somewhat silly but ultimately illuminating night of bondage theater. It was my seatmate's turn now, and to my surprise, she started crying a little.

"I've never had sex," she said. All my conceited, kinky lesbian self-consciousness blew over like a feather. At the risk of appearing like a Vibrating Nun, I had to give her something precious.

"But you just mean you haven't had sex with another person," I said. "I'm sure you've had lots of sexual experiences. Everybody has a story." She didn't lift her head, but she nodded. I touched the top of my head against hers.

I certainly remember the sexual fantasies I spun in my head before a single soul had ever kissed or touched me. They were among the most powerful erotic experiences of my life. There is no such thing as a person who doesn't have a sex story to tell, an erotic autobiography. I feel as if I'm opening up Pandora's *Schmuckkästchen*, her little jewel box, every time I open my mailbox. In the end, I can't feel that bad about the ups and downs of erotic craftsmanship. Speaking truthfully about sex is amazing all in itself—learning the ins and outs of how to put it on paper is just the icing on the cake.

Gorgeous

J. Maynard

When I started high school, it was with a bang. That's right,
first Jeffrey Pavlofsky in the boys' room, which was very
exciting, because after I had my first fuck in a boys'
room stall, he let me watch him comb his hair while I
fumbled on the commode trying to pull my panties off
of my patent leather pumps. But things got better.

I wasn't the kind of girl the boys told their mothers
about, but among themselves, I had goddess status.
They all approached me in awe, stammering and stut-
tering, begging to touch even the hem of my dress when

22

I walked past. No matter how popular they were, I sent them to their knees. I'm not bragging, it's just the truth.

When I showed up at basketball games—which wasn't often because I usually had something better to do—the cheerleaders hated me because all the attention they would normally get went straight to me, Gail Watson, 226 Sycamore Street. If I found an isolated seat in the farthest corner of the gym, every boy would find me; even if his arm was around another girl, I could see him straining one googly eye over the top of some mundane blond bob, or permacurl brunette.

For this, none of the other girls liked me. The pretty preppy ones with their ruffled collars called me trash. The tough girls with leather jackets called me a slut. Even the butchy so-called liberated feminists rolled their eyes when I came around. I mean, gee, if every gorgeous guy in the world offered you his body, what would you do? Say no till you're blue in the face?

Laura Smith, one of the richest, snottiest preppies, stopped me in the hall once, saying, "Can't you even put on lipstick without getting it on your teeth?" and just like that, Jimmy Witherspoon cut in on her and told me all about how he'd been invited to summer school at Yale. He didn't even know Laura was there. I mean, it wasn't my fault Laura was a flat-chested dog. It's not like I said, "Hey, Jimmy, even though I couldn't care less, why don't you come over here and tell me all about Yale summer school." Give me a break. She just set herself up for that one.

I graduated with a B average. Perhaps I would have done better, or perhaps I would have done worse, we'll never know, but Scott Roughman did all my math assignments after school in the parking lot behind the 7-Eleven, and since he was an honor student, he also graded the tests for my class, generally giving me Bs no matter what I did. (One plus one equals love—right Scott?) Sean Fluxbend sat next to me in English and study hall. He was a real writer. He took me out for

malts and whatnot after school. Sometimes we would
just sort of lie on each other on the couch, or in his car
after we did it, till two in the morning. He'd kiss me
and tell me about Kerouac, or Miller, it was all the same
to me, but I generally had a broad enough understanding of things to write something good on my exams.
Once we had to read *The Faerie Queene;* I just couldn't
stomach a poem that long. I mean, please, even the Cliffs
Notes were a drag. So Sean told me the whole story
between kisses. What a sweet boy.

When I was sixteen, Mr. Hexagon, the art teacher
(that's not his real name, but I remember he reminded
me of a two-dimensional figure), had me model for him
while he took pictures of me with my shirt off holding
a bowl of fruit. He lent some of the slides out to one of
his students, and before you knew it, the whole football
team was passing them around. Mr. Hexagon really got
in a lot of trouble for that one.

But it gave me an idea. I called some of the help-
wanted ads in the back of the Sunday supplement that
said things like "Wanted Models, All Ages." The first
few told me that I was too young to work without my
parents' consent, and screw that, I don't want them
meddling with my life, but a lot of people helped me
by giving out numbers of people they knew who spe-
cialized in photographing young women. I made lots of
money by letting them photograph me. They sat me
down on a soft velvet couch with lots of pillows. They'd
give me lots of great food and plenty to drink. They
even gave me all the pot I wanted. Man, if the "cool"
girls could see it! Smoking pot in a circle with a bunch
of sophisticated artsy types! Just the sort of thing they'd
all die for, but it was just thrown on my lap without my
even asking.

When I started college, one of the photographers
told me he was my man. I told him that generally most
men were mine, anyway. He said not like Sean or Scott,
but a man who did manly things, lived a manly life. He

bought me all sorts of exotic clothes and gave me all sorts of wild drugs and did things to my body that I didn't know could be done. It was great. It was wild!

We've been together for months now. He gave me this crazy apartment with shag carpeting, a zebra-skin rug, chandeliers, artwork on the walls, and the walls themselves—one wall is cherrywood, another velvet and gold leaf, another simply white marble and mirrors. He likes variety. He told me it was all mine. It's crazy! It's wild!

We've had tons of parties with lots of different men and women, women like me who are women, beautiful, not preppie but beautiful, not feminists or dykes—beautiful—not cute, not cheerleaders, but goddesses—like me. We've got this whole big scene full of gods and goddesses, and everybody lies down with each other and tells each other how beautiful they all are, and then touches each other and groans with pleasure. My boyfriend says it's better than Rome, so, gosh, I guess I'll never have to go there.

So if there's a moral to this story, you find it. I'm just too gorgeous to have to bother.

C is for Closet, Crevice, and Colossus

Marianna Beck

*Amicule, deliciae, num is sum
qui mentiar tibi?**

Yesterday, I had lunch with a man who confessed that he liked
to lie on the floor beneath a woman while she dressed.

"Yes, of course I know, it's utterly puerile," he said
quickly, "but the excitement it induces in me is nearly
indescribable." I found this statement quite disconcert-
ing. After all, I didn't know him that well, and I was
put off that he'd casually drop a line like that and not

---

*Baby, sweetheart, would I lie to you?

26

expect me to stomp out or hurl some shriveling feminist invective at him. In these cases, you either choke on your food or you keep moving, so I said, "Really? Why's that?"

He actually blushed. I didn't think Republicans blushed. And that brought up another more pertinent and irritating issue. What was I doing out to lunch with a Republican?

I remembered. Now that he was no longer in politics, my acquaintance—he certainly wasn't more than that—had gone into international consulting and hired me for one of his Washington-based projects.

"Sure, there's more to it, but why would you care to know?" he asked.

"I'm big on original sources," I said.

"Well, I suppose, more than anything, it had to do with my favorite German grandmother, Lili. She's the one who slept with her head at the foot of the bed," he began. "She'd started sleeping like that because her husband had nightmares. My grandfather would wake violently and flail his arms and twice had inadvertently broken her nose. Not one to move to another bed, Lili decided to sleep with her feet next to his head."

So maybe this explained how he'd gained a reputation for having an often bizarre, sometimes topsy-turvy management style. Still, it didn't explain how he acquired the predilections of an eight-year-old boy.

"After my grandfather died, Lili moved in with my parents and me, and I ended up sharing my room with her. There were twin beds, and she slept with her head at the foot of the bed just like she always had. With my room crammed full of a lot of her junk, I retreated to the floor of my closet to play."

Oh, here it comes. The closet. I should have known. He probably likes to wear garter belts under his Brooks Brothers suits.

"For hours, I lay beneath a full rack of voluminous housedresses, infused with the smell of rosewater, liniment, and the rancidy odor of her clothes, and played with my toys.

"One afternoon, I was in the closet carefully constructing a battle zone with her shoes when she opened the door and rummaged for a hanger. She stepped right over me, naked except for her brassiere, and provided me with a direct shot of her furry cleft. I froze. Up until then, I'd only heard about these things. My mother had once referred to a woman's *Schmuckkästchen*—little jewel box—in relation to some neighbor who was pregnant. So I naturally thought that females possessed something with a lid which they regularly flipped open to have children.

"What I saw was decidedly much different, something considerably more alive, forbidden, mysterious— something I wanted to touch. I wanted to know what those puffy banks of hair felt like and where that thin, dark crevice disappeared to between her legs. Although I spent every day in that closet for about six months hoping to catch another glimpse, I only saw Lili's furry patch maybe a half dozen times. She never noticed me and I never got caught. Then, we moved to a bigger place and I got my own room again."

He paused for a moment. He'd answered my question, but I admit I wanted to hear more. His answer had seemed honest to me, if not a little touching, and it all seemed rather innocent.

"So that explains it all?" I finally said. "I mean, this is why you like to . . . " I suddenly realized I was asking for more details about a subject I hadn't initially wished to touch with a barge pole. I felt like crawling under the table from embarrassment. But, clearly, he needed little encouragement.

"I don't know that it explains anything other than it provided an impetus for more. Of course it all had to do with those early feelings of seeing something I wasn't supposed to, the fear of getting caught, eyeing the forbidden—all rolled into one thrilling, tidy package. The fact is, I never consciously incorporated any of this into my fantasy life until my first lover, who was a philosophy major, read Nietzsche to me while kneeling over my face and wearing no underwear. I remember gazing at her lips just inches from mine, close enough so that I could see through the tufts of her red-tinged bush and observe the changes in color of her lips—from dark brown at the edges to that lighter, pinkier hue they take on when excitement causes them to part all on their own. It was intoxicating, like the aroma of sycamore trees in full bloom or that tingle you get when you walk into a warm Chinese restaurant and a delicate sweet-and-sour piquancy finds its way to your nose and makes your eyes water."

He stopped to take a breath and I ceased eating.

"I admit there haven't been that many women, including both my former and current wife, who've indulged me in this capacity. I don't exactly understand this because, after all, it seems fairly innocuous. Anyway, I've experienced the whole gamut—from one woman who wanted to turn me in to the police—this after we'd been sleeping together for four months!—to another who threw a drink in my face and called me a pervert.

"But then there was Jan, who took it to a whole other level. Jan was working on her doctorate in Mycenaean anthropology and was studying up on this whole woman-as-earth-goddess shtick long before it got to be a trendy Book of the Month Club topic. While she wasn't exactly what I'd call a lesbian, men to her were basically carbon-based life-forms with a dildo attachment. Her line, I might add.

"One night, stretched out on the floor with a glass of wine at her place, I asked her if she would stand over me while she dressed. She had just gotten out of the shower and was toweling her hair dry, and the look that came over her made my Boy Scout compass point magnetic north."

Nice touch, I thought. At least he's being subtle when it comes to body parts.

" 'Sure, I will,' she said, licking her fingers and sliding them between her legs. 'But you keep your pants on and I'll just pretend you're not here.' She walked over and stood directly over me, and I felt I was looking up at the Colossus of Rhodes. Jan was taller than me, probably six one or two, and her legs seemed to go on forever. Her tiny, pointed breasts seemed to be somewhere in the stratosphere. While her fingers danced a slow rhythm in her pubic hair, she talked to herself. *Probably won't get laid tonight better get myself off now loves to finger me but haven't seen his, nice feelssogood I think I'll wear no underwear tonight see if he notices he probably won't likes to discuss finance a lot.* She talked like that and it made me crazy. Still standing over me, she bent her knees slightly and began to rotate her three middle fingers in a furious circular motion. I swear I had never seen a woman masturbate before. *He likes this I think wonder what he sees if my cunt is bigger to him swollen red can he see inside I'll put a finger in and show him.* Jan slid a finger inside herself and for the first time I noted how red her pudenda was, as she called it when she was being coy. Fra Filippo Lippi opened and bowed in a wet oooooo and then stretched back into a vermilion slit as she spun her fingers at an increasingly furious pace. Every now and then I caught a whiff of her sex, and it was all I could do to keep myself from pulling her down and washing my face in all that warm musky dampness. But I decided to play by her rules for as long as I could stand it. As it was, she fell to her knees over my face at that moment and made this preternatural noise that emanated, I thought, from somewhere deep between her legs.

" 'Okay now, baby banker, lick me dry as if you were a mama cat.' She lowered herself over my face until I was barely able to breathe, let alone get my tongue out of my mouth. I slid around and for the first time felt her pleasure button with my tongue—the size of a big spring pea I might add—from underneath. I stroked and played with it because that's all I could do, given that she had me locked in her favorite Mycenaean goddess submission hold and I was trying to make the best of it. If she wanted me to dry her, whatever I was doing wasn't working because everything was feeling considerably wetter. But it didn't seem to matter. Whatever I did manage to do made her whole pelvis grind into my face so that I could feel her labia in all their slipperiness wash my nose like two little tongues. She pulled away slightly, let me breathe for a bit, and then used my chin to get herself off again. Finally, she stopped, sat back on my chest, and gave me a look that indicated she was extremely pleased with herself. If you can believe it, she actually reached back to feel if I was hard. Apparently, I needed only the slightest touch, because when she pressed me there, I was screamingly erect, and I did what I hadn't done since high school, which was to come inside my pants.

"Hard to believe, isn't it?"

"No!" I said, more vehemently that I'd wanted to, stunned that I'd answered at all.

"Well, that was Jan for you." He stopped talking. What else could he say? For that matter, what else could I say? We weren't exactly going to start discussing profit margins. He sensed my embarrassment and said, "Sorry. I didn't mean to make you an unwitting voyeur, but I guess I have. Let's skip the business stuff and meet up again tomorrow. Same time, same place?"

Without waiting for my answer, he stood up from his chair, paid the waiter, and left. I finally made a motion to leave some ten minutes later, but only after I'd made sure no one saw me flip over the cushion I'd been sitting on.

From
The Same River Twice

Chris Offutt

For six months I worked at a warehouse in the neighborhood,
the first full-time job of my life. I collected clothing orders for a professional shipping clerk with forty years'
experience. His passive numbness frightened me. I was
a gatherer of shirts and slacks; he was a hunter of numbers. The day's highlight was staring at a Polaroid of a
nude woman I'd found on the street. Ancient priests of
South America used fake knives and animal blood to
save the sacrificial virgins for themselves. Up north I
just wanted a goddess to worship.

After work, I saw a tall woman with a huge jaw being harassed by a junkie. I chased the junkie away. The woman smiled and led me to an abandoned subway station with a boarded entrance. A pink dress hung loose on her lanky frame. She pried three planks free and slipped in, motioning down the steps to a bare mattress. She wasn't attractive, but no one else had shown me the least bit of attention. I followed her. A musty breeze from the bowels of the earth fluttered trash along the floor. I felt snug and primal in the dank urban temple. I would become an albino, a blind white harlot in service to Ishtar.

She asked for a match. When I lit her cigarette, she caressed my face and grabbed my crotch, lashing my tongue with hers. I slid my hand down her stomach and between her legs. My fingers hit something hard tucked low against her abdomen. I was accustomed to people carrying guns, and it seemed natural for a woman alone in the city to be armed. The only feasible option was to gain control of the pistol.

I ran my hand up her dress, wrapped my fingers around the barrel, and gave a quick tug. She moaned low and very deep. I pulled again and suddenly realized the gun was made of flesh. My entire body trembled in a fury of incomprehension. I stood, unable to speak. She threw her purse at me and laughed a taunting cackle that echoed in the tunnel. I ran up the stairs, plunged through the opening, and fell on the sidewalk. Two men holding hands stepped off the curb to avoid me.

The following day, I called in sick to the warehouse and stayed in the tub all day. When the water cooled, I refilled it, still hearing that laughter throbbing in my head. I was sure I'd found a circus freak, a hermaphrodite, the only one in the city and perhaps the entire country. At nineteen, it was beyond my understanding that a grown man would impersonate a female. Not all transvestites are gay, I later learned, but mine was. This seemed a crucial difference between the city and the hills—Appalachian men could acceptably fornicate with daughters, sisters, and livestock, but carnal knowledge of a man was a hanging offense.

I ate lunch daily at a diner on Great Jones Street. The joint was a showcase of deformity—goiters swelled throats, and tumors jutted from bodies, stretching gray skin. Hair sprouted in odd places. The owner kept a sawed-off shotgun close at hand. One day a stray woman appeared in a booth. She was short and dark, wearing tight pants, which I studied closely for a telltale bulge. She noticed my observation and I quickly looked away. She moved near.

"Are you a mechanic?" she said. "My car needs work."

"No. I'm an actor. Are you a girl?"

"Everybody I know is bisexual now."

"Not me," I said. "Want to go to the museum on Saturday?"

"Can't."

"Why not?"

"Just can't. Why don't you visit me in Brooklyn on Sunday."

"Where's Brooklyn?"

She laughed and spoke loudly to all. "He wants to know where Brooklyn is!"

The simple purity of Jahi's directions enthralled me: Take the Flatbush train to the end and get out. Walk down the street and go left. Ring the second bell. Finding a place at home involved landmarks such as the creek, the big tree, or the third hollow past the wide place in the road. After the quantum mechanics of lower Manhattan, Brooklyn sounded like simple geometry. I bought a new shirt for the date. That she was black didn't matter—she was female and I was lonely. We were both at the bottom of our republic's fabled melting pot.

Noisy people thronged the streets of Flatbush Avenue. Tattoos covered the men like subway graffiti.

Women wore neon skirts drawn so tight that their thighs brushed audibly at every step. The stores were barred by padlocked gates that reminded me of ramparts under siege.

Jahi's apartment was absolutely bare save for a couch, a table, two chairs, and a bed. We drank wine and passed a joint. After four hours she seduced me because, she later told me, I had not pounced on her all afternoon. She considered me a Southern gentleman. I didn't mention the white-trash truth—every country boy knew city women would breed quicker than a striking snake. Expecting sex as urban custom, I was in no hurry. Plus I didn't know much about it.

When the time came, I pounded into her, spurted, and rolled away. She raised her eyebrows and blinked several times.

"Are you a virgin?" she said.

"How could I be?"

"You don't have to use your whole body. Just your hips."

"I know," I said quickly.

"Look, nobody knows until they learn."

"I've read about it plenty."

"I'm not saying anything against you, Chris. Everybody's different and you may as well learn about me."

She stood on the bed and told me to look at her body very carefully. I'd never seen a woman fully nude before. Jahi had a peculiar frame—strongly muscled dancer's legs, a delightful bottom, and the dark torso of a young girl. Her small breasts sported enormous nipples, ebon pegs an inch long, hard as clay. A few black hairs surrounded them, reminding me of crippled spiders.

She lay beside me and invited me to touch her everywhere, methodic as a surveyor, covering every square inch. Next she explained the complex labyrinth of her plumbing. From its nook she retrieved her clitoris and demonstrated the proper action for maximum pleasure. She counseled me on the rising barometer of orgasm and cued me to a steady drilling until the dam broke. I received a cursory lecture on the soft crest where buttock met leg, the inner thigh, and lastly the anus. I balked, believing this too advanced. With time, she assured me, even that arena would be old hat.

Two hours later I was a sweaty scholar eager to matriculate. Jahi rolled on her back and aimed her heels at the ceiling while I wriggled down the graduation aisle. Propping my weight on knees and elbows allowed her some maneuvering room. The prescribed circular motion reminded me of sharpening a knife on an oily whetstone: apply pressure on the upstroke and ease away, alternating sides for a balanced edge.

To forestall ejaculation, she had suggested I concentrate on baseball. I thought about Cincinnati's Big Red Machine, squirmed my hips correctly, and remembered how the manager always hopped over the sprinkled white baseline to avoid bad luck. The summer I turned twelve, VISTA bused a load of hill boys to Crosley Field for a game. In the parking lot I was astounded to see a black kid, the first I'd ever seen. He was my size and wore clothes identical to mine—jeans and T-shirt. I stared at him so hard that I walked into a streetlight, which didn't exist in the hills either. The VISTA man made me sit beside him the whole game.

Suddenly Jahi was squirming like an epileptic, thrashing her legs and ripping my back. Convinced I'd made a mistake, I slowed the rhythm to a bullpen warm-up. The manager's hand signals blurred to gibberish and she began screaming.

"Fuck me, you white motherfucker!"

Appalled, I pistoned my hips until the dugout began moving across the floor. I went to my fastball right down the old piperino. Hum, baby, hum. I fiddled and diddled, kicked and delivered.

"Give it to me," she grunted.

"I am, I am!"

"Talk dirty."

"What?"

"Talk dirty!"

"Well, hell," I said. "You're a horse's ass."

She clicked into automatic pilot, writhing and moaning, cursing and shrieking. "You like this!" she bellowed. "You like fucking me!"

I loosened my tongue for locker room talk. "Batter up, batter down, who's that monkey on the mound?"

"I'm coming!"

"She's coming around third. Here's the throw. It's in the dirt, safe at home!"

My body twitched, heat surging from my feet and skull to join at the crotch and erupt. The fans shrieked my name. They were leaping from the stands, peeling the artificial turf, ripping bases out of the ground. Pooled sweat like celebration champagne swirled down my side as I rolled over.

"That was great, Jahi!"

"Yeah, you're a natural."

She gave me a postgame pep talk on how to talk dirty in bed. I nodded and thanked her and she sent me out for pizza, her scent covering me like infield dust. I relived the game in my mind, conjuring instant replays of the best parts.

During the next few weeks, Jahi commandeered my urban safari to Coney Island, Times Square, Radio City, and a hundred bars in between. On the Staten Island ferry she climbed over the railing to dangle by her arms. The murky water whirlpooled below, filled with plastic tampon tubes and toxic fish. Jahi grinned at me and kicked the side of the boat.

"Don't jump," she yelled. "Hang on, Chris. Hang on!"

After the crew hauled her up, she began hurling life preservers overboard. "I can't swim," she explained. "I have to save myself."

The angry captain assigned us a guard, whom Jahi

charmed through subtle exposure of her chest. He leaned to the port for a glimpse down her shirt. The boat rocked in the wake of a tug and he stumbled, face red, and banned her from the ferry.

"Starting when?" she said.

"Now."

"Stop the boat!" she yelled. "Take me back." She slapped him across the face. "That nutball grabbed my ass. Help, help!"

Passengers turned away in a slack-eyed city manner, but a couple of burly men advanced. Jahi grabbed them by their belt buckles, one in each tiny hand.

"He's the one," she said, her voice sliding into the plaintive tone of a child. "He's the one who touched me down there."

One of her saviors had two tears tattooed below his right eye. At the base of his hairline were the letters *H.A.N.Y.C.* The taller one had a subway token embedded in his ear hole, the flesh grown around it like a board nailed to a tree.

"Which one?" the tall guy said.

"Don't know," Jahi said. "Can't remember."

"Stomp both," said the other one.

"It was him." The boat guard pointed at me. "He's the freak."

"Rat knows its own hole," the tall one said.

"Yeah," I said. "Smeller's the feller."

The hard guys looked at me and I realized that I'd pulled their focus from the uniform.

"You two are big bullies," Jahi said.

She spread her legs and arched her back, tipping her head to look up at them. Her voice came hard and mean.

"Nervous without your hogs. I'd half-and-half you on the spot if you took a shower. Don't dime me on this fucking tub, boys. Here's the front. The citizen's with me but he's cherry for a mule. The boat heat's a cowboy looking for a notch. You clippers cross the wise and it's a hard down, with no help from your brothers. They took their taste last night in the Alphabet."

The bikers stiffened beneath her onslaught, eyes turning reptile-flat. The tall one eased backward, disappearing among the passengers, his friend following. The boat guard tracked them at a coward's distance. Jahi wiped a sheen of sweat from each temple.

"What was all that?" I asked. "I didn't understand a word you said."

"They did." She brushed her knuckles against my crotch. "You understand this, right?"

I nodded and when the ferry docked across the bay, we crawled into one of the emergency rowboats lashed to the side and frolicked in the bow.

The following Saturday she took me to the nude area of Rockaway Beach, where fat voyeurs trailed ugly women. Men with perfect hair trooped naked in pairs. I remembered my grandmother's opinion of a *Playgirl* magazine my sister showed her one Christmas. "They're just like on the farm," Grandmaw had said. "All those old-fashioned pumps with the handles hanging down."

Jahi chose a few square yards of dirty sand amid condoms and cigarette butts. I've always hated the beach except in winter. The sun's too hot, the sea's too cold, and the presence of humanity spoils any natural beauty still lurking in the sand. Jahi refused to disrobe on the grounds that she was brown enough. We'd never discussed her heritage, and I didn't want to embarrass myself with the stupidity of asking if she tanned. She insisted that I undress. Since I would not lie on my stomach and proffer myself to the steady parade of men, I lay on my back. The sun scorched my testicles within five minutes.

Jahi teased me for days. In the subway she cocked her head, voice loud to draw attention.

"Are your balls still sunburnt, Chris? They must

itch like fire." She addressed the nearest stranger. "Burnt to cinders at the beach. If he's not bragging, he's complaining."

Our public time was a constant duel designed to make me angry, jealous, or embarrassed. As she ran low on ammo against my nonchalance, her improvisations became more outrageous. While waiting for a train, she asked a stranger's opinion of my eyes. Soon she had him leaning close to inspect my face. He agreed that my eyes were slightly crossed, especially the left one. "Yes," she said. "That one has got to go. Do you have a knife? You take it out. You, you, you!"

We rode the subway for hours per day, Jahi's method of rehearsing for her stage career with myriad strangers as her audience. She considered her antics a necessary corrective to my rural background. In the middle of mischief, she'd grin my way, eager for approval. She once stole a ream of paper and opened the bundle on a windy sidewalk. "Oh my God!" she shrieked. "My manuscript!" We watched twelve Samaritans chase blank pages down the avenue. At a topless bar she removed her shirt to bus tables, piling empty glasses on the lap of a drunk who'd been pawing the dancers. A bouncer with shoulders like a picnic table came our way. I stayed in my chair, aware that standing would get my head thumped, trusting Jahi to avert trouble.

"Hey, sugar," the bouncer said to her. "You need a job? We could use your kind of spunk."

"I got a job," she said, pointing to me. "I watch out for him. He's a famous actor."

The bouncer helped Jahi with her coat, then turned to me. "You're a lucky man, my friend."

That evening we lounged in her apartment while twilight pollution streaked orange across the sky. Construction noise had ceased at the nearby condo site where future dwellers would pay extra for the fetid river breeze. Jahi had spent the day trying unsuccessfully to make me jealous on the street. Angry at herself, she told me my acting career was a joke. I spent too much time merely watching, writing in my journal.

I'd never told her about my single audition, crammed into a hot room with sixty guys, each of whom clutched a satchel of résumés. Everyone seemed to know each other, like members of a club. They sparred and parried in dirty verbal fighting until a slow response brought on a death jab. The winner smiled and wished the loser luck.

When my name was called, I stepped through a door and crossed the dark stage to an oval swatch of light. Someone thrust a typed page into my hand. A nasal voice whined from the darkness: "Start at the red arrow."

Twenty seconds later the same voice interrupted to thank me. Confused, I nodded and continued reading.

"I said thank you," the voice said. "Can someone please . . ."

A hand took my arm while another retrieved the script. They led me away like an entry at the county fair, a recalcitrant steer who'd balked before the judging stand. I decided to become a movie actor and skip fooling around with the legitimate theater.

Jahi had surreptitiously removed her underwear from beneath her dress. The thin cloth dangled from her foot. She kicked and her panties arched neatly onto my head.

"Do you write about me?" she said.

"Maybe."

"You should."

"Why?"

"Because I'm alive."

"So am I, Jahi."

"Without me, you weren't. You were young, dumb, and full of come. Now you're just young."

"I'm glad you don't think I'm dumb anymore."

"Oh, you are, Chris. I made you smart enough to know you are, that's all. Write that in your little notebook."

The journal was my combat arena, the final refuge of privacy in a city of 8 million. Each day I saw perhaps two thousand different faces, an enjoyable fact until I realized that my face was one of the two thousand each of them saw, too. My math collapsed from the exponential strain. Jahi wasn't in my journal. Those pages were filled with me. Some of the pages held my full name and place of birth on every line to remind me that I lived.

"Write down everything I say," she said. "Make me live forever."

"Come on, Jahi. I don't even write good letters."

"You don't know it, but you will. You'll reach a point where you have no choice."

"Yeah, and I can be president, too."

"You can do anything you want. You'll reach a point where you have no choice."

"Yeah, and I can be president, too."

"You can do anything you want. You're a white American man."

"Right."

"And I'm a nigger bitch who sleeps with Whitey."

"Goddamn it, Jahi!"

"See," she muttered through a smile. "I knew I could get to you."

I stomped the floor. "I don't care what you pull on the street. Go naked! Start trouble! You're the only friend I've got, remember. There's maybe fifty people who know me at home. Everybody in Brooklyn knows you, and half of Manhattan. I'm the nobody, not you!"

"Not forever." Her voice dulled to a monotone. "I traveled your dreams."

Absolution

John Preston

My little brother knew he was going to have trouble outbutching me when he reached eighteen. That's when he finally realized he was always going to be ten years younger than me. He was always going to be inches short of my six feet two. He'd never have the hair on his chest that I have. He might get my build, but it was going to take a hell of a lot of work to catch up with the years I'd spent in the gym. His prick was always going to be shorter than mine and his balls would never hang as low. And he'd never wear leather the way I could.

But he did try to live up to my example. Little Brother did the only thing that looked like it might work. He joined the Marines.

That made me proud. I never joined the military. I wasn't going to put up with some asshole trying to top me in boot camp. I checked the box rather than put up with that bullshit. But I liked the idea of Little Brother being put through his paces, even if I couldn't be the one who did it. He came back from Parris Island and showed me his new muscles and his close-cropped hair and we went out to have a beer together to celebrate.

Little Brother's Marine career offered us both some insights into the military mind. As I got to know his pals, I learned that most Marines thought they were violent. Really, they never trust their tempers. They are often guys who'd been in trouble in civilian life, high schoolers who were on the track to get a record. The Marines gave them the structure they needed to control themselves. Little Brother was like that. He'd been a hotshot kid. I gave him a lot, but he couldn't get anything more from our family. A bachelor gay brother isn't what a bad-tempered straight kid needed, not all the time, not in all ways. The Marines gave him a place to put his hostility and his rage and find some purpose for it.

Not only did he have a place where he could go and shoot off his testosterone, I had a new scout looking out for my benefit in that cesspool of repressed homosexuality—and masochism. Little Brother never had any misconceptions about my sexuality. When he was old enough to walk, I was bringing men around to the house. He got to first grade thinking it was normal for a big guy like me to have another hairy-chested man in my bed when he'd come in to wake me in the morning. Our parents weren't the most responsive people in the world, so most of his allegiances were with me. That I wanted a man was something he knew; that I wanted one who followed orders and rolled over when I snapped my fingers was easy for him to figure out.

We never had to talk about those things, at least not once he realized I didn't care about his sexuality. If he wanted a girl, that was his business and I didn't give a shit. So when he got out of boot camp and got assigned to a post near my house in Boston, he knew that he had a way to repay me for all the kindnesses of his child-hood—all the Little League games I coached him for, all the advice I'd given him and the money I'd lent him.

He never made an overt offer and I never made a plain request, but little by little he began to bring me some of that hard young Marine flesh. He'd bring home the guys he thought would tumble into bed with me, delivering them the way a happy puppy dog delivers a squirrel to his owner. Just a little payback for all that affection and love.

I had some hot numbers because of Little Brother. I usually got them when he'd bring a pal to the city and they'd stay in my apartment. It didn't take much for the one being introduced to catch on. He had probably been given some clue by Little Brother that there would be magazines and posters and that there were some things I kept in a trunk in my bedroom . . .

But those were only tricks, just little games I played with a couple guys Little Brother knew might like to experiment. The one really important one that I finally got through Little Brother was totally different. He was a whole other story.

It began when Little Brother invited me up to the town where he was stationed for a cookout. I didn't want to go, but he was insistent. My car was in the shop, so he came down to Boston to pick me up. He and a lot of his pals had off-base apartments. They were partial to new pseudocondos that made them feel like they were grown-up. They were all in their mid-twenties then, getting up in rank enough to afford something besides a bunk in a barracks.

I sat around and drank beer with them. The post-adolescent bragging those guys do is pretty boring most of the time, but if you put your mind to it, it can be amusing. They were all boasting about the chicks they'd dicked and the times they'd been drunk. If the conversation was tedious, the talkers were interesting. At my age I've come to really appreciate tight, young flesh, the kind that reminds you of peach skin, no matter what the color. Most of the guys were standing around in shorts, their crotches bulging, their young legs tan and hard with muscles. A few had on jeans. I thought that was a shame. They all wore Marine T-shirts, par for the course. I wasn't going to complain. They showed off the hard chests, the flat pecs with nipples that had the smoothness of nature; a good top hadn't gotten to their tits to get them hard enough to push against the fabric. A couple guys wore tank tops that showed off their biceps even more and gave a good peak at luxuriant armpit hair as well. I shut off their talk and didn't listen at all. I just sat there and drank my beer, letting them put on a fine soft-core porn show for me. In my mind, I could smell their Jockey shorts, damp with sweat, and I could taste the salt on their skin as they sweat in the summer warmth.

Little Brother kept smiling at me, like he knew something was up. I couldn't see it. I didn't have a clue, not until it was time to call it a night and get back to the city.

"Mario's going into Boston tonight. Do you mind just catching a ride with him? It would save me the long drive."

It looked like Little Brother had a plan. "Sure," I said, looking at a shy-appearing jarhead standing beside him. "No problem." Mario looked like he'd be as good a catch as any of them. He was about twenty-five, only five nine. He had the usual buzzed hair and clean-shaven face of a young Marine. He had a butt on him, too. A nice high one, tight against his pants, too bad

they were long-legged denim. He was olive-skinned.
There were slight wisps of black hair over his bare arms,
just enough to really look inviting, not enough to make
him appear nearly as masculine as he'd like. I could taste
garlic and tomato sauce from him. I could imagine a fine
Mediterranean sausage as the main course . . .

Mario led me to his car, one of those overpowered
things that young guys with too much money buy to
balance their fear that they don't have enough sperm.
It was low, a two-door sports model with an engine as
powerful as a fleet of trucks. I climbed in and ignored
Mario as he turned the key and powered up.

Mario kept on trying to pick up conversation as he
drove down I-95 toward the city. All I gave him were
some guttural sounds to let him know I wasn't interested
in mindless talk. If he wanted my attention, he'd have
to work harder for it.

He was shifting into overdrive on a straightaway
when he finally did say something worth hearing. "Your
brother says you're gay."

I wasn't used to one of the jarheads saying something that direct. I just said, yeah, I was. A little bit of
me stood at attention now; I wasn't sure where this
little bastard was going and I wasn't sure I wanted to
hear it.

"I know about that."

This was more familiar ground. Many of the guys
Little Brother had introduced me to had begun with a
disclosure of some playing around in high school. They
usually went from there to admitting a desire to repeat
the performance.

"So?" I said. That was all the commitment he was
going to get from me.

"Well, I never felt good about it, what happened."

"And what was that?"

Mario hadn't looked me in the eye during any of
this. He'd been staring straight ahead. He had one arm
on the top of the steering wheel, the other hand hanging

down the side of his seat, like he'd watched too many James Dean movies. He kept up the pose.

"Some things happened when I was young. In Boston. Where I grew up. Where you live now."

"So tell me." He was going to anyway; I might as well take control of the conversation.

"I grew up in a rough part of town, the South End."

"Not so rough. That's where I live now."

"Yeah, I know. Your brother told me that. But I hung around with a gang then. We were all poor kids, mostly Hispanic, a few Portuguese like me. We never had any money. There was only one easy way to get it."

"You stole."

"Yeah." All of a sudden he didn't want to go on. He concentrated on his driving. "We stole from gay guys," he finally said.

I could feel something moving in my back, something was getting hard and mean. "How'd you do it?"

"My friends . . . we would go to the Fenway, you know the park where they all cruise? We'd go there and get some guy to go into the bushes and we'd roll him."

"Yeah, I bet you did." I flashed on all the guys I'd known who'd been caught like that. They'd foolishly go to the Fenway after the bars; too much booze and too hard a cock would make them take chances they would otherwise have known were stupid. Too often they paid for their foolishness.

"That's why I joined the Corps." Mario kept on going. "Because I could see what was going to happen to me."

"What was that?"

Mario was gripping the steering wheel now. I could see the white of his knuckles. He hadn't made this confession to many people before. Maybe never. I was trapped in the moment; I felt myself being dragged further into something that was going to be real. There was going to be a climax to this story. I was sure of that.

"One night . . . I was with some friends and they

got a guy into the bushes. They got rough. The guy . . . My friends ended up in Walpole. Murder one."

"You got away?"

Mario nodded. There was a tear running down one of his cheeks. "I knew I was on the road to Walpole with them, if I didn't get out of it. The only thing that I could see that was strong enough was the Corps. I signed up . . ."

"As soon as you knew you weren't going to be charged," I accused him.

"I was never seen. No one knew I was there, except my friends. They wouldn't tell."

"And the faggot was dead, so he wasn't going to identify you, was he?" My voice got harsher. I got a picture of Tony, who got his handsome Greek face smashed in at the Fenway one night. And then there was Sal, a barber from out in Scituate who lost one of his balls after a gang of kids had kicked him when he was down, after he'd given them his week's salary. Those scum thought they could bash fags and get away with it. That Mario's pals had been caught was the only real surprise.

"You fucking little son of a bitch." That's all I said. Real soft. Real intense. I really meant it.

Mario sat up quickly, stiffening his own back, and probably his emotions. "I was young. I've made up for it . . ."

Not if you have to tell me now, years later, I thought. I let him drive on. The tear had been wiped away. The emotions seemed to subside. We were quiet for the last half hour of the drive.

Mario stopped in front of my place. He parked the car. He turned off the engine. "Come in. Get a beer," I said. I knew the tone of my voice wasn't welcoming, but I also knew he wanted to follow this one through. There was something we both knew had to happen.

Where there's confession, there has to be absolution.

Mario didn't say anything when I closed the door. He just went over and sat down on my couch, hanging his head and clasping his hands together in front of him. I went and got a beer. Just one, just for me. I stood in the doorway to the living room and took a long draw on it while I looked at him in the faint light coming in from outside; I left the lights in the living room off. Then I started.

"You were the bait, weren't you?"

Mario nodded, just a little bit.

"You were the one they'd put in front of the bushes to get the fags to come to them, weren't you?"

He nodded again.

"A real pretty boy like you must have attracted a lot of guys."

He didn't like that; I could see him flush with anger. But he couldn't look at me, not even then.

"Stand up and show me how you did it." That got his attention. "I'm serious. I want to see how you did it. Stand up. Show me how you got the fags to come to you."

Wordlessly, Mario stood. He spread his legs. He tried to look at me. "I know you did more than that," I went on. My voice had that tone to it that only my most serious bottoms know, the kind of sound that means something mean is going to happen, and probably soon. "You aren't enough to attract anyone like that, like a limp pasta. You had to show them some dick. Let me see how you did it."

Mario moved a hand to his crotch. He kneaded himself, shyly at first, but then more lewdly. There began to be a fire in his eyes; a real flame started to come toward me. "That's right, Mario," I said, my voice lower, even more menacing, "show me how you did it. How you got those fags all hot and bothered."

The pouch of his pants began to expand. I could see a long length of flesh starting to develop down his right leg. As angry as I was, I could still be impressed.

Mario had something to be proud of between his legs, something that would have attracted attention.

As he got harder, he also got cockier. It wasn't just his eyes, it was his posture, his whole way of being. There was heat coming from him now.

"Did you talk to them, Mario? What did you say? How did you get them interested in you?"

"Nothing, man, I said nothing. I didn't have to."

And he was right. His erection was at full attention now and I could just see the guys in the Fenway salivating. I could feel their desire for this young taste of Portugal. They'd walk toward him, quietly, full of hope, just the way I found myself walking toward him now.

I put my hand on his erection, cupping it hard with my palm pressing it up against his belly. "They do this to you, Mario? Did they touch you like this?"

Mario's head moved, but it wasn't the timid nod he'd used before; now he was being seductive, just like some Latin lover in a movie. "Yeah, they'd grab hold of my dick, they'd whisper in my ear what they wanted to do with it."

"What was that, Mario?"

"They wanted to suck my cock." He hissed it out, letting the words flow hotly against my face.

"And you wanted them to do it, didn't you, Mario?"

That broke the spell. He stepped back, tried to push against me. But I had hold of him and I wasn't going to give it up, no way. I squeezed the erection harder, getting a good handful of his balls in my grip at the same time. He let out a sharp cry of pain and then tried to make his move.

That was foolish. I know everything the Marine Corps ever taught him, and a lot more, a lot of it real dirty. The scuffle only lasted a couple seconds, and when it was over, Mario was on the floor, my knee up against his crotch, my elbow pressing down on his windpipe.

"You *loved* it, Mario, didn't you? You loved hearing that they wanted to suck you. You wanted it. Isn't that the real problem? Isn't that what really bothered you?"

He could claim that the tears in his eyes were from his pain, but the real ache was inside him. "How often did they get to swing on your prick, Mario? Did your gang give you grief for that? Did they sense that you really wanted it?"

"I was only a kid," Mario said, his voice soft because of the pressure on his voice box. "I was just a kid."

"You were smart, Mario. You knew how to get it both ways. You could take your gang into the park and you could get your rocks off, and the rest of them wouldn't care. You could say you were only doing it for them, to get the fag into the bushes so they could roll him."

Mario's tears started to flow now. I had him. The nightmares he'd lived with were coming right to the surface, and I had him by the balls. I knew he was going to be mine. I just knew it.

"Stand up, punk." I grabbed him by the shirt and lifted him to his feet. The shirt ripped from the strain, giving me a fine look at his chest, nicely chiseled, just as smooth as I'd hoped, with flat, round circles for tits, nothing more to them than brown flesh.

"I want to see more, Mario. I don't just want to see how you acted when a guy came up to you in the Fenway, I want to see how you hoped he'd act. What did you really want to have happen, Mario?"

I stood back and let him catch his breath. He watched me carefully, diffidently. There was still an element of dare in his expression, but something else was coming to the surface. Mario began to rub his crotch again, provocatively this time. He got hard even more quickly. He cocked his head with a jaunty manner. The torn shirt was hanging from his shoulders in strips, letting me see even more of his torso. I liked the belly the most. It had nice lines to it, going down on either side, and the tightness of the stomach promised there'd be some good abs there, nicely cut, ready to be shown off, given the right position.

"Suck my dick," he said when he'd got his dick at full mast. "Come and suck my fat dick."

I walked over to him and backhanded him across the mouth. He nearly went down, but that Marine training came through. He stood up, blood dripping from the side of his lips. He licked it away with his tongue, making it look like one of the great seductive moves of all time. He let the tip linger at the corner of his mouth.

"You want my cock," he said again, challenging me. "Come and get it."

"No, kid, you got it wrong. I'm the one who's got your number. I don't want to chow down on you. You're the one that's got the taste for my meat. You're the one who's getting down on his knees, just the way you always dreamed of it."

He stopped working his cock then. He stood there, as though he was petrified that someone finally saw the truth. I put my hands on his shoulders and I shoved him onto the floor. When he resisted, I got a foot behind his knee and he didn't have much choice.

His face was right at balls level. I pulled him in. I rubbed his nose against the denim, letting the buttons on my fly scrape him. "Did you ever suck those fags, Mario? Huh? Did you ever get down in the mud of the Fenway and chew on one of their cocks?"

He couldn't answer, but I could feel his face moving back and forth, no. "But you wanted to, didn't you, Mario? Didn't you always want to taste a dick in your mouth?"

His head moved again, but in a different direction. I grabbed the back of his neck and pulled him off my body. I reached down and popped the buttons. I undid my belt. I pulled my jeans open enough to let my half-hard flop out in front of his eyes. My wrinkled foreskin still covered the head, but it was being pulled more tightly as my prick expanded with bloodlust. Mario's eyes looked at it. I saw longing there. I saw lots of things in those eyes of his.

Before he could react, before it got too easy for him, I half-lifted him up and threw him facedown on the couch. I whipped my belt from its loops and wrapped it around my fist, leaving enough of it dangling—buckle out—to do what it needed. With my free hand, I reached in front of a now unresisting Mario and opened his own zipper and then yanked his pants down over his butt.

There was only moonlight and some reflection from the streetlamps coming into the apartment. The shadowy light accentuated the whiteness of his briefs, as though they were fluorescent. The snowy cotton was stretched over that ass of his, the two mounds clearly separated by the deep crevice of his crack. I wanted to linger on the sight, just take it in, just enjoy it, but this wasn't the time.

I took hold of the elastic waistband and pulled hard enough to rip the shorts off him. He shuddered from the feel of the night air on his spread cheeks. I pushed on his neck with my free hand and then I began. The belt sang through the air, slamming hard on his butt, first one side, then the other, then the first one again. He howled with shock and pain and anger, but he couldn't move. His legs were trapped by his pants at his knees; my grip on his neck was too secure for him to escape. I whacked at his butt, taking out my fury at all the punks who victimize and persecute, pounding him with all of my rage . . . and with the righteousness that he needed this, that he wanted it.

I didn't stop until my arm began to hurt. I stood back and caught my breath. He was sobbing into the couch. His back was heaving with his tears. Even in the obscure light, I could see that his ass was covered with welts that were only going to become more obvious with time.

I was ready to make a speech, but I didn't have to. Mario moved, turning around on his knees slowly and painfully. He was still crying. He fell forward and stayed there. I thought at first it was an accident, that perhaps he was really too hurt to even move. But soon I saw that it was just inexperience. He was facedown on the floor, his head against my boots, and there was the unmistakable pressure of a tongue moving against the leather.

He was licking his way up. He began at the toe and then moved along my ankle. When his mouth got to the denim of my jeans, he moved more quickly, ascending the length of my leg until he was at my crotch again.

"I want to suck your cock," he said through his tears. "I want to suck your cock . . ."

I took hold of my hard prick and pointed it at him. I thought he'd be inexperienced and rough this first time, but I forgot to factor in the power of pure lust. He kissed the tip, where the foreskin was being spread tight again by my new hard-on. He just touched his lips to the flap and then used his tongue to move it aside so he could lick at the head of my dick. He licked around that and then down the shaft, nuzzling his nose in my balls.

There was another heaving in his chest, but it wasn't pain and it wasn't tears. It was twenty-five years of repression coming out to the surface. "I'm so sorry," he moaned. "I didn't mean to get them hurt. I just didn't know how to do this . . ."

His mouth worked on my balls, lifting them up with his lips, tonguing the surface. "You're learning real good, boy, real good."

I grabbed hold of my shaft then. I was rock hard by now, and I aimed it at his mouth. I lunged forward. He gagged, thick, viscous liquid pushed up his throat, only making it easier for my hard-on to slide its way down. I started to fuck his mouth, pulling my cock out just enough to let him get hold of his breathing, then shoving it back in, cutting off his air, forcing him to struggle to keep up with me. In and out, back and forth, my dick slid through the slime of his mouth, waiting for just the right time to explode a load of heavy come down his throat.

He tried to rebel at that first taste, but I held tight, pushing myself into him until I could feel the swallowing of my come.

He was exhausted after I was done. Another time, another place, he'd have wanted to jerk off, but Mario was done in. He slumped back on the floor. I thought there might be more tears, but there weren't. He said something, without even looking up at me: "Finally."

Mario didn't need the Marine Corps anymore. He was finished with them after that night. He applied for a discharge and got it. The Marines don't fuck around with you if you convince them you're a fag.

A couple months later, Mario and Little Brother and I went down to Newport, Rhode Island. It's a Navy town and one of the major centers of tattooing in the United States. Little Brother wanted to get a Marine emblem put on his right biceps. I thought that was a good idea. I even paid for it. And the same shop did other work, too. Mario got his own tattoo. My name on the right cheek of his ass.

When the three of us stood together and I paid the bill, having enjoyed watching both of them squirm under the needle, I noticed that Little Brother was eyeing Mario's now sore butt. I imagine he wondered just how the story got told, but he knew better than to ask. He just smiled all the way back to Massachusetts, like a pet that'd finally found the perfect way to please his master.

PG Diary

Linda Hooper

March 15: *Today, Julius Caesar died. Today, I died. I am* dead. My corpse trundles along in a Greyhound bus to hell. In my dead body grows a life, and for that life in me I am buried by the very person who brought me forth from her womb. That evil one, whom I once called "mother," buries me in hell at the end of a Greyhound bus ride. I shall be dead there, until the new life in me is brought forth, ripped from my young body and sold into slavery. Then I shall return to my mother's house. And die again.

I just read over what I wrote. Pretty melodramatic, but it's how I feel. She thinks she can get rid of me this little while and then we can be together as a family again, but she's wrong. I don't want this baby, I'm glad it is going away after it's born. But I hate it that this is her will, not mine. She has wanted to bury me from the day I was born, now she will get her chance. I hate her, I hate her, I hate my life.

Why do they call it "family way"?

Six months, six months, six months, six months, six months, six months, six months, six months.

March 17: I'm here now. It's an old convent, only there aren't many nuns because they all died and no new girls came to take their places, and I wonder why because it's really kinda beautiful here in a real quiet way. There's a yard or a garden out there for us to walk in, and I hope I can read out there, but this room was meant for one nun to live in by herself, and that's sorta creepy to think that there were nuns after nuns living in here and praying only and maybe reading just their missalette or *Lives of the Saints,* and we're living here now just the opposite of what they were, being girls in trouble.

It's a pretty small room, but they crammed two beds in it. There's a statue of the Blessed Mother in a recess on the wall, and the really heavy wood door has a cross and a rose carved into it. Some of the other girls have their own room, but I have to share. She says she's here because her boyfriend is a soldier who died in a helicopter accident before they could get married. How sad. She's read a lot of the same books I have. I think I will like her. I finished *The Scarlet Letter* today.

April 15: I can't write in this journal much. I thought it would be a lot different than it's being. The classes are boring, but I'm with Ellen all the time. We are like Tom and Huck. She's told me four different stories of how she got p.g.—all different. I told her about Jeff and what I thought of the whole thing. We're both showing. I think she's a little farther along than me. Three girls left last week. Will I get that big? It's horrifying. Ellen is so funny. Last night she told me the father of her baby is a Martian. She said he had two things. Isn't that rich?

April 30: I have to write this down, but what if someone found this? No one can know, but I must record my thoughts and feelings on this subject. We were looking at our stomachs and seeing how we were showing, and Ellen said, "I wonder if my boobs are getting bigger," and before I knew it she whipped up her nightgown up to her shoulders. She wasn't wearing her bra, just panties, and I looked. I couldn't help it, I was looking at her and she didn't give me warning. I was looking, so I looked at her and I saw her breasts and I don't know if they are bigger now or not, but when my eyes perceived their open nakedness, I felt a bolt of electricity like a shock from my down there to my heart. It was so unlike seeing bosoms in the Sears catalogs or in art, which I can look at forever. It was so real, and I never knew what maybe boys feel, but now maybe I do.

May 2: I can't help it. I just think about seeing her breasts that one time, and we're still as normal as ever doing our cooking class and English assignments, but every moment I'm replaying that memory in my mind like a skipped record. Even when I'm going to sleep, where I used to think about Queequeg or Anne of Green Gables, I think about Ellen. Now, just Ellen.

May 3: I did something. I did the same thing, to watch her reaction. I wondered what a normal reaction would look like. I lifted up my nightgown to see if my breasts were getting bigger, and she stared and stared.

"Let me feel them," she said. "What?" "Let me feel them, then later I can tell you if they're bigger or not. My fingers will remember." And she walked over and stood in front of the mirror and held my breasts in her hands and felt them all over, but it wasn't like being felt up by Jeff. She looked off at the ceiling like she was memorizing a poem and just felt and felt. She even ran her fingers back and forth over my nipples, and then I felt that shock again. Then I said, "I'll feel yours, too." So she lifted her nightgown and I picked up her breasts and felt them and felt them, and she breathed deep and I thought she wasn't liking it and I started to let go, but she said no, get a good memory of them.

Maybe we can do this every night and really have a good idea of how they're growing.

May 5: We felt each other's breasts again last night in front of the mirror. I had to stop and get right into bed because I just had to. I couldn't look at her, any part of her body or soul. But then we started to talk about how Jane Eyre is really Rochester, too, that Brontë wanted to be like a man, but couldn't, so that's why Rochester had a wife, hidden. I don't know, but that did put thoughts in my head. I'm Rochester and Ellen is Jane, and we live in Thornfield together and I'm gruff at first, and then she sweetly wins me over and I kiss her. I kiss her. What an idea. I want to kiss Ellen, I think.

May 7: So now I have a word for it. Well, something is happening to me, and her, too, I think. Last night we didn't do the breast inspection, but I sat on her bed and we talked after lights out, then I crawled in with her so we could keep talking and we felt each other's stomach. They are poking out a lot now and feel so hard, so full. My hands were under her nightgown and patting her belly, and then she said, "Want to see if my boobs are bigger today?" So I just moved my hands up to her breasts. I just kept touching them and her nipples changed shape. First the dark spot around the nipple was flat, and then it got crinkly. Then she touched my boobs and nipples. I liked touching her at the same time she was touching me, me feeling what she was feeling. I don't know if my dark spot wrinkled up. I could feel her to my bones. Our faces were very close and then we were breathing each other's breath, in and out.

I know that when boys feel up girls' breasts it's a sex thing for them—their penises get hard and then they want to have intercourse. But what does the girl feel? Does she feel what I feel when Ellen is feeling my breasts? I didn't feel anything with Jeff, but I know he felt the sex thing enough for his penis to get hard and want to have intercourse with me.

But what am I feeling? I don't want to have intercourse with her, even if I could. I wanted to kiss her. Our mouths were so close and we were breathing each other's air anyway. I put my mouth open close to hers and she moved her mouth close, and then we closed our mouths in a sort of kiss. Her hands stopped moving but stayed on my breasts. "Janet," she said, "once my mother told me that touching anyone's body that's not your husband's is wrong, and she meant with girls, too." "How did you know that?" She didn't answer and pulled her hands away. She inhaled like a gasp and turned away from me. I thought she was crying, but I wasn't sure. I didn't want to stop touching her. I hugged her shoulders. "Ellen, Ellen, what's wrong?" She asked me something, but I couldn't understand it. "What?" I whispered. "I said," she said, turning on her back and I scooted away, "do you think we're bad to do that?" "No, I was just feeling if your tits were bigger." "Oh, really? Is that all? I thought we promised not to ever lie to each other, and I can't lie to you even if you lie to me, and I was not just feeling your boobs to see if they are bigger, I was feeling them because I wanted to and I don't care what you think but I don't think it's wrong." Then she turned away and started bawling for sure this time and curled herself up. "Ellen, I wasn't being . . . I wasn't just touching your breasts to see if they're bigger. I was touching them because I wanted to and I don't think it's wrong. I don't see how anyone could, what could be wrong with two girls doing this?"

She got a look on her face I'd never seen before. Hateful sort of. "You don't know a lot for reading all those books. Haven't you ever heard of lezbows?" I shook my head. "Lezzies?" No, I couldn't speak, but my mouth said it. "They called me a lezbow in fifth grade and I bet they were right!" "What is it?" "A girl who likes girls." "But what's wrong about that?" "A girl who wants to marry girls, stupid! Like have sex with them, be the man!" "But girls can't be men, they don't have things, you know, and they don't have that sort of, you know, drive."

Her face lost that angry look. "You really haven't heard of it, have you? Not in any of those books, not at school?" "No. Is what we were doing . . . lezbow?" "Yes." "But I don't want to be the man. I want to have bosoms that you touch like you do; how can I be lez-bow?" "I don't know, I'm not the encyclopedia on the subject, you know." We looked at each other and she smiled. "But I've done this with other girls." "You have?" She looked suddenly like she wished she hadn't told me. "No, it's okay," I said, moving back closer to her, "I want to know. I think you're lucky. I never thought about it before. Tell me everything you know." "I'd rather show you."

She put her hands back inside my nightgown and touched my breasts. But this time she also pressed her belly against my belly and pushed a leg between my legs. I let her. Then she kissed me for real and it was the best kiss ever. It was 100% better than any of Jeff's kisses, and not because she doesn't have braces, I wouldn't hold that totally against a person. No, it was way better because her mouth was so smooth and soft. Then she put her tongue in my mouth, not like Jeff would, but she slid it in real slow so I could get used to it and moved it around in my mouth. Our lips were tight together and our tongues moved around inside the caves our mouths made, and I thought this must be Frenching the way it was meant to be. We kissed and kissed and I think we fell asleep still kissing. I woke up this morning in her bed, but she was already up, and we had to get to morning prayers.

May 11: I haven't been able to write much. I'll put in the other news then write about the thing I can't stop thinking about no matter what is going on.

I got a letter from my mom on Saturday and she's acting like I'm at camp or something, just gone for a while having fun, and she puts in news about Tami Turner and her mother, like she doesn't know that Tami is loose and is going to get herself p.g., too.

Patty Barnes must have had her baby by now. She was really afraid. She told us that she heard that they weren't going to let her have it, but her doctor said she was too little to have her baby and he was going to put her to sleep and cut it out of her womb like Julius Caesar, except she wouldn't die. Patty wants to keep her baby but her mother won't let her. I don't want my baby and my mother doesn't want me. It must be passed on down the generations.

School here is a joke. I wish they wouldn't force so many other activities on us though. I hate to sew and Ellen and I have figured out that crochet can just go and go and go and you don't have to do any thinking, it just grows and grows, and if anyone asks you what you are making, you say, "Baby blanket." Oh, Ellen. Yes, it's Ellen I can't, I won't stop thinking of right now; she's sitting across from me reading *Great Expectations* for class. I can see her mouth, her lips. I can see her hands holding the book and I can see her fingers. And that's where my always constant thoughts are. Her fingers. Hands, lips, mouth. Could I truly write it down?

May 12: I couldn't. I couldn't write it. But now I must. This is not sex what we do, but I believe we do together similar things as men and women, but the feeling is not the feeling I've been told. It is not romantic like Romance: I don't want to be her wife, I don't want her to protect me. We are the very best friends. I would die if she weren't here. But plus, we are every night, every night we go to each other as soon as lights out and we kiss and touch each other, and I mean *everywhere*. Everywhere I have kissed her. I can't believe that I have. I know it must be a thing that maybe prostitutes do, but I didn't know what it was, so they say, not until you've tried *everything* do you know the possibilities. And are we the only girls to do this? Ellen said that she had never before. She swore she has only put her hands down there on one other girl, her baby-sitter (who was only three years older than her), but she didn't look and she didn't do what we do.

I didn't want to wash my hands this morning. Yes, it's a strong smell, but I like it. I guess I should write it all down like a story, but I can't. How could words ever say what it is we do together? What she does to me. How could I describe the rapture? How could I describe the feel of her body? The two of our bodies together— other people would point and stare at us, at our age, having the big bellies we do, and hate us. But I like how we look together. Our legs wrap around each other and I look down the neck of my nightgown, and we have our panties off, and our stomachs poke out and touch, and beyond that, our hair down there. And we can touch these hairs together, so black.

I can't write anymore.

May 13: Okay, I have played that memory of the first time over and over in my mind and now I can finally write it. On the day after we kissed, she had to go to visit the doctor and I didn't see her until dinner. We sat together but she wouldn't look at me or talk. I had been so excited all day thinking about her and I thought the day would never stop. And then she cut me like I wasn't alive. So I cut her back and didn't stand with her at evening prayers. And I just got in my bed and she got in hers, but we didn't sleep. I stared at her across the room. I wanted us to be friends again and I didn't know why we weren't. Was she thinking that she was a lezbow again? Finally I said, "Are you asleep?" "No." "Why did you cut me today? Don't you want to be friends anymore?" "How can you be friends with me? I'm a lezzie." "Maybe I'm a lezzie, too." "You wouldn't want to be one." "Well, maybe I only like the kissing part, and not the being a man part. I'm a half-breed." Then we laughed and I went over to her bed and we tickled each other saying, "You lezzie half-breed." "You lezbow." Her hair fell all around us and my hair got in our mouths as we kissed again and couldn't stop. Every time I took my mouth away to say something or look at her, I just had to keep kissing her. It was like a magnetic force pulling our lips together putting our tongues in each other's mouth. I can't believe that: in each other's mouth. But that's not even the good part. The best part. We kissed a lot then. She said, "I feel something queer between my legs, like my period started or something." "Oh, no, you're not losing the baby are you?" "Then I could get out of this dump." "You couldn't leave me here alone, I'd kill myself." "Don't worry, I won't leave you. I'm going to check." And she pulled the covers down and looked between her legs. No stain on the sheet, but it was too dark to tell for sure. Then she put her hand between and lifted them to her nose. "Doesn't smell like blood. What do you think?" She put her hand under my nose. "No, not blood." She put them in her mouth. "Doesn't taste like blood." She put them to my mouth. I opened my lips and tasted her fingers. "No, it doesn't taste like blood. It tastes salty, but not bad or sick or anything." Then I said, "Ellen, I feel sorta wet down there, too." "Why don't you check?" So I put my fingers between my legs. My down there was opened, not stuck together. My fingers went in and touched that place and I jumped. "Did you hurt something?" "No, I touched that place." "Your clit." "My what?" "That bump that feels good. That's your clit." "Really. Does everyone have one?" "Girls do." "You have one?" "Of course." "I thought it was just a thing I had." "Maybe yours is different from mine." "Why don't you check." Then she put her hand slowly down my hair and then put her fingers between the lips. I cannot describe how this felt. It was the smoothest, luscious, softest . . . I breathed in and she almost took her hand away, but I said, "Keep it, keep it there." "I have to feel around to see if it's the same," she said. "Go ahead," I said. So she moved her finger up and down the crack, and she rubbed one side of my "clit" and then the other. It felt so so so so so so so so so so good. I can't say. I grabbed her shoulders. "Don't stop," I said with all my might. "It feels really really good. I don't care if it's different from yours." She kept doing it and then after a while it stopped feeling as good so we both stopped. She stopped her fingers and I stopped gasping so much. Then I said that I would do it to her, and then I put one finger between the lips down there and I held her with my bottom arm, and she put one leg over one of mine, and we kissed as I rubbed my finger on her clit. It felt different from mine, longer I think. She moved her hips in a way and I rubbed back like she moved her hips. Then she put her fingers back on my clit and we did it together in rhythm, till the bed started squeaking and we had to slow down. We took our hands away from each other, then she grabbed me and we hugged so tight and she wrapped her legs around me I thought our bellies would burst. I thought she would pull herself right through me.

But this still isn't the good part. The best part. We started kissing again and I could smell our smell on our hands, and our mouths were so wide open I had a very horrible thought—or I thought it was horrible at the time but I had to say it out loud. I couldn't keep anything from her, it would feel like lying. I said, "I can smell that smell all over our hands." "Yeah, me, too." "I want to kiss you down there." "What?" "I do, I know you think it's sick, but I want to French-kiss you down there, if you will let me." "Don't you think it's yucky?" "No, I put my hand down there, didn't I? Besides, if you like it, then I would like it, too." "Okay." So I slowly, slowly kissed my way down her chest straight toward her crotch. I was so scared, but in a good way. She lay very still. I was kissing her pregnant stomach, up and down the hill, and then I was at where her hair started and I kissed down further and further and she flinched. "Should I stop?" "Not unless you want to." "I don't want to." "Okay." Then I kissed her hair, it was sort of like kissing her head, but the hair was curlier, but softer. I lifted her hair away with my hand and kissed her innermost private part. And I kissed her there. I don't mean just a kiss, I mean I opened my mouth and I put my tongue in and I kissed her like I had been kissing her mouth. I put my tongue all around her. I put it all around her clit, I put it right between and even as far as I could go inside her. I put it everywhere I could and I liked it. She really liked it, too, I could tell, and she told me later it was like flying and swimming at the same time. She rocked herself like she had been rocking against my fingers before and I moved my tongue back in rhythm with her. She started gasping. I wish we didn't have to be so quiet, because she had to choke back some sounds I think. I did this for a very long time, and then she asked me to stop and to kiss her, so I did. And the wetness of her was on my face, and then it was on hers and it smeared all over, and we fell asleep soon after.

June 1: I am a reluctant vessel for a life that is my death. I am a new wineskin with old wine, wine desired by no one, wine unfit for a marriage feast, wine like water, unsanctified by God or Christ. Yet I am a Virgin Mother, but un-blessed. I am alone crying in the wilderness, yet here I find my cousin Elizabeth, who carries her St. John the un-Baptized.

We talked about our babies last night. I don't want to keep mine. I don't want to be a mother of some kid that looks like Jeff. Ellen won't talk, she just says she wants this all to be over as soon as possible. She doesn't talk about her boyfriend anymore. But what will happen when the babies come? How are we going to stay together?

She won't talk about her baby. I'm afraid if she doesn't talk about her baby, she will be too sad and mad. Why doesn't she just say she wants her baby to be with some rich family who can't have kids of their own? I want my baby to go to a rich family, who will dress her in white dresses and teach her high-cultured things and put her in a private girls' school where she can meet only other little girls who like to read all the best of books in all the best libraries. They will drive her to school and back every holiday in long black limousines and drink English breakfast tea served by servants in black coats and made by cooks in white dresses.

June 14: I have known what it is to climax. I have had the supreme feeling of all feelings. Now I know and I must write it all down. We went to bed together as we have been, we had been waiting all day for this. Our hands were under our nightgowns and all over each other as we opened our mouths to the kisses we had been having in our minds the entire day. They now became real. I really like to touch her, especially her belly now. I like it that her hands are all over my belly, all over my skin, touching me everywhere. EVERYWHERE, I mean it. We took our nightgowns off, there was no use in thinking we were going to want them on, in the way, really. Our breasts touched and our bellies touched and our legs touched and our feet even rubbed each other to a good feeling. We kissed and kissed until I felt I was part of her mouth, part of her body, and she was all inside of me. We felt each other's belly and then her baby kicked and I felt it with my very hand. What dear little things we have inside us. I wish she would tell me how she really feels. Why can't she love her baby's new life like I do mine? Does she want to mother it? I think since her mother had her so young and all, by herself she thinks she can, too. That's crazy. Why do what your mother did?

Anyway, we felt her baby kick and we looked at each other with open eyes. "Did you feel that?" I said. "You felt it, too?" "Did your baby kick?" "Yeah, I guess so." "Has it done that before?" "No, do you think something's wrong?" "No, maybe she's a lezbow, too?" And then we laughed and kept saying, "Four lezbows in the bed," just to crack each other up whenever we could remember to do it. So then what? So I guess we were kissing and putting our hands everywhere. We had our hands down between each other's legs and we rocked like that, then she put some fingers inside me and I just had to stop touching her because she was pushing her fingers in and out sort of like when Jeff did intercourse. "Does it feel like a boy?" "No, not really." So she kept doing it; she got down there closer under the covers and really did it steady. Then I felt the most wonderful thing; she put her mouth on my clit and she didn't stop what her hand was doing, the in-and-out, in-and-out. And first my feet started tingling and then there was like a burn on my skin, not a painful burn, but like my skin crawling, but not in a bad way, and then it felt like what she was doing was sending me up and up until I reached the top and I almost made a noise in my mouth, but I couldn't, so I pulled the pillow over my mouth and then the most wonderful unstoppable fire ran through my body from her mouth to the top of my head, and it bounced back and forth like a wave over and over and got slower and slower. She kept pushing in and out, but I said, "Wait," and my voice choked. She said, "Are you okay?" "Yeah, I think so." "Did you climax?" she said. "Yeah, I guess so," but I could barely speak. I wanted to enjoy the feelings of it so I tugged on her shoulders and she kissed me over and over. I kissed her hands, I kissed her hands and she kissed me and my face and I could smell my smell all over everywhere. I don't ever want to stop doing this with her. What will happen when the babies come? I'm not going back home. I must be with her forever.

Four lezbows in the bed.

June 18: Ellen said she started touching herself down there when she was just a little girl. There is not a time when she can't remember doing it to herself. I remember that I started rubbing my clit (though I didn't know the word then) every night before I went to sleep when I was in the seventh grade. She said that she would roll up a sock and press her legs together and rub the top of herself until it happened. When she puts her mouth on me down there, it's only a matter of time before I climax. But when I do it to her, she doesn't climax. She says something is missing, but she can't or won't say what. Maybe I should ask her to try the sock and leg pressing treatment. It seems pretty unfair that I get to climax and she doesn't. I wonder why that is?

August 17: The long, hot, endless summer. Everything in the garden is growing around us. We swell like first the plums, then the peaches, then the melons. Each in its turn cultivated, harvested, sold. Our time will come. To what market will my fruit be sent? And what will happen to me, the fertile field? Who is the farmer who owns me?

This is my first entry in two months. Everything is fine so why write? Ellen and I sleep wrapped up in each other every night. We read, we talk, we're in school.

We get monthly checkups. The babies grow and we grow closer. This is what love is meant to be. When I say "I love you" to her, now I know what I'm talking about. Now I understand the ancients, the romantics, the poets. This is love, and I will never know another. Her face. I can see her face in my mind's eye right now. But not the face that anyone has ever seen; in the dim light of our little cell, her face in ecstasy. It is her face in the highest pleasure a woman can know, and her face is like that because of where my hands are, where my mouth is.

I wonder if doing it is like this for men and women? It must be similar for me, because the poems all seem to describe what I feel. But I have never read a poem by a woman that describes a feeling like this with a man. Maybe I missed something. But what if this with women is one way and doing it with men is another? Now that I've known both, I'd have to say I prefer women. Is this what it is like for men? What they feel when they have intercourse with women? No, it can't be. Because I'm feeling so much like she is part of me, because I know how she touches me, I know how it feels to be touched in certain places, so I know how she feels. And we're not like males at all. We're not grabbing and pushing and we don't trick each other into things. I would just die if I did something to her that she didn't want me to do. What is sex? Is this sex? It feels like how men describe it, but it's not like I've known it, and what else could it be? I have to find some lady poets.

August 30: I went in today and talked with Miss Forbes the social worker about the adoption. I said that I was pretty sure I wanted the baby to go to some nice family and that I didn't want to change my mind. That's how I feel now, but I've gotten kind of used to having it down there. I thought I was going to die when I got here, but now I feel more alive than ever before. I would never have known Ellen, and never known the exquisite pleasure of her and her to me.

But she won't tell me what she's going to do. I wish I knew what to say that would make her know it was okay to tell me. I wish she could feel as sure as me. But now, I have to start worrying about the labor. They tell us things in classes, and it just makes me nervous. I hope they just put me to sleep.

September 15: He said it should come soon. He put his hands in me again and (it is so so so unlike what Ellen does. Just the opposite, really) he said that I was softening up nice, whatever that means. I really like having it inside me now. I can't imagine not being this way, and not living here with Ellen. I don't know how it's going to get out of me. I'm so small down there and my belly is so big. I hope they just put me to sleep.

September 16: Last night we started to kiss but it seemed like Ellen had something on her mind. I'm not surprised it was the babies. It's hard to be anything but pregnant right now. We've gotten pretty used to it, because it's hard to think that we were ever anything but. But last night she was thinking about where her baby was going to go. I said, "Look at how big we are now. I think we're changing shape." "Yeah, they told us we'd drop right before the babies come." "I know, they said that, but I didn't know what that meant." "How come you think you need to know everything before it happens?" "Why are you being cross with me?" "I'm not being cross, I was just asking a question." I didn't feel like saying anything after that. I was starting to get mad, and I didn't want to, I wanted to kiss some more, but there was no way I was going to when she was acting like that. Finally I said, "After the babies come, we'll be able to touch our bellies and our legs and our breasts together just like last spring. I can't wait until it's all over." "Maybe you can't wait, but what will happen to us after the babies come? I can't figure out how we can be together." "Ellen, have you decided?" "Oh, stop it. You sound like a worker." "I don't want to sound like a worker, I was just asking because I thought maybe it was on your mind." "Of course it's been on my mind and my back and my bladder. It's pretty hard to ignore." It was good to be laughing about something. I hate it when she's cross. So I asked her, "Do you want to be a mother now?" "No." She wasn't laughing anymore. "I never wanted to be a mother." "Do you want some nice lady to mother your baby like what's going to happen to my baby?" "No." I was afraid to ask this, but I did anyway because the babies could come any minute and I couldn't wait any longer: "Why not?" "Because I want someone to love me." "Ellen, I love you." "But you can't like a baby can. I want someone who will love me forever no matter what." "I can." "You can't promise that. You're too young. You can't know that. Don't you know about life? Haven't you read enough books to know that you just can't know? But a baby will love its mother no matter what." I realized that she was right. I guess I couldn't know. But I could promise anyway. And so I did, but she didn't say anything.

After a while, I asked, "Ellen, don't you think your mother wanted a baby for the same reason you do?" "My mother didn't want me, I just came by accident. My parents had to get married." "But don't you think it might be possible?" "I guess that might have been part of it, once she was pregnant." "Do you love her now?" "Not like she wants me to. She doesn't understand how I love her. She thinks I'll always do what I want, and that if I loved her, I would do what she wants." "See, why do you think your baby is so different?" The question stopped us both. It was so horrible. Why have children at all? We didn't know. Ellen started crying, but real quiet. "I want someone to love me. Someone I love," she whispered. "I will always love you," I whispered back. "Even if we're separated, even

if we aren't friends?" "I will always, always love you."
"Even if I keep my baby?" "Yes." "Even if we can't be
together?" "Yes, wherever you are, I will always be lov-
ing you, always, always."

"I need to sleep now," she said, and she turned
away on her side. I lay on my side behind her for a long
time, as well as I could, my belly heavy between us. We
didn't sleep or talk. I woke in the night to go to the
bathroom and then went to my own bed.

September 17: It's happening. I can't write much
because Ellen went to tell Sister Mary Thomas that it's
happening, and then I'll be doing it, having a baby. I
had to put down that Ellen told me this morning what
she is going to do. She said she is going to give her baby
away, and then I felt this strong cramp and I knew it
was a labor pain. She looked so sure when she told me,
because she said, "Remember what you said last night"
"Yes." "That's why I can do this. Don't ever forget." "I
won't."

September 21: I haven't been able to write. They
put me under and the baby came and they took her
away. I know she will be living in a nice nice big house
with a nice rich family just like I want her to because
that's what feels right. That's really what is going to
happen, but somehow it feels like a thief in the night
came in and stole something I really needed. But I can't
be so sorry for myself. Ellen had her baby, too, two days
after me. They were going to send me home before her,
but my mom called and said I can't come home until
Friday, so that's when Ellen is supposed to go home,
too, except that we are not.

We will exchange our bus tickets for California. Out
West we can live on our own, on an island near the
ocean. We will build a little house out of driftwood and
clamshells. Ellen wants to be a barmaid, and I want to

be a reporter for a newspaper. We will never get p.g. again.

Now, if you are reading this, you can't tell. I've told you everything up to now that was the very truth, and if you tell anything now, our lives will be on your hands. You know everything in this diary because you deserve to know the things that we had to find for ourselves, but you must not tell and you know why. I didn't know until today that I must leave the notebook behind for the next girl to find. We must keep this going. This is how you can live through all this. You and your roommate will take our places. Keep writing everything down. There's plenty of paper left.

Big Nouns, Unconjugated Verbs

Bart Plantenga

I crossed the park that has no name. I carry a thick notepad in my breast pocket. It covers my heart & can prevent death. A habit begun back when i cared. This is not, however, where i keep my secret phone numbers. & i lug my manuscript in red folder in black rucksack.

I saw 2 kids with lots of letters & words on bright jackets. They were pushing a dog turd with a white stick through the park in the same direction i was going. I hope this won't be the fate of my walking cane after my departure.

I went to the phone near her place. Reached down & in the hem of my jean cuff is a small section where the stitch is slit. In this secret pocket i keep the tight wad of important initials & phone numbers.

Rita Mitsouko is Japanese. I don't know why she's here. She's always home. She's not studying. Not of exceptional beauty or ambition. Not sharp featured. More an image etched in pungent jade soap with which you caress your whole body. A gumdrop face. The mind of a hostage. Patience of a mountain. Persistence of weather.

"Rita? You home?"

"You come?"

"Yes."

"Soon."

"Yes. I am near. At phone outside."

We talked in big nouns, proper nouns connected by unconjugated verbs. Basic things: house, heat, beer, fuck; uncompromised by misleading adjectives.

Smile at door. Like lampshade askew. We sit at kitchen table. Pile of Japanese pop magazines. She points. Faces familiar. "Andy Warhol. You like?" Other pages. Other faces. Other pics of smiles & gadgets.

"Madonna. You don't like."

"Body, yes. Voice, no."

"Hirohito. He not God. He bad, & you?"

"Me bad, yes. Emperors, no like. Never."

"Napoleon. He invent pastry." One hand turns pages. We continue to compose cheap pop haiku. The other hand tunes a radio. A song came on. "You like?"

I twisted the dial of the radio. Then twisted her nipples. "Nipple better." This makes her laugh. Hair shimmers. I think of a man throwing coal ashes into snow.

"Your tits like Napoleon's." My breath was lost on her neck. I licked her nape. The bones that define shoulder at elbows. Feet light like brushes on a snare drum. She always smells like Hong Kong Cocktail.

"Coca-Cola? Want?"

"No. Beer."

"I get." She runs down hall. Gets glass. Enthusiasm. Kitchen. Blouse off her shoulders at elbows. Feet light like brushes on a smare drum.

"Cold." Pours beer. "Nice. For you."

I pull out my baby, 382 pg. manuscript. "See, this is mine. My baby."

"Baby."

"I write."

"You."

"It's a *man-u*-script. Get it?"

"You man?"

"Sometimes." I let a mouthful of beer run down her neck. "Yes, cold." Her nape would make Stradivarius nervous. I drink. She show photo. John & Yoko. Signed: "To Rita, Peace, Yoko."

"Yoko sign. You like?"

"Sometimes."

"I love. She artist."

"Long ago, yes. Bed in."

"Yes, in bed. Artist. Nam June Paik. You like?"

"He okay." As i licked her body clean. Her tiny feet, I surmise, would float. Like toy sailboats. Luxembourg Gardens. June 12. Little tufts of lint between her toes. & a soufflé could never be as exquisite as her belly. Her breath is uneven. Radio stuck between 3 ghostly stations. Her eyes gone.

"Beer good?"

"Great. Refreshing. Quenching. Delicious!"

"You wash now?" Bathroom. Walls white. White tile. White soap. Her white hand through crack of door hands me clean white towel. In mirror i smile at myself. Or is it? Where creams? Where powders? Where clutter of living?

She sitting. Waiting. Edge of couch. Hands clamped between knees. My fingers paint her. To recline. Reclining nude. To floor.

"Pillow." She remove blouse. Lay straight still on futon. I twist her nipples. I remember the eraser caps to put on the end of pencils. We would chew them. Pretend to eat them. Make girls we liked ill. In 4th grade.

"I like. More!" She begins to moan. A wind against dark window. Whatever can we mean to one another?

Wiggle. I shimmy her out of pants. Turn her over. Bite her pastry buttocks. *Les petites religieux.* Small as my kneecaps. Float like a sigh.

The frenzy of ecstasy feeds on its own enthusiasm. Her mouth could barely hold 3 cherries. Or 2 toffees. I try.

"I lately exercise mouth. Stronger. See. I try now." She shows me its maximum aperture.

"Still hurt." She tries to inhale my penis, but can't. Her eyes can't breathe. Wide. Bulge. Licks it instead.

"Like ice cream." & over time i have come to realize I can do anything I want to/with her. This presents a dilemma I have seldom faced in life. Anything! Her trust is amazing. Sickening. Dangerous. She is pliable. Her body folds in half, in fours, in triangles.

"Body origami." I try to go inside. She is laughing. Or how a sigh would laugh. Tight as a knife wound. She insists I thrust. Urges. Wants. Rocks. To. Exhale. Fro. Impale. Glisten.

"Come! Go!" Cunt desperate as begging vase. Her tiny hands fastened to my buttocks. She has orgasm after orgasm immediately. I've only just arrived. A necklace of deep, urgent sighs. Which cut her words. In half. Quarters. Eighths. & i can keep her ears warm with her knees for ½ hour if i want.

"No come inside." Anything—except that. The orgasms don't stop. Like delirious echoes. One feeding another. She is swearing in Japanese. Praising some emperor. Condemning. Not Hirohito. Something beyond. Bigger & then the howl begins. A relentless howl that fills the airshaft. I have to disengage. Her doll legs left stuck in the air. I get up. Close window.

"Cold?"

"A little." I push her head into the pillow. The moan is muted. Not even hers. Someone else's. & finally i come. Shoot up her backbone. All the way to her moist neck. She like.

"I like." I rub it into her body. "Mmmm. Good. You stay?" I have sneakers on still. Pants stuck around ankles. Like shackles. This is so I don't stay. A signal. For her.

"What time?"

"Qua'er pas' 8."

"I go now." Otherwise she folds my clothes neatly. Puts them away. I won't find them. She will wear a nightie. Play house. Watch TV. Head on heaving gut.

"Sleep? Here?"

"No. Gotta go."

"Thirsty?"

"Little." She run. I mean run. Kitchen. Come back. Running. On knees. Serves me. To enslave me with her dedication.

"Cold. Ice." I get up. "Towel?"

"Okay."

& when I leave she watches. From the railing of her staircase. Hand shoving shirttail into her crotch.

"You come back."

"What'm i, a sailor?"

"Okay. Tomorrow?"

"Don't know."

"Soon?"

"Next week." Rita Mitsouko keeps me sane. But at her expense? The way convenience can. Or brandy. Or an accurate weather report. There are no demands, no scenes, no cheap emotion. I give. She get. She give. (Sometimes she gives me mysterious gifts wrapped in rice paper at the top of her stairs. Things of value. Things I can give to my girl. There's something very erotic about giving gifts in this manner.) Yes, I receive. No discount. No fuss. No mess. No hidden clauses.

Love Art

Debra Martens

She should have been locked up, too. To keep going back to him—she was just as mad as Jack. When he tried it on me, calling, "Laurie, come here," and flashing the knife at me, that was it. He wasn't my lover anymore.

He'd always been a bit rough. Throwing me around as if I were a rag doll. Biting me. Like a kid in the schoolyard who doesn't know his own strength. And he had this thing about putting objects inside me. He called it hide-and-seek—let's play hide-and-seek. Over the few months I was with him, he'd inserted a pot handle, vegetables, a hammer handle, cardboard poster rolls, a doll's leg. I let him put bottles in despite the story I'd heard about a bottle getting stuck by suction and breaking inside. I indulged his curiosity. I brought him things to try: an oval stone, hard Italian biscuits, a blunt-nosed umbrella, a bottle brush. But a knife, no way. I didn't wait around to find out what he wanted to do with it.

He liked to cut her skin. Not deep slashes, merely nicks. It was a good sharp knife, one of those wide Henckels. All he had to do was touch the tip of the blade to her skin. Nora's skin was so firm it would break with a whispered pop. I was there sometimes. Yes, the three of us. It's not that easy to say good-bye to a lover. Although I wouldn't let him touch me with the knife, I started looking at women in tight skirts, the flesh pushing against the fabric, wondering if that was the attraction for him, the tension of the flesh pushing against the skin, demanding release.

They found each other at a concert. There were three bands at the old dance hall by the waterfront, the place that burned down last summer. We were dancing together, our gang from the warehouse, and Nora suddenly turned away from whomever she was dancing with and started dancing with Jack. She said something that made him bend down. His dark curls touched her cheek, her neck, as he put his ear to her mouth. He nodded. After he stood up and started dancing, I raised my eyebrows to Jack, to find out what pearls of wisdom had dropped from her red lips.

"Great band." That was it. Small talk. I don't want to sound like a snob or anything, but a lot of bridge-and-tunnel people were there that night. The kids who came in from the suburbs, with their studded wristbands and wide leather belts, with their careful punk attire. Peacocks. Not that I'm innocent; I remember distinctly what we were wearing that night. Jack was dressed like an angel, he always dressed like an angel, in white. Dirty white, mind you, but white all the same: he was wearing white jeans with a leather vest, a white, round-collared shirt with long, loose sleeves, and a cap. I was wearing my purple silk harem trousers, with my orange Hawaiian shirt. Nora was in black, from her tits to her toes.

She might have been a groupie, one of the kids who'd piss their pants if they knew that Martha, the singer in the first band, was a friend of ours. They didn't have Martha's band storing their equipment in the loft down the hall from them, didn't have a band practicing at three in the morning. Don't get me wrong, I love Martha and her band. By this time I'd been living and working in my loft for five years, and maybe that was too long to be in the same space, but I was starting to get work—commissions, and illustrations in magazines. Jack had been painting only a year or so, little burgundy torsos in muddy fields, so he was broke, poorer even than the arts students who hung around, waiting for one of us to die of an overdose or something so they could have the loft.

Not that they would want Jack's loft. He lived at the bottom of the back stairwell of our warehouse, in what used to be a loading area. He'd closed off his space, to make a room around the flight of stairs. Under the stairs was a pile of debris, things that had followed him home like stray pups, things that might be useful for his work. On one side of the stairs was the bed. On the other side, his nest. Here were the castoffs of his daily life. Clothes, dirty and clean together, were heaped with newspapers and books and cassettes and shoes and empty bags and used Kleenex and scarves and coats. The chair, which faced the stairs, was sometimes shaken clear for guests. The bed was the only neat corner of his loft.

I had trouble letting Jack go because I couldn't believe this stuff with the knife. I'd look at him and see my Jack, the picture of innocence, like an English country boy on the postcards you buy in secondhand bookstores. One day he was plain old Jack, and the next, he was turning psycho.

The only words that ever came out of his mouth were kind words, friendly words, curious words. If you wanted to talk bands, he would talk bands. If you wanted to talk dope, he would talk dope. Or art or food or friends. If you didn't talk, he wouldn't talk. We in the warehouse swapped personal horror stories, but Jack never talked about his past, unless you count the funny stories he told us about his shrinks. Yet no hate came out of his mouth. No words that resembled his paintings.

If anyone seemed like they would greet their lover with a knife, it was Nora. She was deeply and quietly angry: her black clothes and studded belt were surface signs, the way an ooze of oil on the ground was evidence of a toxic dump site below. She was a small thing, and her blond hair was close-cropped, spiked. She was no groupie: she sang. She'd cut hair and waitressed her way through singing lessons, and now she was getting paid to sing. And she could. She could sing. Even if she couldn't sing, she would've become a singer, she was that determined.

Around her, he hardly talked at all.

He liked to nick her skin so that when they made love, her blood would leave marks on the sheets. When he started with the knife, he cut her at the back of her neck. After they'd made love, the first time he cut her skin, he stood over the bed, gazing at the patterns the blood made on the sheets. He'd rolled Nora out of the way, as if she were a log obstructing his view. He called the stained sheets love art.

Over the weeks, his cuts moved around to the front of her neck, slowly down past her collarbone. Before she let him put the knife near her breasts, though, she made him do her limbs first. He was happy with her arms and legs for a long time. Their lovemaking tousled the sheets; it hardly mattered what position he fucked her in, or where the nicks were, as long as there were some front and back.

In the mornings, he'd throw her out of bed. She'd go around the corner for coffee and Danish, bring them back warm from the bakery. She'd dawdle on the way, talking to the people coming out of their lofts. While she was gone, he'd make the bed. He'd pull the sheet tight across the mattress and admire the old and new bloodstains. He'd shake out the top sheet, let it billow over the mattress, pull it smooth, and admire.

I liked Nora almost right away. The night of the dance, she came home with Jack. Because we still thought she was one of those suburban jerks playing at being tough, that she wouldn't last, Henry made a point of walking in on her when she was using the toilet down the hall the next morning (the door barely closed, never mind locked). Later that day, she came upstairs to visit me. Right away, she saw my books—Gertrude Stein, Brautigan, Hesse, Nietzsche. Most people who came to my loft simply didn't see the books and certainly never talked about them or asked to borrow one. She offered to lend me hers—Robbe-Grillet, Marquis de Sade, Anaïs Nin. Only after she saw the books did she go to look at the feathers.

A friend of a friend told me where I could pick up thirty flats of antique feathers. I bought them not knowing what to do with them. They were for hats, for costumes. I thought they were beautiful. After they sat in their flats in my loft for three days, I painted all the walls in my loft white, and I painted the ceiling and the floor black. I chose the wall across from the windows for the feathers. I drilled a zillion tiny holes, spiralling outward from a small wing shape, and I stuck the feathers into the wall, close together. All of them together made a giant multicolored wing on the wall.

That's what people see when they come to my loft; they see the feathers, not the books. They have to ask about the feathers. Where'd you get them, what'd you put them up for, aren't they dusty, don't they take up too much space sticking out, aren't you afraid you'll get paint on them, great shadow on the wall, and so on.

Nora had a good long look at them. She turned to me, where I was sitting at the table, and said, "Why'd you paint the floor black?"

White came out of Jack's mouth, too. White lies. Jack never told Nora about the shrinks, that he was being checked by the shrinks all his life. When they let him out of the loony bin, where he'd disappeared for a while, not much changed. Nora came back. Come to think of it, no one knew where she went to, either, or where she lived before she moved in with Jack. When she wasn't singing or waitressing, she was at his place. His mound spread to cover more and more of the floor, as her things got mixed in with his.

The only daylight came from the skylight above the door at the top of the stairs. They stayed down there, living and fucking like rats. We kept an eye on them. Made sure they ate. Sometimes opened the door at the top of the stairs to look down into their nest. He told me his shrink told him to seek out normal human intercourse. Jack wasn't sure what this meant (he told me like it was a joke), and neither was I. I thought maybe it was eating and talking.

One morning, on my way out, I heard Jack shouting. He was chanting, "Talk, so talk, talk, so talk." From Nora, the sound of gagging. I opened the door of the stairwell landing and looked down. She was lying half on the floor, half on the wall. Her legs were up the wall, but her head was below her torso, at the bottom of a mound of clothes. Jack was pushing the neck of a bottle down her throat, jerking it in and out in time to his chant.

I hollered, "Jack, take it out, Jack, stop."

He did, as if he had been woken from a dream. But from her mouth came a bloody froth, and laughter. She laughed.

She was in love with him because he didn't try to protect her. She was sick to death of men who tried to take care of her, tell her what was good for her, claim her as their own, as if they were her fucking parents. Jack didn't do that. He let her come and go. He didn't even have a telephone number to call her when she wasn't there. He would watch her sing, but he wouldn't interfere. She said he was the only guy she knew who seemed not to have one ounce of jealousy in him. All the same, she thought Jack was fragile.

And I think he was besotted by her love. She was the first lover he'd had who didn't pick fights with him for not calling, for not seeming to care. When they were in public, you couldn't tell they were together. If he left the room, say to get a beer, and if he passed her, he never touched her. No stray caresses. He never reached for her hand when they walked together. One night, at my place, Henry insulted Nora, and Jack didn't say anything; he watched Nora to see what she would do, like he was watching a play, like he'd never met her before.

Around this time she let him start nicking her torso. Up to three nicks a day. The nicks were two finger-widths apart at first, as he worked down from her collarbone. He stopped short of the nipples and made tracks around to the back, where he worked his way up to her shoulders, and then down, rib by rib, to the small of her back, to her buttocks.

One of the nicks was too deep. She sat down to dinner at one of the upstairs lofts, and when she got up, there was a stain on her pants where no stain should be. We argued about whether to call his shrink. It was only because I liked Nora that I convinced them. Jack was locked up again. Nora disappeared.

I didn't tell anyone about Nora, about her being as bad off as him. Jack used to be my lover. He was happier with her than I'd ever known him. She made him happy. I could see that. I thought maybe she was playing at Anaïs Nin, you know, her erotica. I was afraid she'd let him put the knife to her cunt next.

The shrink suggested that Jack might be able to control himself if he had order in his life. Between me and the other warehouse people, I managed to find some of the stuff I needed to clean Jack's place.

The mound had spread. I found the bed only because I knew where it should be. Under the dirty clothes, the sheets were neatly tucked, and blood encrusted. The love art was taking on the contours of an oil painting.

I shook the apple cores from pockets, chips from creases. I shook all their clothes into plastic bags and took them to the Laundromat. I swept. I put out garbage. I folded all the clothes and put them neatly into milk crates stacked along one wall.

I didn't wash the sheets. I didn't touch the bed.

When he came back, Jack asked for Nora right away.

She was there the same day, with a package of new sheets. How did she know he was back? He stripped the bed. And then, if you can believe it, he pulled an iron and ironing board out from the junk under the stairs, and he ironed the sheets. Then he hung the old sheets up on the wall. As if it were a finished work.

They tried hard to be good. The knife was gone. They made love in a clean bed in a neat room. The sheets were only bloodied when she had her period. He was painting, and she got to her studio on time; she was putting together a record. We stopped keeping an eye on them.

Some months later, a little mound of shed clothing began to grow. At first, only some socks and underwear. Nora was too busy waitressing and singing to do the laundry, and Jack never had the habit. A few more socks in the corner. By that time, I had stopped coming down to see them. Gradually, they took up where they had left off. She brought a knife home from the restaurant, not as good as a Henckels. He had to press harder. New blood patterns started.

You see the stains on the floor, on the walls. When he pressed the dull knife into her vital vein, did he do it on purpose? Had he made love to her while she bled to death? Their bodies slippery with blood, blood flying off in every direction as they moved. As if he were trying for a Pollock effect, clots and rivers of blood on the messy canvas of the bedsheet. Blood soaked through to the mattress, spilled over to the floor. And then Jack trying to warm her body, holding her in his arms, bracing his slit wrists against her back. Everything slick with blood. The sheets, the bed, the floor, even the walls. Them. Nora. Jack.

That's how I found them, the morning I came down, drawn by the butcher-shop smell.

After their bodies had been taken away, I put all the sheets into the incinerator. The love art was not for public viewing. Everything else, I left as it was, for the time being.

Better Safe

Michael Lowenthal

Safe sex is the best thing that's ever happened to me. It has turned my secret fetish into the moral high ground, making my lifelong fantasies suddenly PC.

You see, I am a condom queen. A certified latex addict. These days people are always talking about this or that dysfunction being the last closet, the final taboo. You get three people together on "Oprah" and suddenly you've got a new oppressed minority. I don't want to stake a claim to any special status. I'm as tired as the next guy of hearing about equal rights for vampires or inclusive language for lesbians with facial hair or whatever the latest "last" taboos are, but I can certainly sympathize. I know all about closets within closets.

I came out with a bang. Nineteen seventy-four. New York City. I was twenty-one years old. My hair was long, my shorts were short, and I was ready for action. I knew there were faggots into just about everything—enemas, tit clamps, piss-drinking, and more—so I was sure I would find a community of condom fetishists without much problem.

Naive baby fag that I was, I plunged headfirst (pun intended) into the scene. I would go down to the Village in my cutoff jeans and fringe vest, swivel my hips a little bit, and I'd have a man in my apartment in no time. But as soon as I would bring up the idea of using a rubber, the other guy would pull away, horrified, and look at me as if I'd just suggested we not fuck on the first date or something equally unimaginable.

"That shit's for the heteros," I heard more than a few times. "What kind of self-hating faggot are you?"

It seems that condoms—like marriage, courtship, and sex with people whose last names you knew—were a hindrance to be borne by the puritanical straight oppressors, something that we freedom-loving, unrepressed queers could do without, thank you very much.

This rapid string of rejections came as a rude and painful shock. I had assumed that other gays, of all people, would accept me for who I am. My condom fetish is an essential part of me, just as natural as my being gay. In denying my preference, they were denying my very being. In fact, my obsession with rubbers began even before I was conscious of being attracted to boys.

I was twelve. My parents had just divorced, and my dad had moved into a genuine bachelor pad a few miles from our house, where I spent weekends even though he was hardly ever there. One Saturday morning when he was gone as usual, I stalked into his room and started poking through his stuff. His room was a mess, which I guess isn't a big surprise considering this was the first time in his life he'd had to clean up after himself.

I waded through a heap of dirty socks and underwear on the floor, past an avalanche of mail between the night table and the bed, making my way to the dresser against the far wall. I'm not exactly sure why I was drawn to it. I just had a hunch I'd find something: a stash of M&M's maybe, or my father's emergency cash. What I found, of course, was better than anything I'd imagined.

I knew about condoms in a vague, naughty kind of way. (It's not like we had sex ed back when I was in junior high.) I think I'd seen a dispenser in a truck-stop bathroom once on a family vacation. And I'd heard that my best friend Tommy's big brother had been dumped by Barbara Mason because he refused to use one.

But here, in the top drawer of my father's dresser, under the boxer shorts and his little-used jockstrap, was the real McCoy. The box itself was a thrill: a soft green color with a blurry romantic picture on the front, and on the back, full directions for use, complete with a diagram. I just held the box for a little while, turning it in my sweaty hands.

After a minute or so I worked up my courage and opened it. I took out a small foil packet and squished the contents from one side to the other. It felt almost fluid inside, and a tingle shimmered through my stomach as I imagined all the moist places this was meant to go. Finally I tore open the packet and squeezed the condom halfway out. It was definitely wet, but in a different way from what I had imagined, slippery but also kind of tacky. Rolled up at the edges, the rubber was a dull muddy yellow, the color of a fading summer tan. But in the center, where there was a little nipple poking up toward the ceiling, the rubber was clear as cellophane.

I held the condom up to my nose and smelled it: musty and fresh at the same time. A little bitter, but not in a bad way. The smell was intensely familiar, but it took me a minute to place it. Then a rush of memory flooded over me: my mother, towering above the tiny four-year-old me at the kitchen sink after dinner. Her yellow dishgloves teasing me, tweaking my nose, the latex squeaky-smooth and smelling clean like just-folded laundry. Then ducking to get away from her hands, pretending to be shy, nudging up against the back of her heavy wool skirt, to the soft chalky skin at the back of her knees.

I let my pants fall to the floor, and without even bothering to step out of them I grabbed my stiff dick. The rubber rolled on as if it were meant to be there all along, a missing body part that now finally made me complete. As I pushed the tight circle of rubber all the way to the base of my dick, I felt the blood being forced to the tip. I couldn't believe how much bigger the rubber made my erection. The veins swelled like thick purple vines wrapping around a post. It was like looking at my dick through a magnifying glass.

I ran my finger lightly over the smooth surface of rubber. My own touch was electrifying, sending shock waves of pleasure up and down my spine. Somehow the tightness of the latex made my finger seem like ten fingers, its gentle beat the burn of a blazing fire. I grabbed my dick just below the tip and made a fist. I didn't even have to pump it up and down the way I normally did. I just held it there, enjoying the sensation of having every square inch of my dick squeezed in its tight rubber wrapping. With the other hand I took hold of the clear nipple at the top of the condom. I pulled it as far out as I could without tearing the rubber and then let go. It snapped back against my piss hole with a cold sting. The pain made me wince, but I noticed that my dick swelled even larger. I stretched the nipple again and let it whip back, then again and again. The pain was like an ice-cold needle being stuck down the middle of my cock, but at the same time my balls were tingling with pleasure. The rubber was tight all over me, the acid smell of the latex filing my nostrils like a drug. I snapped the rubber nipple one more time, and the muscles in my groin gave way. I fell to my knees, shooting a solid stream of sperm into the latex capsule, watching the clear nipple swell with my milky whiteness.

After the first time, I was hooked. I went back to my father's bedroom the next weekend, and the next, and the next. . . .

Pretty soon I was spending all my allowance on rubbers. I found a drugstore on the other side of town where the clerk didn't give me a hard time. I experimented with different kinds: ribbed, lubricated, foreign brands. Sometimes I would wear a rubber all day in school, hiding my hard-on under extrabaggy pants.

It wasn't long before my fetish became a genuine addiction. I had to jack off at least once a day into a rubber, usually more like two or three times. I couldn't get off unless I was wearing one.

You can see why it was so painful when I finally came out about my fetish, only to be ridiculed by all my potential partners. But I won't bore you with my tales of misery. We can just fast-forward for a decade or so after my disappointing debut. I was your better basic, run-of-the-mill Manhattan queen. I went out dancing, marched in the pride parade, changed my wardrobe with each fashion wave. Your standard-issue faggot . . . except for the small issue of sex.

I still had sex every now and then, but it was hardly worth the effort. I was as turned off by the men as they were turned off by condoms, and the act itself caused me as much tension as it relieved. After so many rejections I stopped letting myself even bring up the subject of rubbers. It was like being in the closet all over again.

Imagine my surprise ten years later when everybody started talking about safe sex. Suddenly the same self-righteous queens who had shut me out in the seventies were telling me with equal conviction that using rubbers was my duty to the community.

In the next few years I was surrounded by condoms. Drugstores put them out in the aisles with all the other merchandise, and right up front, too, not tucked away with the feminine-hygiene products and hemorrhoid medication. Rubbers were on posters, in magazines, on the sides of public buses.

I'll never forget the day I came home from work, turned on the news, and there's the Surgeon General of the United States urging everybody, gay and straight alike, to indulge in my long-hidden fetish. I could have kissed that sweet old Republican!

Don't get the impression that my sex life changed overnight, because it didn't. In fact, as condoms became more and more socially acceptable, I had less and less sex. As elated as I was by the change in attitudes, I couldn't quite get up the courage to go out and take advantage of it. When your entire life has been based on denial, the prospect of satisfaction can be somewhat overwhelming. On top of that, with so many friends starting to die of AIDS, it would have felt wrong to gain so much pleasure from the very circumstance that was killing them.

I'm not sure what finally turned me around. Part of it, as the eighties ran into the nineties and we'd been living with the plague for almost a decade, was watching my infected friends reclaim their sexuality. What I saw them learning, and learned with them, was that with so many forces out there to destroy us, we should get everything we can out of life while we have the chance. If that sounds kind of carpe diem hokey, so be it. When you've seen twenty-six-year-old men on their deathbeds, talking about all the things they wish they'd had time to do, it's all too real.

But the bottom line was, I was *horny*. I'd had almost no sex for a couple of years, and I had still *never* had the kind of sex I wanted. Now that sex with condoms was happening all around me, it was simply too much to bear.

I get giddy just thinking about what happened next. I'd like to be able to tell you it was spontaneous— maybe then I'd seem less like the vulture that I am. But the truth of the matter is I meditated on my plan for weeks. After almost two months of plotting, the perfect opportunity arose and I knew I couldn't pass it up. It was then that I executed the first of what by now are many similar conquests.

It was January 1991, the country in a yellow-rib-boned hysteria. With almost half a million American troops standing poised in the Persian Gulf, an equal number of citizens gathered at the Mall in Washington, D.C., to protest the imminent war. Some had traveled ten hours or more—from Michigan, Florida, and Maine—to stand up for justice and truth.

And why was I there, pushing my way briskly through the crowd? Why had I taken the Metroliner down from New York on a weekend when I should have been at home catching up on correspondence? Because I knew ACT UP was going to have a large contingent in the march, and what better place to meet a young, horny, safe-sex fanatic? (I had considered going to a regular ACT UP demo in Manhattan—and eventually I would—but for this first time, this experiment, I needed the safety of being in a city where I was totally unknown.)

The Mall was jam-packed with people. There didn't seem to be any order to the way groups were lining up, but the ACT UP contingent was not very hard to find.

I simply followed the chant: *Suck my dick. Lick my labia. U.S. out of Saudi Arabia.*

I hovered around the edges of the group for a few minutes, trying to blend in. I had worn my oldest pair of jeans, the ones with holes in both knees, and a plain white T-shirt under the big leather jacket my friend Steve had lent me. I had carefully affixed stickers to the arms and back of the jacket: MONEY FOR AIDS, NOT FOR OIL; SODOMITES FOR SADDAM.

Nobody gave me the hairy eyeball, so I figured the uniform was pretty authentic. I kept a low profile and scanned the crowd, searching for the perfect victim. There were probably a score of safe-sex radicals to choose from within fifty yards of me, but one stood out above the rest. He was tall and extremely thin, a male Olive Oyl. He was dressed about the same as I was, except on the shoulders of his leather jacket, in place of studs, he had glued strips of condom packets: blue, green, and red. The jacket was unzipped to reveal a SAFE SEX IS HOT SEX T-shirt that pictured two naked men tangled in a wild fuck.

As he walked closer to me, I saw that his face was smooth and sharply hewn, tapering to a solid, slightly cleft chin. Even more appealing was his shining strawberry-blond hair: crew-cut, but still somehow endearingly disheveled. His sideburns were sculpted precisely, creeping down below his ears and then jutting inward like two furry maps of Italy.

He wove through the crowd with graceful ease, as if he could sense all the gaps. "Die-ins are at Twelfth Street, Fourteenth, and in front of the White House," he chanted to everybody he passed. "Die-ins at Twelfth, Fourteenth, and the White House."

He must have shouted the same line two dozen times, yet each time he repeated it with wonderful conviction. If he took all his assignments seriously, I knew he must follow the rule book on safe sex down to the letter of the law. This was definitely my man.

"Die-ins at Twelfth—" he started the mantra again.

"Fourteenth, and the White House," I deadpanned before he could finish.

He looked startled, and then embarassed. "I guess everyone's pretty much heard, huh?"

"I think that's a safe bet."

He looked down sheepishly and fiddled with the zipper on his jacket. It occurred to me that underneath all the radical-crusader paraphernalia, he was just a kid, probably no older than twenty.

"You think it's okay to stop, then?" he asked.

So he was the type who needed orders. This would be even easier than I'd expected. "Listen," I said. "You did a great job. Maybe now you should take a new assignment."

"Sure. What needs to be done?" He was *so* eager-beaver it was frightening.

"You don't have to if you don't want to. But I'm from out of town, and I don't know a single person here. I could really use some company for the march. You know, like a local escort."

"Oh, well, I'm from here," he said. "I mean, I guess I could do that. Sure."

I extended my hand. "I really appreciate it. My name's Jerry."

"Arlo," he said. "Good to meet you." As he held out his hand to take mine, I noticed for the the first time that it was sheathed in a latex glove.

When the march moved out into the street, we walked together through the seas of people, trying not to get separated. Arlo lived up to his activist image right away, shouting all the ACT UP slogans with the conviction of a Baptist preacher. When one chant died down, he was always the first to start another.

After a few blocks we passed a small group of counterprotesters, mostly prudish-looking women whose

husbands were serving in the Gulf. Arlo said we had
to stop and slipped the backpack off his shoulder. I had
no idea what he was doing as he reached inside and
then flung his hand grandly in the protesters' direction.
To the women's absolute horror, dozens of miniature
packets of lubricant showered down on them, glim-
mering in the winter sun like so many giant snowflakes.

"Safe sex is for Republicans, too!" Arlo shouted.
"Spread love, not AIDS."

Arlo's activist adrenaline was really pumping. I
began to imagine the kind of sex we could have. I knew
it would be extreme, like everything about this kid.

When we all "died" in the middle of Pennsylvania
Avenue, Arlo took the metaphor seriously. He gave up
all control of his muscles and collapsed to the ground,
150 pounds of dead weight. I know because he died
right on top of me. It was such a wonderful feeling to
have him pressing on me, covering me with his skinny
length. One of his gloved hands fell across my face, and
I just couldn't help myself. I took his pinkie into my
mouth and sucked it like a calf at the teat, letting the
bitter dryness of the latex spread over my tongue.

When the rally was over, I asked Arlo what he was
doing next.

"Well, they're making posters over at Mark's house
to publicize the big action next week. I thought I'd go
over and maybe help."

Even after my finger-sucking routine, he didn't get
it. This generation has no appreciation for the art of
seduction, I thought.

"Arlo," I said firmly. "I've really enjoyed being with
you today."

"Me, too, Jerry. I had a really good time."

"Good, I'm glad." I was going to have to make it
even clearer. "I'm kind of pooped, so I'm going back to

my hotel. I was hoping you might want to come with me."

Arlo flinched and looked quickly into my eyes, as if he wasn't sure he'd heard me correctly.

"Oh," was all he said. *Now* he got it.

We didn't say anything on the way up to the room. I watched Arlo in the mirrored walls of the elevator. He seemed nervous in a way he hadn't been before, rubbing his sideburns obsessively and scuffing the carpet with his shoes. The radical activist's bravado had disappeared.

We stepped off at the twelfth floor and followed the maze of hallways to the room. Our leather jackets creaked awkwardly with each stride, punctuating the silence between us. I was beginning to wonder if I should go through with this after all. Maybe I should level with Arlo about my motives. But we were already at the room, and I figured if he hadn't freaked out by now, he wanted this as much as I did. He'd had ample opportunity to run away.

As I was fumbling to slide the credit-card-like key into its slot, Arlo touched me gently on the shoulder. "Um, Jerry? Can we be clear about something before anything happens?"

"Sure," I said, leaving the key in the lock.

Arlo looked into my eyes with a devastatingly serious expression. "I'm safe," he said plainly. "Totally. I mean, that's the only way I'll do it."

I'm safe. Totally. The words raised the hair on the back of my neck. I wanted to ravish Arlo right there in the hallway, to shove my throbbing hard-on into his earnest face. But I suppressed my desire and tried to match his serious demeanor. After a sufficient pause I leaned forward and pecked him dryly on the cheek.

"I wouldn't feel comfortable any other way," I said.

"That's what I like about you younger guys. You've got that commitment."

A wide smile bloomed on Arlo's face and the swagger returned to his air. We rushed into the room and he immediately tossed his backpack onto the giant bed. Neither of us said anything, but with some kind of telepathy we moved so we were facing each other, about five feet apart. The rules were clear for this stage: no touching, just looking.

First we both stripped off our leather jackets. Then Arlo pulled his T-shirt over his head and I saw that his long torso was smooth except for a small patch of reddish hair just above his solar plexus. His nipples were hard, small burgundy cylinders rising out of his otherwise flat chest. I yanked off my own shirt quickly, wanting to keep up with the kid without missing any of the show. I'm proud of my muscular chest, but Arlo hardly seemed to notice me. He was concentrating intently on the removal of his own clothes. He slipped off his shoes and socks, and I did the same. I wanted to let him think that he was calling the shots.

Then Arlo moved his hand to his belt and paused, staring directly into my eyes. This was clearly the centerpiece of the ritual. Taking in a big gulp of air and holding it, as if even breathing would destroy the sanctity of the moment, he undid his button-flies and in one smooth motion stepped out of his jeans and his Jockeys at the same time.

At first I was so overwhelmed it was all I could do just to look at his legs. They were long and lean, not a millimeter of fat. His skin was pale, with just the slightest wisps of curly hair. He looked almost frail, in need of protection. It was more than I could have hoped for.

Finally, I steadied myself and raised my eyes to his crotch. His circumcised dick was just like his legs, long and thin. In fact, it was about the thinnest cock I'd ever seen, hardly bigger around than my thumb. It hung limp in the wide space between his legs, its squarish knob well below the sac of his balls. But then as I watched, it twitched to the side and then lurched upward in small bursts, filling with blood until it stood straight up to his belly button. It must have been eight inches long, and still hardly as thick as a hot dog!

I took a step back and admired the bare fullness of him. He was completely naked now, all except for the latex gloves that he'd been wearing since the moment I laid eyes on him. Something told me he didn't take those off.

Now it was my turn. I unhooked my belt and lowered the zipper slowly, trying to look in control. I pulled off the jeans deliberately, one leg at a time, folded them, and placed them on the dresser. Then the excitement of the moment got to me and I couldn't keep up the charade any longer. I yanked off my underwear, ripping it in the process. My bulging cock protruded like a lightning rod in front of me, as long as Arlo's but more than twice as thick.

We stood there for a few moments, ogling each other. Neither of us had said a word since we'd entered the room. Nor had we touched. This was so different from the frenzied groping and exaggerated "I'm gonna fuck your tight ass" talk that I had experienced as sex in the seventies. With Arlo, everything was calm and controlled. He was all concentration, like a surgeon about to enter OR. The restraint was driving me wild.

Just when I had decided I'd have to make the next move, Arlo reached over to the bed and got his backpack. He unzipped the main compartment, and an army's worth of safe-sex paraphernalia spilled out. He tossed me a pair of surgical gloves identical to the ones on his hands.

"Boy, you're serious," I said. I knew the rationale, but I was hoping I could get Arlo to explain it out loud.

As if he could read my mind, he said, "Most people

have small cuts in their cuticles, all around their fingers. Even putting a condom on somebody else could be dangerous if you're not protected. What if some precome leaks?"

I began to swoon just from hearing Arlo talk that way. I stretched the translucent latex over my fingers and let it snap tightly on my wrist: the sound of a palm slapping flat on a bare ass. Then the other hand. Smack. I realized as I wiggled my fingers in their tight new covering that our roles had reversed. Despite his youth, Arlo was the experienced one here.

Arlo grabbed a rubber from the pile and ripped open the foil packet. "I have to put this on myself now," he said. "It's kind of tricky with—" and he looked down at his thin cock. When he stretched the condom over his length, I saw what he meant. The rubber hung too loosely on his thin prick, clinging only in a few places. In all my fantasies about rubbers, I'd never even thought of this.

Then it got even better. Arlo reached again into the backpack and pulled out a small, blue rubber band. He looped the band carefully around the head of his dick. He twisted it once and then lopped it over again. Then again. And once more before rolling the band down to the base. He winced a little as he pushed it along, but I could tell from the way he sucked in his breath that there was pleasure mixed in with the pain. It was tight all right, so tight that the veins in his dick pumped to almost double their previous size. My own dick bulged, too, as I watched the display.

"There," he said casually. "I'm all set."

My heart was racing. My hands and arms felt like jelly. I was too buzzed to think straight, let alone maneuver a rubber onto my own cock. I picked up one of the foil packets from the pile and handed it to Arlo. "You look like an expert. Why don't you dress me in my armor?"

He *was* an expert. He tore open the package and pulled out the rubber, holding it up like a prize. Kneeling before my crotch, he grabbed the base of my shaft firmly with one gloved hand. The touch of the latex sent a wave of warmth through my tight stomach. My knees weakened and I almost fell back onto the bed. With the other hand Arlo positioned the rolled-up rubber on the tip of my cock, and suddenly his mouth was on me, sliding down, tight and warm and wet, although I knew I must be imagining the wet because he was covering me with the rubber, stretching it over my length with his teeth, miraculously getting it on me without ever having touched my bare skin with his mouth or tongue.

Now I did fall onto the bed. I took Arlo with me, tackling him and kissing his chest, gnawing at the tiny island of hair just above his sternum. His skin was as tight and smooth as the rubbers we were wearing. Slowly, I worked my way up to his neck. I licked around his Adam's apple and pretended to take a bite. Then I put the whole bulge in to my mouth and sucked on it the way you would someone's ball sac. Arlo loved it. He ran his gloved hands frantically through my hair, creating waves of static that lit my scalp on fire.

I moved back down the center of Arlo's chest, leaving a trail of hickeys that bloomed on his skin like a polka-dotted necktie. I lingered over his belly button, rimming it gently and then plunging its depth with my tongue. At the same time I reached up and squeezed his rock-hard nipples between my rubber-covered fingers. Arlo shivered at the touch and squirmed under me, whimpering unintelligible phrases.

Finally I made my way down to the prize. In its clear wrapper, Arlo's cock glowed in the bright hotel-room light. It lay elegantly on his pale belly, like an exquisite centerpiece on a banquet tray. I lowered my mouth and took a tentative taste of his encased shaft. He was wearing a mint condom! The fresh tingle of the mint and the bittersweetness of the latex mingled on my tongue, and I sloshed my own saliva around in my mouth like a sip of fine wine. I took another lick, longer this time, up the full length of his prick. It jerked in response, lifting a full inch off his body. Then I lost any hint of self-restraint. I began lapping at the shaft wildly like a dog at a bone, nudging it all over Arlo's belly. I rubbed my lips against the velvet-smooth rubber, reveling in the touch of latex against skin. This was better than any of my fantasies.

I climbed back up Arlo's body and brought my face level with his. As we started to kiss, he reached down between our bodies and circled my cock with his fingers. He pumped a few times, forcing more blood into the already swollen head. I thought my cock would burst right out of the rubber. Arlo jerked me again, and the friction of latex against latex produced a loud squeak that was pleasure-pain in my ears.

I was already close to coming, so I took Arlo's hand and guided it away from my crotch. He seemed to get the message, moving his hand up gingerly along my chest. But when he got to my shoulder, he grabbed suddenly and rolled over, pinning me to the bed. There was a shocking strength in those thin arms of his. I took the maneuver as a sign that he was ready to fuck. I started to ask him if he wanted to, but as soon as I spoke, he covered my mouth and nose with his hand, not letting me finish the sentence. When I tried to breathe in, all I got was the latex smell of his glove. I was immediately drunk with it, the aphrodisiac scent of my years of fantasy, of all the men I'd dreamed of having. I wanted to tell him how good it was, but Arlo held his hand there, squeezing tightly, and the lack of breath was like a dagger in my lungs. I squirmed, trying to get out from under his grip, but I was losing energy fast, my empty throat burning. I was sick with dizziness, about to black out, when suddenly he released his hand, and as I drank in a mammoth intoxicating gulp of air, my cock opened with a rapid-fire of come. I groaned loudly as I shot out more and more, thick gobs of sperm that filled the tip of the rubber and then oozed down, surrounding me with my own warmth.

Arlo saw that I had come and grabbed his own cock. He circled the base of his shaft with one hand, holding the tight rubber band. With the other he jerked himself wildly, so fast that his hand was a pink blur before my eyes. It only took a few seconds. Arlo shuddered a few times and let out a sharp grunt. I saw the tip of his rubber swell with fluid, and then he collapsed on top of me and panted into my ear.

We lay there together for a few minutes, letting our hearts and lungs slow down to normal pace. I breathed in deeply, enjoying the bittersweet tang of another man's sex sweat. I felt as if a whole new world had opened up for me, as if this had been my very first time. And in a way it had.

When Arlo was dressed, we kissed unromantically for a few seconds and then I showed him to the door. He seemed so blasé about the whole situation, and I couldn't help wondering if somebody like Arlo took it for granted that this was what sex was, or if he had any idea what things were like before AIDS. Just as he was about to step outside, I asked him if he'd ever had un-protected sex.

"God, don't I ever wish." He laughed. "But it's just not worth the risk."

"Do you think it will always be this way?" I asked.

Arlo nodded emphatically. "Even if they come up with a cure, it's not like AIDS is going to go away. Yup. Safe sex is here to stay."

My whole body felt buoyant, as if a heavy weight had lifted.

Arlo stepped into the hallway, but after a few paces he turned and looked at me strangely, as though he were seeing through a wide expanse of distance and time.

"It must have been a blast in the old days, huh? When you didn't have to do everything through a layer of latex."

"Oh, I don't know," I said as he disappeared down the hall. "Every age has its good points and its bad."

Slow Dance on the Fault Line

Donald Rawley

Faith has not spoken for weeks. Not to the nurses or her husband's doctor, her mother, or closest friends. Since Ted's heart attack, people knew not to call; she would pick up the phone and only listen, then quietly put the receiver down. Now when Faith walks into a room, there is the acute exhaustion of her silence. She is there to listen, nod her head, understand. There is nothing more for her to say.

She is silent with terror. She has felt the succinct, flat drop of abandonment for the last five years, and now it has assumed form. Faith is forty and her husband, Ted, is forty-one. She reasons she is young, that she had never foreseen or predicted anything. She is still beautiful and now deserted.

One month ago Ted had a heart attack, and the doctors now have given him days, a week at most, to live. Faith can only remember their shoes, never raising her head to the incorrigible hospital white that has followed her now for a month like a hot ending, where light obliterates breath and water and flesh.

It happened at dinner, at a nothing little place in the Valley they had stopped at after a screening at Warner Brothers. It happens to everyone just like this, Faith had thought. You are sitting on the toilet, having dinner at a fast-food restaurant, putting bleach into the washing machine, and you go, or start the slow process. He had slumped onto the food, his hand pushing chow mein onto the tablecloth. She had gone wild, remembering nothing until after the sedation, when Ted was lying in bed at home, next to a nurse, the stink of his dying crawling through the long halls.

Ted was an agent at William Morris and Faith was an agent's wife. She had never worked. She was addicted to a certain amount of Valium and Percodan; they softened the edges. She had coped for twenty years to make sure she was everything Ted wanted her to be. Valium helped. Perfection helped. A smooth face. A smooth house.

Ted had big-star clients and a big house and they were in astonishing debt. There were two mortgages and payments were late. Their matching Jaguars were bought on time and letters had come in for repossession. Out of seventeen cards, only three were not at the limit. No health insurance. No life insurance. No savings. She had paid for the hospital with a credit card. She was drawing money on the last credit cards to pay for the nurses. She had put the Jasper Johns up for sale, but the dealer explained it was a minor piece and there were no takers. She kept her jewelry. She wouldn't sell her jewelry. Now she wore as much of it as she could.

Neither had any family, children, good friends. Faith had stopped talking when she realized at his death she would be left with nothing. Maybe her clothes. The days were a game; she shut everything out, helping with Ted's catheter and bedpan, cleaning the mucus running down to his lips, under his pink upturned eyes and calcimined lids. Ted's organs wouldn't work. She would touch the sponge to the pale ash of his skin, falling inward like dry rotted wood, then walk past the nurse into the bathroom.

There she would wash her hands repeatedly with liquid soap, spray herself with Chanel No. 19, redo the makeup on her face several times. Once she masturbated with the nurse in the next room. The makeup had to be right. She tried to speak to herself in the mirror, but that's where the numbness was. Now it was three Valium a day, sometimes four, and the wait.

She only noticed the sky, began to study it each evening and tried to reeducate herself on color. She noticed her face, the immediate world before her, where her feet walked, how to close a door quietly like it had never been opened. Every evening she got into her silver Jaguar and drove along Mulholland Drive, watching the sky. Certain dusks it was bewildered, questioning; other times, impatient. It made her feel like a child in her deadened flesh; it made her feel something.

She remembered as a little girl watching skies and asking things her parents couldn't answer. Then, as an adult, she hadn't paid attention for over twenty years. There were stars, and sunsets. Each moment became an aphasia and a halt. Winds would shift and stutter, smelling of other lives.

It is her birthday today, and this October in Los Angeles is over one hundred degrees. There have been brush fires destroying new construction in the northern Valley mountains, and the Santa Anas have begun to light the sky with the char of oil and bundled wood. It is an arsonist's sky, Faith thinks, sore, inflamed, and livid.

Storm clouds are coming in fast, leaking wet lavender and coarse gray violets into the edge. She sees aubergine and peach light in the west; a blue she remembers on Mexican tile. She takes the curves of Mulholland slowly, staying close to the yellow line. On her car radio she hears there will be an electrical storm tonight; no chance, no percentages, the storm is already here.

She parks on Mulholland and lights a cigarette in her car. Her hands are numb and her left leg has fallen asleep. She will wait for the thunder and lightning. She has all the time in the world.

It begins with heavy, dusty drops of rain and the sound of the elements colliding, rumbling, like an elevator dropping. Then white light in veins, like the veins of a man's arm running from the wrist to the shoulder, then nothing. If God is a man, then these are his arms; if God is a woman, then these are her lover's, Faith reasons.

She wonders if, at this moment, her husband has died. If she should be there, or here to see him rise. She wonders if the nurse is frantic and cursing her. No one knows how tired she is, and in her soothing air-conditioned car she tries to cry, thinking the storm will let it out. It is dangerous sitting on the top of a mountain in a car during an electrical storm. It is dangerous not to be able to feel.

Faith massages her leg and decides to drive down into the Valley, from here a shallow pond covered with fireflies and damp air. At dusk she will drive through alleys full of pillowless couches, dead plants, and stacks of magazines. She understands why pretty things get thrown away.

Faith has driven for an hour, past tract houses and sex stores, magnolia trees and carpets of ivy. The storm is getting stronger. Lightning frames inconsequential things she normally wouldn't see when she drives: plaster elves and birdbaths, dogs turning corners, women counting money in glassed-in motel offices, the moments when streetlights turn on.

Children stand on front lawns and gape at the storm, then squeal, running around in circles. People are driving strangely, making wide left turns and almost hitting curbs, stopping for no reason and yelling at the driver next to them. Faith is hungry, thinks she should stop for a taco, but there are too many fast-food stands for her to be able to make a decision. The possibilities of taking one firm step in any direction are endless; she will keep driving tonight until the car runs out of gas. She doesn't know what else to do.

She is on Victory Boulevard headed into the flat gape of the West Valley, when, just out of Reseda, she sees a carnival on a vacant lot. It's a cheap one, with ten or twelve rides, and has been set up overnight. Each ride is lit with blinking lights and moving up and out into the sky at a different angle and rhythm. She thinks of big bands in the forties where men stand up and point their horns up and down, tapping their polished shoes, polished as Ted's doctor's shoes walking down deliberate and well-understood corridors.

She puts on a tape of Harry Connick, Jr., and drives onto the dirt lot where she can park and watch the carnival. She turns the air conditioner off and rolls down the windows, letting the tropical blast of night air clean the car out, make it part of the scene. She turns the headlights off and watches people move in the dark toward the lights of the carnival.

The odor of smoke hovers in the trees, distilling the blinking neon. It is the burnt oil from the giant, rocking machines. There are no families here, only some scattered Mexican couples and women she reasons are just like her, walking through the electricity, stumbling to the lights, the rock and roll, the cotton candy and chili dogs. They are alone, walking toward anything that gives light, anything that carries a pulse.

And then there are the men. They stand by parked cars, just beyond the streetlights, combing their hair with one knee up, attentive and silent, their silhouettes dark bronze and featureless.

They are homosexual, Faith thinks: I've seen them before. Two days ago, she had been at . . . she had been at a park at dusk, driving, stopping and thinking, when she had seen them, hanging around rest rooms under palms and at the edges of orange-tree borders, absolutely still. Then combing their hair and checking their watches, walking in and out of the rest rooms in a monotony, into other men's cars where their heads would disappear, then back into the scalding Valley sun. She had watched for hours that slow evening, falling asleep, then waking up when a bum had knocked at her window.

It was a hunt. She wondered if tonight she was hunting, if carnivals like this are made for the hunt, where people who are lost come to eat. She only wanted the numbness to last forever. She would go on every ride twice, there was enough money. Today.

This is an October of fire that travels by wind and men she cannot see. Faith looks in her purse for Valium, cigarettes, and money. Checking, checking. Her lips must be repainted. It's her birthday. She takes a Valium and lines her lips, runs her hands through her hair and realizes she can't feel her hair, lights another cigarette and slowly gets out of her car.

She does not know why she is here except she cannot sit in Ted's room anymore with a nurse she will never see again. The house will be taken away from her, put up for sale, and there aren't even pictures of it, or scrapbooks. They never kept scrapbooks, considering it unsophisticated. There would be nothing by Christmas. Only a sense of something torn, drawers emptied and new cities, hotel rooms, and planes.

Her high heel catches on a rock and she falls down, then gets up and steadies herself. The men in the shadows say and do nothing. She can only hear the shifting of boots, a car door quietly closing behind her. The wind of the storm pushes her beige silk dress against her body. There is no front gate, no entry to focus us; the rides are scattered and form a messy line that reaches to the back of the dirt lot.

She thinks of all the places she's never been to, of living naked in the trees, sleepwalking through gardens and beaches and trains with private rooms. She realizes she has never traveled with her husband to a destination that is completely foreign. At the front booth of the first ride she hands the girl ten dollars for ten dollars' worth of tickets. There are no smiles, and Faith assumes they are both silent women.

The half-empty carnival is full of color and movement, defying the regular flashes of lightning. God is taking pictures tonight, Faith thinks. Each ride has its own music playing, and Faith decides not to choose, but walk to the first one and keep going down the line. Until she reaches the last ride. That one she will ride until her money runs out. Then she will drive until her gas runs out. Then she will lie down and sleep.

Faith walks past revolving, empty kiddie rides; scratched teacups, tiny boats, and sports cars in Day-Glo glitter under dirty pink and yellow tents. They are attached to the motor by chains. There isn't a carousel with beautifully painted horses, or anything remotely innocent here. This is a carnival for children used to chipped toys. And they are home tonight, listening to the thunder.

She gives a ticket to a freshly scrubbed man with jowls and gin blossoms, pink as a pig. He runs the Tilt-A-Whirl and straps her carefully into the red oval chair. She feels secure now. Complete and ready. She will spin hard in a silence until there is no world around her. This is good.

She feels she is on the edge of the Pacific, her face the hue of cold mist. Her feet tense. She can feel something. Of becoming another element, of tasting salt and anything that gives life, controls the moon, and eats away cliffs.

It is at this moment that she sees a man staring at her. Standing against the ticket booth to the Octopus, a black iron, pink-lit spider ride, he is ugly and damned and he smiles. The ride heaves and sways in jagged stretches, like any animal used to crawling on ocean bottoms, drinking the life around it. The tiny cars at the end of each of the Octopus arms spin under the electrical storm, up and down to the Rolling Stones' "Sympathy for the Devil." She can see there is only one couple on the ride. The woman has curly, jet black hair and it is falling in her face. She is screaming, exquisitely frightened, and her boyfriend or husband or brother is laughing, his arm around her and his hand massaging her breast.

Faith feels like a fool sitting on the Tilt-A-Whirl, numb and dazed in her beige silk dress with her hands in her lap and her legs crossed as if she were at a cocktail lounge. But this is what she wants; to be out of place, foreign, traveling in circles. She focuses her eyes so she stares past him but can watch him without effort.

The man staring at her doesn't have a shirt on and his shoulders are dirty, watery from the sudden shift of rain that breaks the static in the air like urine. She wants to watch this man and knows she can. The fat man is making her sit here, strapped in, until more people show up for the ride.

The man staring at her is the most muscular man she has ever seen. Not a bodybuilder, but just huge and hard, with tattoos crawling up his scarred arms. She discerns women riding dragons, skulls and hatchets and clouds covering his shoulders. There is an eagle in flight across his chest, one of its wings touching his nipple, which is pierced. She looks at the ground, then looks up again, sees he is still watching her.

She sees his eyes, sable brown and feminine, almond shaped with thick lashes. The rest of his face is horrible, as if he's been in an accident. The kind of accident men get into when they get loaded and fight each other. His nose is flat and flared, smashed up and broken, and his lips are bulbous, crooked under a pencil-thin moustache. He is bald and pockmarked with over-size ears that point up at an obscene stance. His head is too small for his body and his eyes are too large for his pitiful face. His arms and hands are immense, muscular, and he is swaybacked. She knows he is younger than she is. He doesn't make sense to her. She is used to men who are easy to decipher, size up, control.

He spits, stretches his arms above his head in a sudden wave of rain and lets his muscles flex, then yawns, scratches his armpit, and grins at her. His two front teeth are silver. One of his eyebrows is half-singed off. Then he looks down at his crotch and up at her, licking his lips. Faith is not frightened. She is surprised. She watches him from across the dirt lot and is entranced, thinking of the same fascination she experienced watching her first pornographic film, for those beginning minutes, until the repetition began to bore her. It's those beginning minutes when everything is alive, Faith thinks. She realizes he has broken through. She is too tired to smile.

The Tilt-A-Whirl begins to gyrate and wheeze,

spining in half circles, undecided. The Mexican couple
are in the car next to her. The ride picks up and she
suddenly likes the way her back is slammed against the
metal, the circles that hit hard. What is the music? Bon-
nie Raitt is singing "Tangled and Dark," but only the
pulse of the song comes through as the wheels of the
Tilt-A-Whirl mainline and spit sparks and oil. She likes
the incoherence and cacophony. She understands it. She
wants everything she can understand.

When she gets off the ride, her legs are weak. He
is at the gate. Smiling as though they are friends.

"You are one beautiful woman. And that car blows
me away. I saw you come in, you know. I watched you.
You going on all the rides tonight? I can tell. Got nothing
better to do, do you? I'll go on them with you."

Faith walks by him. This silence is making her mad.
Nothing will form in her mouth. Her vocal chords sting.
She turns around and stares at his chest, his arms, and
pockmarked cheeks. His bald head, covered with drops
of rain.

"Bet you think I'm a carny, don't you? I'm not. I
live around the corner. I'm easy to find, baby. In the
trailer park around the corner. There's only one."

Faith tries to breathe. Her chest is tight.

"Let's go on the Fire Wheel. You want to. Come
on. Maybe lightning'll hit us. Maybe you'll touch me.
Maybe I'll tell you poetry men tell women who are lost
at night. Come on."

His voice is soft and basso hoarse. He effortlessly
puts his arm around Faith and walks her over to the
Fire Wheel, almost lifting her off the ground. For some
reason she closes her eyes. Then she knows. It is to
feel another man's arms around her, record the sensation.

"You're stoned, aren't you? Bet it's some kind of

rich lady's drug. You got a couple for me? Give me some later and I'll fuck all night. Dare me."

His muscles are surprisingly soft or it is soft skin wrapped around stone, she is not sure. The Fire Wheel looks like an angel-food-cake pan with leather straps and caged sides. Faith can see it turns around furiously and glues people to its sides. Centrifugal force. It is orange and withering black, children's Halloween colors. Candy corn and papier-mâché.

She doesn't know why this man is touching her or his name or if Ted is dead. She is completely disconnected, a visitor to eight-thirty at night, a place that will be gone in the morning. She is not frightened. She is going on all the rides.

He grabs two tickets from the roll clutched in her hand.

"You're going to like this. You're going to like me. I want you real bad, lady, I got a hard-on right now and you're not saying a word. You let me around you and I like that. When we get on, I want you to let me touch you."

Faith stares at his giant's back, at his ass when he pushes ahead of her like a child.

"Come here. You can use the straps if you like. Nah, don't use them. I want to be able to crawl all over you. Look, we're the only people on the ride."

He positions her next to him. Faith feels dizzy from the fourth Valium she has taken in the car. She might faint and suddenly she doesn't care. She knows she will be picked up. This unnamed man's shoulders are a foot higher than hers. He looks down at her and smiles. He strokes her hair. She stares straight ahead.

"You're soft."

His hands are huge and cracked; the calluses and blisters on his palms catch in her hair. He lets go and she closes her eyes again. When she opens them, he is rubbing his chest with slow even strokes, pinching his nipples and then rubbing his chest again, rapidly. He doesn't look at Faith, but whispers in a musical tone:

"Feel the eagle on my chest. Touch him. Can you feel his wings? Can you feel his feathers? He's flying. Feel him."

He takes Faith's hand and places it on the center of his chest. She doesn't feel anything except the coarseness of tattooed flesh and his heartbeat. He takes his hand away from hers as a taunt. She quietly leaves her hand there.

"Feel my nipples. Each one. Slowly. Do it."

The ride begins to lurch and slowly rotate. It builds its speed with a precision that takes Faith's breath into spasms; a cancer that is colorless and suffocates. She is thrown once again against the cage wall. One of her shoes has come off and has inched up toward her shoulder. The man has pinned one arm and leg over her; she can feel his erection on her hip, extravagant and moving with the same force as his limbs.

"See how it feels, baby. To be pinned to a wall and not be able to move. And I'm right here on you, around you."

The Fire Wheel has tilted up at a forty-five-degree angle, and they have lost gravity at the cut-rate carnival. Rain comes, then a white endurance, electric and brief, and they continue to spin, stuck to the wall, and he keeps whispering in her ear, things she cannot understand.

She does not know where he will take her, if he will be violent, if he is diseased and rambling. She is shaking her brains, she is having a good time, she is young.

"I can keep you this way forever if you like. I can keep you against a wall, allow you only your breath. We don't have to leave. We can stay this way all night, curled in midair, anything you want."

It is almost one A.M. and they have been on every
ride: the Paratrooper, the Round-Up, the Tilt-A-Whirl,
the Zipper, the Fire Wheel, the Cliffhanger, and the
Octopus. She doesn't remember the rest. He has whispered obscenities and hung them like doves at her neck.
He has held her like a father, made her touch his genitals, and touched her vagina through her briefs, rubbing her pubic hair with his immense hands until it
hurt. He's licked her brassiere through her silk dress
until there are great spots on the front that stink of his
breath. He has made her close her eyes most of the
night.

On solid ground her legs give way. He buys her a
beer with quarters out of her purse and she does not
care. She takes another Valium, thinking soon she could
be someone else. He lights a cigarette and holds it to
her lips. As she smokes through his hand, she smells
semen and tobacco and an utterance of night that can
cure, the perfume of men and chants she has suddenly
heard, as if they were delivered.

Then they are dancing in the parking lot, her Jaguar
door open, Harry Connick, Jr., singing on the tape deck.
She does not remember putting it on. The men in the
shadows are there, watching, sitting on their cars. Certain cars are rattling where they are having sex. He is
holding her against him with both arms and her feet
are dragging the ground. She is coherent and calm. She
is listening.

"I'm the poet, baby, who's waiting for you."

He's ugly as a tropical flower with overwaxed leaves
that fight for sunlight in the steam. She wonders if there
are tattoos on his penis, if he sat, drunk, in front of the
tattoo artist, keeping it hard as he wiped tiny dots of
blood away as the ink went in.

"Baby, I can take you to a place where there's an

earthquake every day. In the desert between the Salton Sea and the Mexican border, where rocks move and men make women shake."

He lets his mustache brush against her earring, then along the ridge of her ear.

"I'll fuck you so hard and so often the only smell you'll know is me, the only God you'll know is me, the only food you'll want is me. I'll keep you wet all day and crying for me at night. I'll lick and clean you like a dog and I won't let you out of my sight."

His breath smells of tequila and chocolate mints. Faith can feel it on the fine hair of her cheek. He brushes his lips against hers and she smells marijuana, motorcycle exhaust, flames. The storm has not let up, the fires have not ceased, and the carnival is still buzzing in the pitch.

"I'll teach you how to suck my beautiful big cock and lick my balls. I'll teach you over and over until you get it right. I'll save all my come for you, baby. I'll fuck you in the ass and eat your pretty pussy while I'm fucking you. I'll comb your hair while you sleep and play with your titties while you dream of me, so you're wet when you wake up."

Faith rolls her head and looks at the sky. She must look at the sky. It will have answers. It will explain to her what season it is, why she is still alive, where she is.

"I'll make you laugh. I'll feed you snakes and wild birds. I'll make you jewelry from Indian heads and quartz. I'll teach you how to slow dance on the fault line, with fire under our feet, where we could drop in if the earth shifts. I'll teach you the music of rivers and canyons. I'll drink your sweat and paint you in the sand."

Faith almost speaks. Then closes her eyes.

"I'll take you to Mexico and South America and we'll get lost in towns with four-room hotels. We'll put on shows and teach the whores how to do it. We'll travel only on nights with no clouds so we can see the moon. I'll love you."

Faith begins to back away from him. He becomes rapid. His voice a growl. His chest becomes tight. He squeezes his cock through his pants.

"Look at it. It's yours. I live in a trailer park. I eat out of cans and write poetry on paper towels. I need money and I need you."

Faith watches this man, this child animal with a broken nose and pierced nipples, and she knows he is a narcotic, the hesitation before the rush, and she is waiting. Waiting to feel it on her skin, waiting for the blood to seep through Ted's brain and then into his lungs in the ancient language of lightning.

"So what do you do, little lady with a silk dress and a silver car? I'll give you everything. Stay with me tonight and don't go back. I'm desperate and alone. We're all alone. Forget where you came from. Let me fuck the words out of your throat."

She can hear the gasp of two men in the shadows. A car has stopped shaking. Thunder.

"What's the matter? Can't you talk? You're not deaf. Or mute. You're just playing with your own little balls of shit."

"My husband's dying." Her own voice surprises her. It must belong to someone else. It sounds hollow and pinched like a Hollywood woman, an old woman who cannot be taught. Faith reasons she is already a widow and has been for many years. She steadies herself and pulls away completely from him.

"Let him die. Kill him. Kill him for me. Put the son of a bitch out of his misery. I'll give you my address. I'm easy to find. If you want, I'll kill him for you. I'll be gentle. You want me to use a pillow, a gun, a knife, just let me know. I'll fuck you after. I'll fuck you so hard you won't care. You won't be afraid anymore."

Faith listens to the silence, staring at him. He looks like a child.

"I got nothing to lose, lady, and there's only one thing I want. I want a woman. I jack off all day long. I can do it for hours. I don't care what I have to do to get you. I'm lonely and I want a woman to love me. You."

The lights of the Octopus and the Fire Wheel are being turned off. The storm is focused east, and the sky is still lit at intervals, but it has become a warm glow, translucent yellow. Faith is aware of the streetlights, of police lights at another end of the lot, and she gets into her car. She has her keys somewhere, the ignition of course, they have to be in the ignition for the tape to play. The men in the shadows have become distant and they, too, are dispersing.

She could go home now. She can talk, feel the blood in her neck. The man is still standing in the middle of the parking lot.

She had expected him to grab her hair and pull her into the dark. She would float. But he didn't. He just stood there as she got in the Jaguar and slammed the door shut.

"I want a woman to love me."

Faith turns the ignition key.

"Come back to me when he dies."

It is her birthday. Faith checks her lips in the rear-view mirror and slowly pulls out of the lot. She will have to remember where she is.

A week later Ted is dead. Two weeks after that Faith has bought two tickets to Cancun, converted her jewelry into dollars and pesos, put the house up for sale, and declared bankruptcy. She now talks, only about business, facts, essentials. Los Angeles is covered with the linen of crisp winter flowers and a warm midday sun, the haze of the Pacific and the sense that things are real, if only for a matter of days.

She has bought an extra ticket for the man at the carnival. If she cannot find him, she will cash it in at the airport. She has everything she owns in one bag, has bought a supply of Valium that should last a month or more. The Jaguar has been turned in and she has a rental car and she is driving through Reseda, trying to remember where the carnival was, which allotted dirt park was singed by it.

There is no trailer park. She keeps driving, looking for something that would be part of him. She is driving too fast. She rolls around a corner and suddenly finds it. It is early, and dawn comes in a henna flame. She has watched the sky every day since Ted's death and she has promised herself she will watch it in Mexico. It is now her companion.

Faith considers what will happen in Mexico. That one day she will wake up with this man, whose skin is a childhood taste, like sickness and cough syrup. That it will end. He will walk into the jungle, wait for another woman, and hunt. She will start swimming in the Caribbean and not stop. Or maybe not swim at all.

The trailer park is just as he said it was. Around the corner, but there were a hundred vacant lots. She drives slowly down the narrow trailer-park drive, past Chinese lanterns and tiny fences. She stops the car and gets out and walks in the early A.M. shiver. He said he was easy to find.

She sees a sleeping blanket with a mass huddled in front of the office trailer. She walks over to it and looks down. She kicks it. She doesn't care. As the bundle moves over, she sees his face covered with blood that has dried. He has been fighting.

They will sleep in Mexico, clean and oiled. She will rub his body in the sun, watch the eagle writhe under her thumb, the woman on the dragon glittering on her palm. She will absorb his desperation until they are both without language or thought.

He opens his eyes and looks up at her. He is naked under the sleeping blanket. He has lost his clothes. He smiles.

Cool and Clean and Crisp

Mark Butler

My friend shook me awake. "Get up, get up! Get up before it's too late!" I didn't understand. This was the beach. It was *never* too late to get into the volleyball game. It went on forever. Then I realized there was something in my hand. It was a can of beer. It felt cool and clean and crisp. She must have put it there. My God, this girl . . . already nurturing me! I sat up and watched the game. The players were lean and athletic and moved with grace and skill, and every one of them held a can of beer as they leaped and dove and spiked. And they never spilled a drop! The rock and roll you grew up with blasted out of a stereo you couldn't see. The sun was warm but not hot, and there wasn't one drop of dirty sweat on one single person on that beach. Beautiful bikini-clad women carefully positioned in beach chairs gazed out at the water through mysterious dark designer sunglasses. They all held cans of beer. The game went on but she wasn't in it and I panicked. My friend was yelling gibberish in my ear. "Get out of here! This isn't *real!* Get a life!" I took a swig of my beer. It was cool and clean and crisp.

We had argued about this before. He didn't seem to understand: this was the life. The people who created this were creating the life. And here I was, in the life. My friend wasn't making much sense. He thought it was all fake. He thought it was one big commercial. Maybe it was. So what?

He was always talking about depth. Life and depth. I wasn't exactly sure what this meant, although it sounded like a cool title for a surfing movie. But I didn't have time for this. She was missing. I looked around the beach; I looked in the water. Nowhere. Then suddenly a warm ocean breeze brushed my cheek, and I knew it was her. I looked up to the sky, and there she was—the breasts of the universe swooping down on a parasail over the clear blue sea. Huge round nipples protruded through her wet beer-slogan T-shirt: one nipple through Cool, the other through Clean. Crisp was superimposed over her lintless belly button.

My friend was in front of me, waving his arms in my face and screaming. I couldn't hear a word, and worse yet, he was blocking my view. I got up and moved, but he moved, too. I started to go around, but he stuck his hip out, bumping into my beer can. Aaaah! Somehow, miraculously, I kept the can balanced and didn't spill a single drop. I pushed him aside and squinted into the horizon. Where was she? *Where was she?* Wait! There! There she was! She swooped!

She dipped! She was a bird! A bird in a shoelace bikini! She maneuvered the parasail expertly. With one hand! Her other hand was poised with her can of beer. Then it happened . . . she saw me! Taking a swig of beer, she let go of the parasail (no hands!) and waved, her breasts shimmering in the golden sunlight. Cool. Clean. She was suspended in midair for a split second. Time stood still. The volleyball players dropped to their knees. A guitar riff filled the sky. A passing priest in Bermuda shorts uttered extreme unction as he sipped his one-calorie cola. The lifeguard wept, unashamed. I had to have her again. I took a step toward the water. My friend grabbed me by the shoulders and shook. *"This is not real! This is not real life!"* I subdued him with a stun gun I had picked up that morning at the 7-11. This was no time for his fruitcake philosophy.

I continued to walk, never taking my eyes off her. She saw me again and smiled. Oh! The sun lurched suddenly toward her glistening white teeth, confounding the solar system. The earth shifted out of its orbit. The ground shook violently. Volcanoes erupted. Giant crevices split the sand. We lost a six-pack. I sidestepped the oncoming tidal wave and kept my balance, spilling nothing. It was game point, her nipples were still hard, and I quickened my pace. My quivering friend pulled himself out of a crevice and pleaded with me to stop. I wasn't listening.

She was soaring higher and higher. The clouds gave way. Planes stopped in midair. A bewildered seagull announced his retirement to a packed press conference. I was at the water's edge. My friend tried to talk, but his mouth was full of sand. He was gesturing wildly. His face was red, his hair was on end, and I finally understood.

He was an idiot.

No matter. I was wading now, knee-deep in the water. I reached up to the sky. Then I heard a click behind me and turned to see my friend, with a perfectly legal semiautomatic assault rifle. He pointed, aimed, and started to squeeze the trigger as tears streamed down his face.

"This is for your own good!" Suddenly out of nowhere came the volleyball, cracking him in the skull like a rock. He dropped onto the sand, facedown and out cold. I looked over at the game and there they were: the players, the dudes, the babes, my comrades, my buddies to her bosom. They were blond and lean and handsome or blond and lean and beautiful. Some were sandy blond. They were the rebels. So the group of them laughed and gave me the thumbs-up as they chugged. Nice shot, guys.

Then the old crew came over, and one by one they stepped on my friend's head, giggling. They dared each other to mush his face further and further down into the sand, playing. They built a campfire, roasted weenies, told stories, shed a few tears, hugged, belched, buried him upside down to his ankles and held burning matches to his toes. Bonding.

Then they all slapped me with a high five as I started my climb up the golden rope to the parasail . . . to the sky . . . to her, and when I got there, she smiled that smile, balanced me on her beer can, and maneuvered us into a cloud. She ruled the wind. Then we did it, like we had done it so many times before. Only this time we did it in space, floating at the end of the string like a cosmic kite with two tails, and in the interest of safe sex I pulled out at the last second (ending the local drought), but of course leaving her completely satisfied as usual. Her orgasmic scream was so intense that it actually broke the sound barrier, and very nearly disrupted the new volleyball game.

I don't think my friend's my friend anymore. He

just doesn't get it. He wants to think. He wants to talk. There's nothing to think about. There's nothing to talk about. Watch man . . . watch. You can't talk with sand in your mouth. Sand belongs between your toes.

Now I hang out where the sun always shines, while he sits there and waits for the rain, and he can't even handle his beer! Hah! Hates the beach, but I knew as soon as we got here that this was the place for me. This was the place for a person to be and this was where I was. And when we got here, we drank all day and all night and laughed and danced and sweated clean sweat and never argued. And these were the most amazing people; no matter how much they drank they never got drunk, and no matter how many days in a row they drank they never got fat. And they didn't seem to work although they occasionally talked about having spectacular modern jobs in shadowy creative offices.

I knew if I stayed long enough, I would become one of them. That was the day I waiting for.

But suddenly the sky got dark so we had to move. The sinewy young men slipped into their torn T-shirts, and the lean, luscious young women slipped onto their sinewy young men, and they jumped into their Jeeps and I jumped with her into the back of a 1994 all-terrain vehicle driven by the guy who always brought the Frisbee and the dog that everyone liked.

We got into the Land Rover just as the storm hit, and she caught just enough rain to make her hair so sexy wet that we just had to do it one more time, so I strapped her down roughly in the backseat with the safety belt as she pouted. Invitingly. The aesthetic rain drummed down on the cloth convertible roof, and a completely appropriate moody-but-just-rockin'-enough song played on the stereo. All right, Mr. Power Ballad! How on earth did you know?

Finally, as we rolled on down the highway, I mounted her as she squirmed rain-wet slippery silly under the bondage of state law, moaned, "Oh, what a feeling!" and balanced our beer cans on her breasts. Then, as I drove her perfect willing ass into the soft Corinthian leather, I looked out the back window toward the beach and saw my friend, in the downpour, upside down in the sand with his wiggling toes aflame, and the only thing I could think of was "Who cares?"

Unsafe Sex

Pat Califia

Malcolm loves me for myself. If I put on fifteen pounds, he worries—not because it's unattractive, but because it's not good for my health. I'm sure Malcolm doesn't jack off in a frenzy, yanking on his tits while he visualizes isolated parts of my body—my dick, quivering to hold itself up, my asshole spread wide with both my palms flat against my cheeks, the little smear of hair that decorates my booth-tanned crack.

In fact, I'm not sure he jacks off at all. But wouldn't it be peculiar if he didn't? Malcolm probably masturbates just often enough to be well adjusted. Then I bet he gets up and changes the sheets.

No, what we have is a mature, adult gay relationship. As k. d. lang says, "Sex is an important thing, but it is not *the* thing." It is my whole self that engages Malcolm. He is patient and considerate, thoughtful and kind. He never forgets anniversaries, birthdays, or holidays. He even sends out cards to my parents for Mother's Day and Father's Day.

I am the perfect other half of this perfect relationship. Malcolm and I live in a midtown-Manhattan co-op. Every square foot of it cost a few thousand dollars, and we deserve it. We've decided it's okay to take good care of ourselves. We need our home to be a haven, a retreat from the dog-eat-dog, mercenary atmosphere of the business world. We can afford security. That's because we work hard at our respective professions. Malcolm is an attorney; I own a travel agency. We have health insurance, medical powers of attorney, and wills that we update every two years. We are each other's beneficiary on our life insurance policies. Our prosperity counselor has helped us to create a safety net for our old age.

Malcolm and I do not use words like *fabulous*. We do not own pets. There is nothing more ludicrous than grown men slobbering over small, fluffy dogs. We do not go disco dancing (although we did when we were dating). Only 10 percent of our video library is porn. We keep the K-Y and the condoms in the bathroom. Sexual paraphernalia on display in the bedroom is just a little gauche, don't you think? We had our six weeks of mating frenzy, but we're safely past the honeymoon phase now, thank God. Our relationship is held together by much more than just fucking.

We walk with Dignity in the annual Christopher Street march, but we would never be caught dead at one of those poorly planned, inflammatory temper tantrums that the little boys with the nose rings and the Doc Martens are so fond of staging. Do they really care about anything besides getting on the evening news? I don't think gaining personal notoriety is necessary to promote social change. Malcolm's family in Connecticut would slit their wrists if we got ourselves on the front page of the *Daily News*.

We make an annual donation to the Gay Men's Health Crisis because we have to take care of our own. Malcolm and I would really love to find some time for volunteer work. But if we had time to volunteer, we wouldn't be able to afford that sizable contribution, would we? Oh, and we don't give handouts to panhandlers. The taxes we pay to provide welfare are quite enough, thank you. I'll grant you, the homeless are a terrible problem. They make it so hard to get into the subway stations. So I give my spare change to cabdrivers instead. At least they're working. Although you'd think if they planned to stay in this country, they'd have the courtesy to learn to speak English.

Like so many other hardworking men who just happen to be homosexual, all Malcolm and I want is our little piece of the American dream. We have to take responsibility for proving that the stereotype of the promiscuous, narcissistic clone is false. We are men first, gays second, but we don't want to make a fetish out of our masculinity, either (although Malcolm needs to add a few more squats to his routine to build up those flabby calves). Oh, and you should have seen the look on his face when I told him I wanted a diamond ear stud for our last anniversary! I must say, I was more than happy to take this Rolex instead. We don't want to be bitchy, but we deplore those members of our community who continue to live out mainstream America's flamboyant and perverse images of the gay lifestyle—the Queer Nation kids in their kilts and pierced eyebrows, the tattooed leatherboys, the diesel dykes on bikes. I will admit it makes us a wee bit resentful that their freedom to slander the rest of us was won at our expense, through the efforts of decent, ordinary men like ourselves.

But you shouldn't think we're dull. We try to keep the playful and spontaneous spirit of our limerence phase alive. We don't want to lose touch with the child within. We have our wild and crazy side. We're even thinking of buying a Miata.

Malcolm is working late again. I wonder when that new assistant of his is going to get the hang of the firm's filing system. It's too bad Malcolm's not trying to teach him his numbers instead of his letters. They could use Malcolm's dick for a yardstick, then they'd only have to go up to six.

When Malcolm phoned with this news, I told him I might not be in when he gets home. I have to take care of a sick friend. And it's the truth. How could I ever lie to sweet, decent, open, trusting Malcolm? Let's be real. My dick is the sickest friend I've got. If I asked him, I'm sure Malcolm wouldn't dream of trying to isolate me within our relationship. Outside interests enhance a couple's intimacy.

Tonight, I want somebody who does not love me for myself. I want somebody who does not love me at all. And I want someone I can adore blindly. Someone to worship. It has to be just the right person. Not everybody can be an icon, even for the ten minutes it usually takes for me to suck them off. No, it has to be a big man with a hint of brutality, more than a hint of the animal, the bestial. Somebody strong and domineering who will be deaf to my comfort or my history, somebody who doesn't care about my taste in restaurants or the location of my seat at the opera. But he can't be too smart. I don't want to talk to him, for chrissake. And no kissy fags who will ask me for my phone number. I don't want to found a cult, y'know, I just want to throw myself down, grovel, get used, and get up and go home.

I take a cab to the meatpacking district and walk

around. They closed the Mineshaft a long time ago. I have no idea what took them so long. But honestly, what do they think went on there that doesn't go on now in the alleys and culs-de-sac that surround that foul pest-hole, that shit-encrusted and semen-drenched toilet, that firetrap that was probably saved from going up in flames only by the hundreds of quarts of piss that were sprayed upon it every night?

Most of the streetlights are busted. The streets are paved with brick and cobblestone and garbage. Mud and less palatable things clog the storm drains and gutters. It isn't dark yet (I'm not that much of a fool), but the hookers are already starting to stake their turf.

I can't help but stare at one whose starved-looking midriff is a moon crater between her metallic silver halter top and a cracked, black vinyl skirt. I can tell she's a girl because she doesn't have any cleavage, just an exposed collarbone and knobby shoulders. The only ones who still have tits are the queens on hormones. Boys or girls, their stockingless feet are crammed into thrift-store high heels. All of them wear a score of rubber bracelets and probably have a tattoo. Some of them come out in tattered lingerie. It makes you wonder what on earth they change into to go to bed—if they ever sleep in a bed.

Why do whores put all of their makeup on their eyelids or their lips, and nowhere else? It makes the ornamented part of the face jump out at you. The effect is rather frightening and carnivorous. How can anybody let that into a car with them? I can only believe that the act of paying is much more important to their johns than the indifferent blow jobs they will get from these strung-out crash cases.

I give up trying to figure out which ones are really girls and which ones are boys. They might as well all be fish to me. When I see them, I don't feel that pull in my gut as if somebody were trying to make violin strings out of my intestines. I don't feel my teeth set on edge and grow points. I don't feel my knees tremble and my throat get thick with the phlegm I'm about to be forced to cough up.

Still, the hookers glare at me. They fold their arms, plant their feet, and give me looks as sharp as the razors in their ratty wigs. Tricking for free offends their morality. Little do they know what I am willing to pay for this evening's adventure.

Then I see him. It never fails. I have sometimes wondered why the fates always send us out together, me and the object of my desire, and how they manage to guide us so that our paths will cross. He is a big, black man wearing boots and leather pants, a police shirt, and a Sam Browne belt. No badge. That's good. Phony police badges are such a turnoff. His leather cap is pushed so far back on his head, he must be a little drunk. His face does not move to acknowledge my presence. But he hesitates a split second before stepping off the street into an alley, and once around the corner, he makes enough noise to let me know he has stepped behind the first Dumpster.

I come upon him pissing up the wall. The yellow jet is so fierce, I imagine he will hit the fire escape. It is quite honestly one of the biggest dicks I have ever seen. He smiles at me, obviously expecting me to be impressed. I have a master's degree in sociology from Columbia University. What kind of brainless twinkie does he think I am, to be swept off my feet by that old chestnut, that tired staple of stale pornography, the muscular, mean, black hunk with a monster piece of sex-meat?

One of my knees lands on something mushy and wet. There is a piece of gravel under the other. I shift to avoid both of these unpleasant trifles and shuffle (crawl, really) onto blessed dry, dirty brick.

"Why, lookee what we got here. We got us a cute little cocksucker, just look at the doggie hang his tongue out and beg. Wanna chase this bone, white boy? Wanna get force-fed some real man-stuff? This is gonna make you pant for sure. Open wide and show me you want it, white boy. Beg for me."

While he is saying all this, I am making the appropriate whining noises. I've never done this before, but I discover that I know how. It's a latent ability, sort of like my talent for collecting on delinquent accounts. He reaches into his jacket pocket. The only way out of this narrow back street is the way we came in. I wonder nervously what the hell he has in there. A knife? Tear gas? A stun gun?

Something much, much worse. A condom! I can't believe it. I actually back away half a shuffle.

"What the hell do you think you're doing?" I say. Actually, I'm afraid I snarl. It's not the best way to encourage a topman, but my libidinous dreams are going up in latex-scented smoke.

"Wrappin' my joint," he says matter-of-factly, as if this were a natural part of what we are about to do with one another.

"That's really not necessary," I say.

"Who asked you? You think I want your white-bread fag disease?"

This blatantly homophobic remark from a leather freak who is so obviously queer in his butch drag compared to me in my casual J. Crew clothes makes me choke. I like being called a cocksucker and a fag as well as any other man fortunate enough to be born with a throat like an Accu-Jac, but this is too much. I wonder what he'd do if I called him the *n* word?

He continues to put on the rubber. "Oh, come on, it won't even go all the way up!" I protest. "Look, it only covers a third of your dick."

"Tell you what, if you can get anything besides the head of this big banana in your mouth, I'll peel it for you, baby. Now get over here and do your job."

Before I can tell him this is not safe, sane, and consensual, he is fucking my face. I squirm and twist, but he has me by the hair. All this resistance means that his erection isn't getting enough traction. "Stop that," he says sharply, cuffing me, then grabs me again. "I'm gonna kick your nuts up around your ears if you don't cut that shit out and suck my dick, you pussy-face fag. You know you want it, and I'm gonna make sure you get what you want and a little bit more."

He is wearing heavy boots. Their steel toes can probably do all the damage that he promises. When rape is inevitable, you might as well relax and enjoy it. I try, I really do.

"Don't like the way that tastes, do you, punk? Tell me what you like, you scum-sucking cunt. Do you like uncut dick that's gotten really raunchy, grown itself a real crop of cheese? Or would you rather drink rank bitter piss out of truck drivers' hoses? Or is your thing just plain old spunk, huh, white boy? Seems to me a gourmet like yourself ought to be relieved to have nothing on his breath after he gives a blow job but a clean old condom."

I'm trying to prove that he was wrong about how much of his dick I could get down, but it's hard to point out my success when he's so busy enjoying it. I'm losing my tonsils to the Roto-Rooter man. But nobody wants a piece of rough trade who's using protection!

"I wanna fuck you, baby. You got a cute ass for a white boy. That's a nice little bubble butt that's restin' on your heels. Bet it's even tighter than your throat, ain't it, cocksucker? Drop your pants, bend over, lemme see that tiny pink hole."

I'm only too happy to oblige. But I make sure I position myself facing the main street, so he is not between me and an exit. Surely now, I think, now he will want to plunge all the way into my aching furrow, and he will have to dispense with that ridiculous barrier. But when I hint at this, he says, "I'm getting real tired of your bullshit, princess. Whatchoo want me to do, tear you a new asshole? Let's just go for a ride and you quit your bitchin'."

I make one more attempt to get what I really want, and he slaps my butt. Hard. So hard it takes my breath away. I hate that. Of course, it also makes my asshole open up like an umbrella. He's a marvelous fuck. It takes a lot of skill to drive something that big. Too many well-hung men think all they have to do is the old in-out. But this man is teasing me, stroking all points of the compass, doing everything inside me except turn cartwheels. I wish it were enough, I really do. But I know he isn't going to lose his stinking, filthy load in me, really use me, soil and despoil me. And without the fillip of that violation and defilement, I can't let go.

"You like come so much, I wanna see yours," he pants. "Get it out and jack it off, boy. Show your master how much you love making his hard dick."

The stupid thing is hard, of course. It apparently doesn't realize we aren't having a good time. I told you it was my sickest friend. So I dutifully beat my meat, agreeing with everything he says, echoing the names he calls me, swiveling my butt as if I were Catherine the Great and this were the last member of my guard who could still get it up. He is sir, he is daddy, he is my master, and he owns my ass. I am a dirty bitch, a high-pocket slut for hard cock.

"Don't you dare come without permission," he hisses, but it's too late. I flood my palm and the ground below us. He shoves even further into me, which gets him close enough to grab my wrist. He forces my hand up to my face and smears my sticky fingers across my nose and mustache. "You like jizz so much, lick that off your lips," he sneers. Then he yanks on my hips, bucks three times, and comes.

There isn't even time to say, "I hate you." I see them coming long before he does—a small gang of undernourished urban youths carrying baseball bats, car antennas, and what looks like a brick tied in a pillow-case. I have to get away! I push him and all the disappointment he represents away from me and hear him fetch up against the Dumpster as I bolt out of the alley. I sprint to the corner, whistling and yanking on my trousers. A cab miraculously pulls over. There is no time to look back, only time to throw open its door and escape.

During the ride home, I brood about how safe I will feel once I am back in my own space with its Persian rugs, Shaker furniture, and David Hockney prints. I mustn't forget to take my Elavil tonight. I will brew a pot of chamomile tea and listen to Debussy. Do you think it's really possible that Malcolm loves me for myself?

Elegy for Andy Gibb

Danielle Willis

When I was ten or eleven, my friend Miriam and I would sit on her bed reading *Tiger Beat* magazine and making out with the pillows. Her pillow was Scott Baio and my pillow was Andy Gibb. At that time, everyone was divided into bitter factions as to whether Shaun Cassidy, Scott Baio, John Travolta, or Andy Gibb was the most gorgeous guy in the world. There were some girls who liked Leif Garrett, but the general consensus was that he was too faggy. And the girls who liked Rod Stewart or Mick Jagger were definitely total sluts.

As far as I was concerned, Andy Gibb was the one for me. When my parents weren't home, I would steal my father's *Penthouse* and masturbate to the letters in Forum, imagining that the protagonists were me and Andy Gibb, except that I skipped over the oral sex because that was gross and besides, I knew that Andy Gibb would never want anything as disgusting as a blow job anyway. I could tell that just by looking at his picture. He was so much cooler than the other Bee Gees.

One night while I was masturbating, I had my first orgasm. My hips jerked upward and my vaginal walls started contracting violently. I was sure I had done myself an internal injury. I ran to the bathroom and sat on the toilet seat until the contractions stopped. Later, I confessed everything to my mother, who then yelled at my father for having *Penthouse* lying around where I could find it. She made him have a talk with me. He sat on the edge of my bed looking at the floor and explained that dirty old men like himself got turned on by magazines like *Penthouse* and that I shouldn't let it affect me. I told him I got turned on, too. He adjusted his glasses and went and got my mother.

My mother closed the bedroom door and whispered that masturbation was okay as long as I didn't stick anything inside myself. I could hurt myself that way, she said. Eight years later when I was seventeen and having my first lesbian affair, she took me aside and told me that a man could like my pussy as well as a woman. I asked her if she'd ever made a trial comparison, and she told me not to talk like that. She also used to have my father check on my little brother in the bathtub to make sure his penis was developing correctly. Anyway, back to Andy Gibb.

Shortly after my mother's warning about phallic objects I began to fuck myself with shampoo bottles and Mitchum deodorant sticks. I wouldn't use carrots or cucumbers because that would be a waste of food. I'd lie there plugging away with myself imagining that

Andy Gibb and I were fucking under a table at a crowded restaurant and that afterward we were going for a ride in his private plane. I could just see his pale blue, wide-collared, satin disco shirt fluttering in the night breeze as we boarded the Lear jet from atop his penthouse apartment.

I was a slob even back then and I never washed my shampoo bottles and deodorant sticks. I kept them hidden under my bed where they soon acquired a thick linty fuzz. I started getting yeast infections and decided Mom had been right and turned to God. Our housekeeper was a Jehovah's Witness who was only too happy to steer me down the path to salvation. I brought the Bible to school with me every day and read it during lunch period, and every night I prayed that I not be tempted to abuse myself. I even threw away all my *Tiger Beat*s.

This lasted until I saw *The Rocky Horror Picture Show* a few months later. The sight of Tim Curry in full makeup wearing nothing but a garter belt, a leather bustier, and a pair of rhinestone platform shoes was enough to ruin me for both Jesus and Andy Gibb for the rest of my life. I got myself a fresh shampoo bottle that I actually took care to wash after using and the years went by. I went to high school and started fucking girls and cutting classes on Fridays so I could take the Long Island Railroad into the city and go to the East Village. I was very avant-garde. I dressed like a medieval page and my favorite movie was *Eraserhead*. I listened to the Velvet Underground and wrote experimental poems with titles like *Love/Death/Dissolution*. My ambition was to become a performance artist.

When I graduated I went to Barnard, the same school as Laurie Anderson. My roommate was a Southern Baptist named Sorina, who I later found out was also a former Andy Gibb fan. Now she was into Michael Jackson even though he was black and she didn't believe in interracial marriages. When I told her I was gay, she dressed in the bathroom for a week. Later we came to the agreement that I could have my girlfriend Jean sleep over every other weekend as long as we didn't make "kissy-kissy" noises. That would be against her religion. I used to enjoy silently finger-fucking Jean in the dark while Sorina said her prayers in the next bed.

Later that year Jean and I broke up. I had a nervous breakdown and was asked to leave Barnard until such time as I could provide written statements from two different psychiatrists that I was stable enough to continue my studies. I went to live with my parents for a few months where I was prescribed a great deal of psychological medication and hung out with science fiction nerds who practiced witchcraft and had group sex to Glen Campbell records. Eventually I moved to San Francisco and started dating transvestites and working as a stripper. I dyed my hair black, went through a can of Aqua Net Extra Super Hold every day, fucked myself with dildos to songs about necrophilia, and published a book of poetry called *Corpse Delectable*. Nobody suspected that I had once entered a contest whose grand prize was a fifteen-minute phone call from Andy Gibb.

Anyway, the day he died I was sitting in a torture chamber in Berkeley crossing and uncrossing my legs in agony because my golden-shower client was almost twenty minutes late. I reached for the newspaper to distract me from my now almost uncontrollable urge to run to the bathroom, and there on the front page of the entertainment section was the headline "Andy Gibb Dead of Natural Causes at Age 30," along with an airbrushed photo of Andy in his heyday. He really was cute.

R.I.P.

Finally, a Coherent Explanation of Straight White Male Sexuality

Sigfried Gold

I want to be all over the place at the same time. I can't stand being locked up in one little perspective, in one little train of thought. I'm a man, though. I think linearly. It sucks. It makes me very uncomfortable. I was just talking to a boy, a young man, Ray. He works at this coffee house by here, and we've known each other more than a year. He's an archconservative. He's learning history and philosophy and literature now. He wants to be a writer. He wants to leave something behind. He wants to justify his existence. I tried to tell him it was impossible. There is nothing a straight white man can say in this time that makes the slightest bit of difference. Especially if he just wants to follow in the tradition of all the other great straight white guys. We've been having these discussions for a while. I think he used to think that he was just greater than me, and I only didn't believe in greatness because I would never achieve it for myself. At least now he thinks I'm smart, because the more he reads, the more he realizes how much I've read. I am quite a powerful man, almost a great man, because I've read a lot. I want to get fucked up the ass. And I really want a girlfriend. Lately I've been fantasizing about a girlfriend fucking me up the ass with a dildo. Does that make me gay? Probably not. I did call a man to ask him on a date tonight. That's more gay, I suppose, but I really don't want him to be my girlfriend. Although I wouldn't mind him fucking me. But I'm such a prude that I would probably never let him fuck me unless we were going steady. And I don't go steady with men. Well, maybe I would. I wish I had breasts. I would definitely go steady with men if I had breasts. I think about this kind of stuff all the time. Does that make me gay? Queer, anyway. Or a mild sort of pervert. Maybe I should be like one of those weird straight white crossdresser men who go on the Montel Williams show with their wives. And their wives say, "My husband certainly likes women. I can vouch for that. [Looks suggestively at husband; husband looks virile in prim white dress and pumps.] And I don't mind when he wears my clothes, I have plenty of clothes." Maybe I'm not one to talk, but I think those people are weird. I'm sure next year or the year after they will be organized and it will be very politically incorrect to say they are weird, that's why I'm saying it now, while I can still get away with it.

But I don't want to be a married man who wears his wife's clothing. Maybe I have mild transsexual tendencies, but there's no way in hell I'm giving myself to a surgeon to carve me out a vagina. I want God to give me a vagina, like he did the mad Dr. Schreber. And then I want God to fuck me, like he did the mad doctor. I want to be a woman. I want to have a cute girlish butt that I can wiggle on the street. If I had a cute girlish butt, I'd sure be a lot more flamboyant with it than any of the girls around my neighborhood. I want a petite, breasty figure and I want to be held in a man's strong arms. I want to be kissed by his steely lips and fucked by his authoritarian cock. But since I'm an awkward, overweight man, I want to have my clumsy head held against a woman's large breasts. See, I don't have a gay bone in my body. My imagination is purely heterosexual. It's just that I don't want to be the man. The man gets the short end of the stick in heterosexual sex. I want the long end of the stick.

When I face the fact that I'm a sad, lonely, desexualized male, I only want to rest against a woman's large breasts. I want the woman to hold me like a baby and kiss my feverish head. I want her to rock me in her arms until I feel safe. I want her to say, "There, there. You'll always be my little baby." Then she will take my little wee wee in her hand, and suddenly she will transform into a hard-muscled man, and I won't feel safe anymore. He'll be holding me, soft and vulnerable in his arms, and I will see him looking down at me with desire, and I won't feel safe at all. I will tremble with anticipation, my sphincter will turn to Jell-O. I will feel his cock harden against me, and I will be so scared of it that I have to gobble it into my mouth and cry as it strikes the back of my throat and spill my tears in his pubic hair.

I wonder why I'm not attracted to Ray. He's very cute and young. I guess because he's straight and kind of a jerk. He has a friend, Jack, whom I had a crush on, but Jack might as well be straight, he's such a jerk, too.

They're both total conservatives, but they look totally hip. Jack is into these Mortimer Adler triumph-of-the-great-white-man-type books. Talking to Jack about philosophy or literature is like squeezing your head in a vise, but otherwise he is quite adorable and has a nice sense of humor.

I should explain my prejudices about gay men and sraight men. See, as a straight man myself, it is perfectly within my rights to think that all gay men want to fuck me. All straight men think that. I'm well aware that most women don't want to fuck me, and I don't suppose that all gay men want to fuck all other gay men, but it's a special thing about being a straight man that when you meet a gay man, you can just take it for granted that he wants to fuck you. (That's why you can't have gay men in the military.) Well, personally, I find the thought of all those gay men lusting after my little jewel of a virgin asshole quite flattering, and that's why I like all gay men. And of course I can't stand straight men: they don't lust after me, I don't lust after them, so what's the point? All they want to do is win arguments with me or beat me at pool. I don't need that shit.

Pardon me, I got sidetracked. I was talking about getting fucked. About how my bright red cherry lips would pout and beg for the taste of his rigid cock. How I would push him back on the bed, my hands sliding up his bare strong chest. He's still wearing underwear, his erection straining against the waistband, struggling to get out; and I say, I want to feel your beautiful cock in my asshole, but first—I lick my glistening lips—first, can I look at it? Can I take a little peek? He's too virile to answer, but I know he means yes. I trail my red fingernails down his smooth stomach to the waistband of his underwear and slowly work my fingers under it. I glance quickly up at his face and see that he is transfixed. He is paralyzed and pumped with lust at the same time. If the mood falters for an instant, I see, he will rape my face with wild abandon, but for now I have him under my spell.

I lift the elastic of his underwear, and there is the throbbing head of his red, brown, purple cock, the color of warm meat, engorged with blood and pulsating, uncircumcised, and utterly irresistible. I moan. I wiggle my ass to show him how much I want him inside of me, and I plunge my hands into his underwear to take his balls in my hands. I want to take his cock slowly into my mouth, but I cannot, I have to have it all. The head alone fills my mouth. I push forward till it hits my throat, but I've never done this before. My big green eyes water as I look up at him, wanting his entire cock but not knowing how to get it. He pulls my head into him. I gag and cry out in pain. He furiously throws me facedown on the bed and shoves his angry cock up my ass. Oh, please, I moan. Oh, thank you. More. Deeper. Please, please, please. I come tremendously and he comes, in my ass and on my back, and I faint with pleasure.

As you can see, I really am a straight male, raised on straight pornography. Sexual pleasure mostly only comes to me through my dick. I have only ever orgasmed through friction on my dick. But my dick is actually beside the point. The reason we straight men are so obsessed with our dicks is because of our violently repressed thirst for dicks in general. I seem to care only about my dick, but I need the vision of glistening red lips to distract me from the fact that it's *my* dick. I see my dick and her lips, when what I really want is his dick and my lips. That's why we straight men are always bragging absurdly about our lusty fourteen inches, because of our profound disappointment of every day seeing the same piece of flesh protruding from our own groins and that's all we get, we never get our lips around the bigger, harder, other cock. We want the name-of-the-father phallic superduper man-meat in our mouths where we can taste it. Then somewhere in this thicket of cocks and lips, lipstick makes its appearance, convincing us utterly that these lips are hers and not ours, and through this deception, the redness of the lips produces its own excitement. But we don't need to fool ourselves anymore. Straight men need to suck cocks. That is the hidden mystery of the universe.

Intercore

M. Christian

It was the fall of 2010, and my world wasn't safe; so much out there to catch—or catch you. The forces of law and order were coming down hard, blaming us for a world passing them by.

That, and there were always new strains. Only my dead or missing friends had names. The userid's cybersez.

The sender was a flaming-hot number in the cybersea, a dominatrix icon that played games with the boys' heads, and played it ultimately well, and safe.

She'd earned, not taken her id: *bytebitch*. She wasn't a girlie milking her tits for all the drooling boys. She was a hard dealer—no-nonsense and straight. They didn't like that, expecting sugar and spice, not razors and sure, clear percentages. They'd stuck her with her license plate, and she'd kept it: honesty is the best policy.

Straight player to another, she invited me into her parlor, stripped that hot icon down to something molten and perverse. We exchanged digitized images of our faces. She was a bowl-cut of darkshade hair, pool-brown eyes, plush lips, and cheeks to cut and die on—a mix and match from somewhere Asian and someplace African.

Then that message in alt.sex.freak.: *location* (here), *time* (now), *and the deal* (—was this). *Oh, and bring your Toshika.*

And there I was: Not really a street, an alley. The sun eased itself onto jagged skyline teeth; the impalement a pollution-red sunset. Cool shade, the perfume of urban life (piss and wine), the corpses of cars picked clean for their valuable meat and metal. Pools of water and oil, not mixing on cracked streets. Saw no one, but that didn't mean anything—kept my hand in my pocket, wrapped around the cool mean of my little Zilk automatic.

InSane Frisco, Ringold Alley, South of Market—didn't have to live in the city long to know the association: I stood before the gates to Stud Paradise, a graveyard full of memories of gloriously gay alley sex. I found the spot, lit an over-the-counter joint, and waited. The amplified THC mellowed the scene, and for a while I lost the stench and took it all in as a painting: *Portrait of the End of the City*. I waited, appreciating my drug work of art so much I almost missed her.

She walked with purpose down Ringold. Black plastic raincoat, cheap leather boots, a purple, threadbare Zo/courier bag—showing what her last straight job was—coal-mine eyeshades. Invisible in the SOMA turf, she was average enough not to catch a second glance.

But I knew her—we'd fucked. But never in the flesh. Cybersea fucking: interactive chat and visuals. Breasts just the right size for filling hands, she said. An electric cunt tight enough to rip condoms off, she said. We'd fucked so many times, but I'd never seen her in the flesh, and I'd never asked for her real name.

Trust.

bytebitch saw me. Didn't smile. The brown eyes behind the shades might have, but I had no way of knowing. On the corner with me was the picked-clean carcass of a Saab. She moved to its pitted fender and propped herself against it. *cybersez: get comfy.* Dropping her bag into the grimy alley muck, she pulled a cig out of one of her plastic pockets, lit up with the finger-thick flame from a self-defense Hotpoint lighter, and took a long drag of amplified tobacco. Then a quick flick into a puddle of mostly oil, and it came to a hissing end. My joint followed, and as she pushed off the fender, I got out my camera—

—my beautiful Japanese Toshika, direct-to-disc job. Small and light, straight to read/write CD. In my other hand was that little German automatic, with its clip of detonator-nylon rounds: in case of trouble. No extra hand for my dick.

Her SOMA-standard, black-latex-gloved hands were on either side of her SOMA-standard, black plastic coat; she arched and tugged—the first three snaps letting loose, showing in a flash her valley of pale tit, the start of those "hand-filling breasts." Hint of something firm and black holding them up. Leaning back against the Saab's one intact headlight, running black-gloved fingers over that slope, eyes hidden and safe behind those black shades, I let my little Toshika focus itself and started to tape.

The bra was black cloth, simple with no stays. One gloved hand scooped down into the right cup, came up with a white mound of tit—red dot of nipple at the tip.

She letting it fall outside the bra. Red nipple, wrinkled and angry, pointed at me and my lens. I focused as she gripped it between black fingers and twisted, pulled. Those glasses still on, she hissed and arched backward, glass headlight pressing into her ass—the one she'd said was "strong enough to crack balls and walnuts."

I taped.

More abuse to that tit—pulling and twisting, holding it straight out from that gleaming black plastic coat by a nipple. In my fine Japanese sight, black-lacquered fingernails flashed, showing what was under the glove (and it flopped to the ground, dead bird) and traced the sculpture of that tit. A pinch of soft skin, another hiss.

Still taping. Zoom out—

The pair were out to play. Twin mounds of soft white skin, rosy pinpoints out and up, erect. She leaned against the autocorpse, both tits out to the cooling night air, held up by the useless bra. Black fingernails dipped into a plastic pocket, dug around and came up with nasty surprises. The first clothespin, intimate pink plastic against pale skin, just above her left nipple. The next followed, part of the pattern, a cheap blue plastic one. Slowly, she clipped each plastic clip after the previous, slowing working her way around her tit.

A circle of plastic, hard-toothed clamps ringed that one tit. A flower with the hard button of a ruby nipple in the center. Hand a little unsteady, holding a black one this time—special color for a special place. When she let go, it sank its plastic mouth down *hard!* onto this already hard button, and the hiss that worked its way between her perfect plastic teeth turned from moan to scream in the urban asshole of Ringold Alley.

Left followed right: a hand dipped into a pocket and paraded another line of clamps. Soon two flowers stared at my fine lens, two flowers of plastic clamps around perfect conical tits. The one for the center of the left was SOMA-standard black, too. As it bit down, echoing the right, her scream echoed off and through the postindustrial wasteland. As I focused and watched that last one go on, night threw itself down on us. The streetlight hummed and winked on.

Nailed by hard light, *bytebitch* staggered back against the pain of her self-imposed torture. Panting, she gripped one side, then the other side of the plastic raincoat—

Snap, snap, snap, snap.

No underwear. Bare crease, cleft of a smooth, polished cunt. No stubble—industrial shaving for her. She was wet, and she shone and gleamed in the streetlight's hard arc stare. Her cleft was a reflective streak between a soft, valentine mons. She leaned back on the fender and rubbed a palm against her cunt, pressing hard and up, touching palm to clit. A rough, ham-handed masturbation. One foot anchored and she hoisted herself up onto the remains of the headlight mount. Braced, she spread her legs, one booted foot on either side of the car—one against the grill, one against the greasy guts of the brake assembly. Legs spread, she cupped her cunt with one black-nailed hand.

I taped. I taped. I taped. Black like a beetle's back, those polished fingernails went around the red bead of a hard, hard clit, then up inside *'bitch's* cunt. Back and forth, back and forth, a liquid action, repetitive and slow. I taped and taped as her hand got wetter and wetter.

Beautiful shot, her hand, her wrist, her arms reflecting the shine of the streetlight, wet from her juice.

bytebitch pushed off, turned, and I caught it all. She whipped around, the black raincoat flying, wrapping itself around her. Her ass walked backward, toward me. Her legs, pale and white—boots scuffed, looking like little black cats playing in the junk. She moaned, like a deep-throated kitten getting a barbed dick. The raincoat flipped up and over her.

Bare and perfect, her ass was full and round, and with her legs spread, everything was there for the cold night and the colder lens of my camera: twin cheeks curving up and down and around to a pair of velvet, wet cunt lips. The glow was real and wet under the hard lights, her lips were parted, churning with her rough jerking off. Three? Four? Was her hand in there? Fisting herself in the harsh light? I saw and taped her lips squirm and bubble with pussy juice. Her moans became hard and quick, forced and stubborn. She grunted while jerking off, deep, masculine sounds. I thought her cunt was going to swallow her, black-lacquered, and all.

I focused and watched. Focused and watched, precise crosshairs on a wide, wet cunt, foamed and slick from her juice. Thighs shimmering, clit—a perfect shot—a red marble when she pulled back her pointed collection of black fingertips. I taped, numbers flowing; light levels a rocking bar-graph; flickering, fluttering digital time.

Taping, taking—

Her moans changed, like changing shots. I noticed it, the way you suddenly realize how dark it's gotten. Blink, blink, night. Blink, blink, her moans were restrained, corked.

An acrobatic flip. Flashes of white and other colors from the mother-loving clothespins still on her tits. I caught, perfectly trapped, her mouth stuffed with black plastic cock. Saliva ran down her chin and added gleam to her cleavage. Then slowly, she drew inches and inches of fat plastic sword from her mouth, its head slipping past her lips trailing threads of spit.

It went between her legs—all the marvelous details: one leg went up, one hand fished between her wet thighs, for the lips of her wet pussy. As she spread her lips, the other hand snaked the wet dildo in.

Inch, inch, inch—it went up her, her original moans and cries back again with full rutting volume. *bytebitch* bent for the camera, leaning back, away from me, eyes still unreadable behind darkshades, mouth open and panting as she swallowed the plastic dick with her cunt mouth.

One hand stayed between her legs—details lost behind the black coat, you could see in the final footage after tweaking and reenhancement what she was doing—rubbing and stroking, and pulling on that red marble between her wet cunt lips for all she was worth. The other hand was fucking herself with the dildo. Sitting in dark safety later, with my cock and drugs, you could hear her—the rutting bitch—and the sound of her self-fucking. (Good sound quality, those Japanese.) A chorus of wet slaps and sucks perfectly muted and transmogrified by the flesh of her cunt and ass.

No sound track needed.

As her cumming came, she rolled off the car (and I tracked and followed, taping) and crouched down, squatting above the Ringold filth, all there for me, for the camera. Shielded eyes up and pleading to the audience, she parted the cloak to show it, show her speared by her plastic pal, in all its magnificence. Ah, the details: dark cherry clit, like a wet blister between her slick lips. Black plastic cock in and out, in and out, still driven by her other hand.

Perfectly timed with her shuddering moan, it flopped out of her cunt like a beached fish. It slapped onto the dirty asphalt and rolled into the gutter, picking up dirt, grit, and that sparkling sand made from ground-down bottles and broken windshields. She came again, moaning deep and spastically batting away the clothespins—snapping them off like hungry, stinging flies she'd suddenly realized were all over her. When the ones on her nipples finally let go, they went zinging into the chain-link fence and clinking against the dead Saab.

Exhausted, deflated, she collapsed. *bytebitch* slid down onto her black raincoat, legs kicking straight out from under her. She sat there, for some time, panting, tits going up and down, up and down, beads of sweat raining from softening nipples.

Got it all.

When she had recovered enough, when she no longer saw lights in front of her eyes, and when she was together enough to stand, button her coat, grab her bag, pick up her gloves, adjust her hair and shades, she started off down the severely lit street. I waited to make sure none of the shadows followed her.

Then I checked my Toshika, watched it all in the tiny viewfinder. All there. Every last bit.

Late tonight, in code, disguised as trivia, as something hopefully below examination, it will go sailing out onto the Sea—profits being split between the star and the crew. She trusted me to do a fair deal.

There's the bottom line: trust. She needed someone to hold the camera, put it together, and do nothing else. She was trusting me to do it—and share the profits—from the only game left in town.

Full Metal Corset

Anne Tourney

Aileen calls the room where she works the "fluorescent nunnery." All day the breath of machines stirs her hair; she suspects she is dying fast in this climate. The skin on her breasts and inner thighs has grown tough. Her hair is dry and won't reflect sunlight.

She supervises thirty women who enter data from endless reams into their computers. Aileen sees the hieroglyphic figures everywhere. Data stream out of wine bottles, turn up in her food, and pump out of her husband's cock.

At her desk, Aileen can make herself come in twelve seconds. She can make her cunt muscles pulse in and out like butterfly wings until her vulva clenches in four creamy spasms.

When she isn't masturbating, Aileen watches the employees. A new typist has caught her attention. She gazes at the ream with mystic concentration, as if the data were a formula for ecstasy. Aileen doesn't like this woman. She doesn't respond to Aileen's progressive attitude. She wears smocks that whoosh around her, raising dust. Except for her speeding fingers, she moves with a nun's slow serenity.

Aileen prefers the girls who make crass jokes in the rest room, sneak soda cans under their desks, and fake car trouble so they can stay home an extra hour in the morning and fuck their boyfriends.

"It's Laurie, isn't it?"

The girl stands before the bathroom mirror, clenching her teeth as she adjusts something under her smock. Aileen washes her hands rapidly.

"Lily. The name was given to me."

Of course it was given to you, idiot.

Suddenly the girl lifts her smock over her head. Aileen stares. She feels an unexpected twinge between her legs. The girl is wearing a cruelly elaborate corset, laced so tight that her waist disappears between her bulging hips and bosom. The fabric resembles black leather, only it is much less yielding. The top covers the girl's breasts, slicing into the flesh, but holes have been cut out to expose the nipples. The laces, which cross at the front and tie in the back, obviously restrict breathing. The material creaks as the girl reaches back to loosen its fastenings.

"Could you help me?" she whispers. "I've got to take this off."

Aileen reminds herself that she is hip. She has seen

porno magazines. She knows about S&M. But she doesn't move.

The girl finally releases herself and lets the contraption fall. She winces, rubbing the network of red lines across her torso. Marks from a series of pointed studs inside the corset pepper her waist.

"That's barbaric," Aileen breathes.

"Oh, no," the girl protests. "It's beautiful."

"What the hell would posses you to wear something like that?"

"It was given to me."

Aileen is getting angry. "That's the sickest thing I've ever seen!" she exclaims. She has forgotten that she is cool, open-minded.

The girl smiles. "Why don't you try it on?" she suggests. "I won't lace it all the way. They never make you do that the first time."

Aileen wants to scream, but she reminds herself that she is tolerant. She is also a practical supervisor. This girl never misses a day, arrives five minutes early every morning, and does the work of two ordinary typists—all while wearing a garment straight out of a torture chamber. Aileen recalls the expression on the girl's face as she enters the mounds of data. She moistens a paper towel in cold water and presses it to her forehead.

"Back to work," says the girl cheerfully. She hoists the corset off the floor and refastens it. While the girl envelops herself in her blue smock, Aileen stumbles into a stall. She wants to vomit, but between her legs she is thoroughly wet.

Aileen now despises Lily. With the other employees Aileen is friendlier than ever, using their slang and chatting with them about their sex lives. The girls laugh at Aileen's jokes, then mock her behind her back.

When Aileen accidentally glances at Lily, she sees the corset. When she hears Lily sigh, she knows the girl is in pain.

One morning Aileen's phone rings. All the women look up. She motions for them to on with their work, but they keep staring. Aileen decides to entertain her audience. She poses on her desk and picks up the receiver.

"Hell-loooo?" she says smokily. The women giggle.

"I'd like to speak to Lily," says the voice. It is a man's voice, smooth as a plum.

"Lily?" Aileen recoils. "Employees can't receive calls here," she says coldly. "Talk to Lily on your own time."

"It's essential that I speak to her."

The voice gives Aileen no alternative. Lily has already risen from her desk. When the girl takes the phone, Aileen snatches her hand away. The girl listens for a moment, then puts the receiver down.

"I have to go," she says. Her tone is conspiratorial, as if Aileen should understand why Lily has to depart at the summons of a phone call, with no prior notice, in the middle of the morning. Aileen won't let her leave.

"I'm sorry," says Lily, walking toward the door. The other women stare after her.

The company has given Lily an unprecedented raise. She will return tomorrow, five minutes early, and she will continue to do so, except when a voice on the telephone orders her to do otherwise.

Aileen is furious. She sits at her desk and tries to look over some documents, but she can't read. With shaking hands, she yanks a pack of cigarettes from her purse and stalks out of the room. She lights one in the hallway, then enters the rest room.

Sitting on the floor, propped against the wall under one of the sinks, is the corset. The sinks have new, ultramodern faucets; water flows, without the help of knobs or handles, whenever hands are extended for washing. Beneath these water-saving miracles lies the corset, a medieval nightmare.

Aileen reaches out to touch it. The material is untextured and cool, but Aileen pulls her hand away as if burned. She drops her cigarette in the sink and lifts the corset with her fingertips. It is lighter than it appears, but heavy enough so that it would eventually become a burden.

She strokes the studs lining the garment, then pulls the corset experimentally around her waist, noting the sharpness of the metal teeth. A strap dangles from behind; apparently, this fits between the legs and fastens in the front. Repelled, Aileen realizes that her crotch is damp again. She should take this thing to the incinerator. Better yet, she should take it to the cops. Instead, she finds herself laying the garment down and undressing.

Standing nude, she laces the front and pulls the strap through her legs, buckling it above her crotch. She can still breathe comfortably, and the studs' pointed tips barely sting. She pulls the laces tighter and rebuckles the crotch strap so that it really digs into her. Undulating her hips, she groans at the combined sensations: the edges of the corset biting into her flesh, the studs pricking her waist, the strap abrading her pussy lips. With her palms, she rubs her exposed nipples. She grasps the strap between her legs and jerks it up and down until she comes—so intensely that she soaks her thighs.

Aileen wears the corset back to her desk, certain that someone will see the black garment through her ivory blouse. She sits down, but she can't work. The pain has worsened. The studs pierce her skin, and the stiff garment won't let her breathe. She panics; she has to remove it.

I can't stand it. Oh, God, I can't stand it.

Then she thinks of Lily, with her beatific expression. She forces her body to accept the pain. Closing her eyes, she gives in to it, becomes it. She focuses on the agony of the strap cutting into her pussy. Soon she is excited again.

She tells the typists she is leaving early. Indifferent, they continue typing. Aileen leaves without her jacket or her purse. She can't imagine why she would need them.

In the streets she walks stiffly, but with an undefinable urgency. Walking in the corset brings her to a new level of pain and arousal. Soon she has to stop. The agony is unbelievable. Leaning against a parking meter, she breathes deeply, but the studs are fiery points against her rib cage. Her entire torso is blistered and raw. The strap between her legs feels excruciating.

A car pulls up at the meter. Someone gets out and lifts her, putting her into the car.

Inside, hands remove her clothing and work at the corset. As each lace is unfastened, Aileen takes a drink of air. She has never felt anything as sweet as the removal of that garment.

"You fastened it too tight," her rescuer chides her. "The first time, you should lace it no more snugly than a life preserver."

The car's interior is large, lush, and dark. Tinted windows guard her from the outside world, and another window separates the backseat from the front. Her savior strokes ointment into her flesh. His fingers tell her that, though he is now ministering to her pain, he can also inflict it. His face is scarred and pitted; he has earned his privileges.

His touch arouses her. She leans against the seat and is preparing to ride to orgasm when he stops.

"From now on," he says, "you won't take pleasure before I do. Whenever I want you, wherever you are, you will come to me."

"What if I don't?" Aileen starts to ask, but the look on his face makes her say instead, "What if I can't?"

"If you disobey me, I'll find you and weld you into the corset. No instrument can cut through that material. It can't even be burned. It's indestructible. Can you imagine how it would feel to be trapped in the corset?"

"Yes," she whispers.

"You can't go back, now that you've put on one of my corsets. You do want to wear it, don't you?"

She can only answer yes.

"You'll continue your life the way it's always been, with two exceptions. First, you will interrupt any activity when I summon you. Second, you will allow no one but me to touch you."

His face is triangular, with silver eyes—a wolf's face. A face that demands worship. Aileen bows her head.

He unzips his leather trousers, and his cock leaps out, radiating heat. She sucks lightly on the tip. Grasping her hair, he directs her to move faster, and she takes the whole shaft into her mouth, using her muscles to massage his cock to the beat of its pulse. She tastes the ripe flavor of groin sweat. When she feels him swell suddenly, she produces a steady pressure with her lips, tongue, and throat. She accepts the explosion, all salt and cream.

He turns her on her back. Still erect, he rams into her, coming after a few bullish thrusts. He sits back and replaces his cock in his trousers. Aileen moans, wildly unsatisfied.

"Do you remember what I said?" he asks. "I'll please you only when I want to."

Her cunt walls clench like a fist. Rebelliously, she tries to touch herself, but he takes her hand away.

"This time, I'll reward you," he says.

He seizes her knees, spreads them, and leans down to cleave her lips with his tongue. Removing his tongue from her steaming hole, he spears her clit with it. She comes in seconds.

"There's a war against this kind of worship," he says when they are finished. "The corset won't just transform you, it will defend you. Whenever you wear it, you're free to surrender yourself to me. No one can prevent you. I'm giving you a rare opportunity."

He eases the corset onto her and laces it around her nude torso so that its studs barely caress her wounds.

Sweating Profusely in Mérida: A Memoir

Carol Queen

The Boyfriend and I met at a sex party. I was in a back room trying to help facilitate an erection for a gentleman brought to the party by a woman who would have nothing to do with him once they got there. She had charged him a pretty penny to get in, and I actually felt that I should have gotten every cent, but I suppose it was my own fault that I was playing Mother Teresa and didn't know when to let go of the man's dick. Boyfriend was hiding behind a potted palm eyeing me and this guy's uncooperative, uncut dick, and it seemed Boyfriend had a thing for pretty girls *and* uncut men, especially the latter. So he decided to help me out and replaced my hand with his mouth. That was when it got interesting. The uncut straight guy finally left and I stayed.

In the few months our relationship lasted, we shared many more straight men, most of them—Boyfriend's radar was incredible—uncircumcised and willing to do almost anything with a man as long as there was a woman in the room. I often acted as sort of a hook to hang a guy's heterosexuality on while Boyfriend sucked his dick or even fucked him. My favorite was the hitchhiker wearing pink lace panties under his grungy jeans—but that's another story. Long before we met him, Boyfriend had invited me to go to Mexico.

This was the plan. Almost all the guys in Mexico are uncut, right? And lots will play with men, too, Boyfriend assured me, especially if there's a woman there. (I guessed they resembled American men in this respect.) Besides, it would be a romantic vacation.

That was how we wound up in Room 201 of the Hotel Reforma in sleepy Mérida, capital of the Yucatán. Mérida's popularity as a tourist town had been eclipsed by the growth of Cancún, the nearest Americanized resort. That meant the boys would be hornier, Boyfriend reasoned. The Hotel Reforma had been recommended by a fellow foreskin fancier. Its chief advantages were the price—about $14 a night—and the fact that the management didn't charge extra for extra guests. I liked it because it was old, airy, and cool, with wrought-iron railings and floor tiles worn thin from all the people who'd come before. Boyfriend liked it because it had a pool, always a good place to cruise, and a disco across the street. That's where we headed as soon as we got in from the airport, showered, and changed into skimpy clothes suitable for turning tropical boys' heads.

There were hardly any tropical boys there, as it turned out, because this was where the Ft. Lauderdale college students who couldn't afford spring break in

Cancún went to spend their more meager allowances, and not only did it look like a Mexican restaurant-with-disco in Ft. Lauderdale, the management took care to keep all but the most dapper Méridans out lest the coeds be frightened by scruffy street boys. Scruffy street boys, of course, is just what Boyfriend had his eye out for, and at first the pickings looked slim; but we found one who had slipped past security, out to hustle nothing more spicy than a gig showing tourists around the warren of narrow streets near the town's central plaza, stumbling instead onto us. Ten minutes later Boyfriend had his mouth wrapped around a meaty little bundle, *with* foreskin. Luis stuck close to us for several days, probably eating more regularly than usual, and wondering out loud whether all the women in America were like me, and would we take him back with us? Or at least send him a Motley Crüe T-shirt when we went home?

Boyfriend had brought Bob Damron's gay travel guide, which listed for Mérida: a cruisy restaurant (it wasn't) and a cruisy park bench in the Zocalo (it was, and one night Boyfriend stayed out most of the night looking for gay men, who, he said, would run the other way if they saw me coming, and found one, a slender boy who had to pull down the panty hose he wore under his jeans so Boyfriend could get to his cock, and who expressed wonder because he had never seen anyone with so many condoms; in fact most people never had condoms at all. Boyfriend gave him his night's supply and some little brochures about *el SIDA* he'd brought from the AIDS Foundation, *en español* so even if our limited Spanish didn't get through to our tricks, a pamphlet might).

Damron's also indicated that Mérida had a bathhouse.

I had always wanted to go to a bathhouse, and of course there was not much chance it would ever happen back home. For one thing, there were all closed before

I ever moved to San Francisco. For another, even if I dressed enough like a boy to pass, I wouldn't look old enough to be let in. But in Mérida perhaps things were different.

It was away from the town's center, but within walking distance of the Hotel Reforma. Through the tiny front window, grimy from the town's blowing dust, I saw a huge papier-mâché figure of Pan, painted brightly and hung with jewelry, phallus high. It looked like something the Radical Faeries would carry in the Gay Day parade. Everything else about the lobby looked dingy, like the waiting room of a used-car dealership.

Los Baños de Vapor would open at eight that evening. They had a central tub and rooms to rent; massage boys could be rented, too. I would be welcome.

The papier-mâché Pan was at least seven feet tall and was indeed the only bright thing in the lobby. Passing through the courtyard, an overgrown jumble of vines pushing though cracked tile, a slight smell of sulfur, a stagnant fountain, we were shown up a flight of concrete stairs to our room by Carlos, a solid, round-faced man in his midtwenties, wrapped in a frayed white towel. The room was small and completely tiled, grout black from a losing fight with the wet tropical air. At one end was a shower and at the other a bench, a low, vinyl-covered bed, and a massage table. There was a switch that, when flipped, filled the room with steam. Boyfriend flipped it and we shucked our clothes; as the pipes hissed and clanked, Carlos gestured to the massage table and then to me.

Boyfriend answered for me, in Spanish, that I'd love to. I got on the table and Carlos set to work. Boyfriend danced around the table gleefully, sometimes stroking me, sometimes Carlos's butt. "Hey, man, I'm working!" Carlos protested, not very insistently, and Boyfriend went for his cock, stroking it hard, then urged him up onto the table, and Carlos's hands, still slick from the massage oil and warm from the friction of my skin, covered my breasts as Boyfriend rolled a condom onto Carlos's cock and rubbed it up and down my labia a few times and finally let go, letting it sink in. He rode me slow and then hard while the table rocked dangerously and Boyfriend stood at my head, letting me tongue his cock while he played with Carlos's tits. When Boyfriend was sure that we were having a good time, he put on a towel and slipped out the door. Carlos looked surprised. I had to figure out how to say, in Spanish "He's going hunting," and get him to go back to fucking me, solid body slick from oil and steam; if he kept it up, he would make me come, clutching his slippery back, legs in the air.

That was just happening when Boyfriend came back with David. He was pulling him in the door by his already stiff penis, and I suspected Boyfriend had wasted as little time getting him by the dick as he usually did. He had found David in the tub room, he announced, and he had a beautiful, long *uncut* cock. (Boyfriend always enunciated clearly when he said "uncut.") David *did* have a beautiful cock, and he spoke English and was long and slim with startling blue eyes. It turned out he was Chicano, second generation, a senior at Riverside High who spent school breaks with his grandmother in Mérida and worked at Los Baños de Vapor as a secret summer job. We found out all this about him as I was showering the sweat and oil off from my fuck with Carlos, and by the time I heard that he'd been working at the Baños since he turned sixteen, I was ready to start fucking again. David was the most quintessentially eighteen-year-old fuck I ever had, except Boyfriend's presence made it unusual; he held David's cock and balls and controlled the speed of the thrusting, until his mouth got preoccupied with Carlos's dick. David told me, ardently, that I was beautiful, though at that point I didn't care if I was beautiful or not, since I was finally in a bathhouse doing what I'd always wanted to do and I felt more like a faggot than a beautiful *gringa*.

But David was saying he wished he had a girlfriend like me, even though I was thirty, shockingly old—this actually was what almost all of Boyfriend's conquests said to me, though I suspected not every man could keep up with a girlfriend who was really a faggot, or a boyfriend who was really a woman, or whatever kind of fabulous anomaly I was.

Then someone knocked on the door and we untangled for a minute to answer it, and there were José and Gaspar, laughing and saying we were the most popular room in the Baños at the moment and would we like some more company? At least that's how David translated the torrent of Spanish, for they were both speaking at once. Naturally we invited them in, and lo and behold, Gaspar was actually *gay*, and so while I lay sideways on the massage table with my head off the edge and my legs in the air so I could suck David while José fucked me, I could watch Boyfriend finally getting *his* cock sucked by Gaspar, whose black, glittering Mayan eyes closed in concentration, and I howled with not simply orgasm but the *excitement*, the splendid excitement of being in Mexico in a bathhouse with four uncut men and a maniac, a place no woman I knew had gone before. Steam swirled in the saturated air like superheated fog, beading like pearls in the web of a huge Yucatán spider in the corner; David's cock, or was it José's or Carlos's again, I didn't care, pounded my fully opened cunt rhythmically and I wished I had her view.

You know if you have ever been to a bathhouse that time stands still in the steamy, throbbing air, and so I had no idea how long it went on, only that sometimes I was on my back and sometimes on my knees, and once for a minute I was standing facing the wall, and when Boyfriend wasn't sucking them or fucking me, he was taking snapshots of us, just like a tourist. The floor of the room was completely littered with condoms, which made us all laugh hysterically. Rubber-kneed, Gaspar and David held me up with Carlos and José flanking them so Boyfriend could snap one last picture. Then he divided all the rest of the condoms among them—we had more at the hotel, I think that week we went through ten dozen—and got out his brochures. He was trying to explain in Spanish the little condoms he used for giving head—how great they were to use with uncut guys 'cause they disappeared under the foreskin—and I was asking David what it was like to live a double life, Riverside High to Los Baños, and who else came there— "Oh, everybody does," he said—and did they ever want to fuck him—of course they *wanted* to—and did he ever fuck them—well, sure—and how was that? He shrugged and said, as if there were only one possible response to my question, "It's *fucking*."

When we left, the moon was high, the Baños deserted, the warm night air almost cool after the steamy room. The place looked like a courtyard motel, the kind I used to stay in with my parents when we traveled in the early sixties, but overgrown and haunted. The Pan figure glittered in the low lobby light, and the man at the desk charged us $35—seven for each massage boy, four each to get in, and six for the room. Hundreds of thousands of pesos—he looked anxious, as though he feared we'd think it was too much. We paid him, laughing. I wondered if this was how a Japanese businessman in Thailand felt. Was I contributing to the imperialist decline of the third world? Boyfriend didn't give a shit about things like that, so I didn't mention it. In my hand was a crumpled note from David: "Can I come visit you in your hotel room? No money."

From *Stone Butch Blues*

Leslie Feinberg

The loneliness became more and more unbearable. I ached to be touched. I feared I was disappearing and I'd cease to exist if someone didn't touch me.

One woman in particular turned my head every morning: Annie, the waitress at the coffee shop near my job. When she brought me coffee, it seemed she didn't notice me. But then she'd catch my eye and turn away from me, wrapping my attention around her like a shawl. She was as tough as a gangster. God, I liked Annie. She treated every customer like a trick. She worked them for a tip and didn't let them drop till they left it.

I sat at the counter and watched Annie relax with her coworker, Frances. The men in the restaurant seemed to think the women's attention only existed for them. If they had seen how intimate the women were with each other, the men might have been jealous. But they didn't notice. I did.

Annie saw me at the counter. "Hey, sweetheart, what's shaking this morning?"

I laughed. "How are you, Annie?"

"Finer than a frog's hair quartered, darlin'. Whatcha havin'?"

"Coffee and eggs over easy."

"You got it," she said over her shoulder as she swung away from me. Her body demanded I pay attention.

Frances and Annie showed each other their kids' school photos while they waited for their orders from the grill.

"Can I see?" I asked Annie as she brought my eggs.

She eyed me warily as she handed me the photo. "Don't see why not."

Four rows of sweet children's faces looked back at me. "Which one?" I asked. Annie wiped her hands on her apron and pointed out her daughter.

"God, she's great," I told her. "She's got your eyes—smart and angry at the same time."

"Where do you see that?" Annie demanded as she snatched the photo from my hand. She stormed off. A moment later she brought my coffee and slammed it down so hard it sloshed over the rim of the cup. Then she lifted it up, wiped the counter, and spilled it again. "Next time you want to read a book, go to the goddamn library." She spun on her heel. I put down a tip, paid the cashier, and left.

The next day I brought her a single flower. "I'm sorry I got personal," I told her.

"Aw, well, I don't mind you gettin' personal, darlin'. Just take your damn sweet time about it, okay?"

"Agreed," I said.

"What kinda flower is this anyway?"

I smiled. "A mum for a mum."

She frowned. "Oh, I get it."

Annie's body language was very reserved with me. But as soon as Annie and Frances got together, she loosened up. They whispered. Frances smelled the flower and put her hand over her heart. Annie smacked Frances on the shoulder.

I wanted to spend time with Annie when she wasn't working. It was no secret now.

Annie brought me a white paper bag. "What's this?" I asked.

She shrugged. "Coffee and a cherry Danish."

I was confused. "I didn't ask for it."

"I didn't ask for no flower either. It's on the house," she shot back. "It's fresh. The Danish is fresh."

I smiled, left a tip, and paid the cashier for my breakfast. Then I came back to the counter and tried to get Annie's attention. She made me wait.

"Whatdya forget?" she asked.

"I wanted to know if you . . . " I hesitated. It could be a big mistake to go out with someone who knew my coworkers. She could make real trouble for me if she found out; I'd have to quit my job. But I was desperately lonely.

"If I'd what?" She sounded suspicious.

"If you'd want to go out with me sometime?"

Annie put both her hands on her hips and looked me up and down several times. "Ask me again sometime." Somehow I thought that was a good sign.

Our serious flirtation began the next morning. It was fun. It felt good. It reminded me of the old days between femmes and butches. But this was not between women. At least that's not how the world around us saw it. And, I reminded myself over and over again, that's not how Annie saw it.

The amazing part was that this courtship dance could take place in public and everyone—coworkers and strangers alike—encouraged and approved. Meanwhile, Anita Bryant was thumping the Bible in a well-publicized campaign to overturn a simple gay rights ordinance. I wondered how human affection could be judged so differently.

When I finally got up the nerve to ask Annie out again, she wiped her hands on her apron and answered, "Sure, I guess. Why not?"

Friday night I knocked on her door. It took a long time for her to answer. I heard her yelling something. I got a funny feeling in the pit of my stomach. Annie only opened the door partway. "Uh . . . ," she started. I could see a child wrapped around her legs.

"It's okay," I interrupted. She wanted to cancel. I tried to conceal my disappointment. "Maybe another time."

"Wait." She opened the door all the way. "I mean if you want to come in, I could make you some coffee or something." I did want to come in.

The three of us stood awkwardly in her living room. "My baby-sitter, well, it's my sister's kid actually, she got sick, so I have Kathy home tonight and she's running a little fever."

I raised my hand to stop her. "It's okay. I can see you've got your hands full. Relax!"

Annie unwound a notch. "Sit down. Would you like something to eat? I could make us something."

"Aren't you sick of serving food?"

She laughed. "It's okay. I don't mind."

"Want me to sit in the kitchen so you can function in one room?" She smiled and nodded.

I set the small canvas bag I'd brought on the floor near the couch, out of sight. Maybe bringing a dildo had been too optimistic. Then again, being caught without one could present its own crisis. I tried to breathe past my anxiety as I followed Annie and Kathy into the kitchen.

"Can I help?" I offered.

She looked surprised. "Naw, that's okay."

Kathy clung to Annie's leg with one arm and clutched a stuffed rabbit with the other. I smiled at Kathy. "Does your rabbit have a fever, too?" Kathy looked at the rabbit and then at me without answering.

"Later," I told Kathy, "if you think your rabbit has a fever, I'll take its temperature. Is it a girl rabbit or a boy?" Kathy held the rabbit up in the air as though I could determine its sex.

"Ah, it's a girl," I surmised. Kathy looked up at her mother.

"Go show him your rabbit," Annie urged. Kathy shook her head violently and clung to her mother for protection.

"You like macaroni and cheese?" Annie asked. I hate macaroni and cheese.

"That would be great," I answered.

Annie served up three plates of sliced ham, macaroni and cheese, corn, and white bread. The first plate had small portions with pictures of the Flintstones still visible underneath. "Is that mine?" I asked Kathy. She shook her head and squeezed her bunny tighter.

Annie set my plate in front of me and sat down. Kathy held up an empty glass. Annie jumped up to fill it with milk. "Want a beer?" she asked me while the refrigerator door was open.

"Sure," I said.

"Need a glass?" I shook my head. She smiled.

Annie brought two beer bottles to the table and sat back down. We lifted our beers in a toast. Kathy tried to do the same thing. Her glass tipped over, pouring milk all over the table. Annie immediately tried to mop the milk off my plate with her napkin. I jumped up and came back from the sink with a sponge. We got most of it.

Annie looked tense. "Your meal's all spoiled."

"Naw," I said, "milk's good for you."

Kathy seemed ready to cry. She hugged her bunny tighter. I smiled at her. "Sometimes when I drop something, I think everybody is gonna be mad at me," I told her. "I'm not mad at you." Kathy narrowed her eyes as she checked me out, just the way her mother did.

"Would it make you feel better if I spilled my beer?" I asked her. Kathy smiled and nodded emphatically.

"Don't you dare," Annie warned me with a hidden smile.

The rest of the dinner went much smoother. After dessert Kathy thrust her bunny at me. "Take her temperature?" I asked. She nodded.

"This wabbit needs to go to bed soon," I told her. "I think she's got a cold." Kathy weighed the information and nodded. "Does your wabbit need a bath first?" I asked. Kathy shook her head from side to side.

"Oh, yes, she does." Annie laughed and scooped up Kathy in her arms.

"I'll clean up," I told Annie. "Take your time." Annie eyed me suspiciously.

I was washing the last of the dishes when Annie came up behind me. She grabbed a dish towel off the refrigerator door. I washed the pots while she dried the dishes. It felt good. But the longer Annie dried dishes, the angrier she seemed to become. "What's up?" I asked her.

She threw down the towel and glared at me. "I'm not an easy lay, you know. You guys know a woman with a kid's been fucked before, so you figure you can get whatever you want, right?"

I rinsed a sponge under the faucet and walked over to the kitchen table to wipe it off. "I got what I wanted at dinner," I told her.

She looked stunned. "What, macaroni and cheese in milk gravy?" We both laughed.

"I just wanted to spend some time with you when we're both off-duty, you know."

"Why?" She measured me with those keen eyes again.

"I like you. I guess I really like tough cookies, and God knows, you are one."

She shook her head. "I can't figure you out."

"So what?"

"So a man you can't figure out is a dangerous man," she told me. She came closer. My body turned toward hers. It was happening.

"I'm not dangerous," I promised. "I'm complicated, but I'm not dangerous."

"Whatchya lookin' for, darlin'?" Annie ran her fingers lightly through my hair. Oh, God, it felt so good.

I sighed deeply. "I've been hurt. I'm not looking to get married, I'm not looking to disrespect anyone. I guess I just need some comfort."

"That's it?" she probed. "Like a one-nighter?"

I shrugged my shoulders. "I don't know," I told her honestly.

Annie weighed my words carefully in the scales of her own need. She turned away from me, but I knew after a moment it was alright to touch her. I kissed the closest cheek. My lips brushed her ear and traveled down her neck. I could hear her breathing change. She turned and looked at me for a long moment before offering me her mouth. We kissed deeply, but still carefully. Slowly we began to move against each other. I could feel how she offered her body to a man as a test. I was gentle. I was slow. Gradually her body became aware that my tempo was slightly behind hers. Her face flushed with heat. She pressed her pelvis against mine and looked at me quizzically. We both knew I didn't have a hard-on.

"Mommy!" Kathy called from upstairs. Annie looked apologetic. I nodded toward the sound of Kathy's voice. Annie was gone for a few minutes. She came back into the kitchen and filled a plastic Cinderella glass with water. "I'll be right back," she said hoarsely.

I remembered the bag I'd left in the other room. Now was definitely the right time to get it. I grabbed the bag and raced into the bathroom. I locked the door and took off my pants and BVDs.

The harness and rubber cock fit nicely in my briefs. I pulled my pants back on and checked my wallet for a condom. I heard Annie call my name from the kitchen. I flushed the toilet, ran the tap water for a moment, and came out to meet her. I was out of breath.

"What were you doing in there, running?" She laughed.

It would take time to get back the feeling. I ran my fingers through her hair.

She closed her eyes and parted her lips. The phone rang. We both laughed. "Forget it," she said. It kept ringing. I pulled her close to me. She pressed her pelvis against mine. This time she smiled.

She pulled back and searched my face with her eyes. I leaned against the sink and waited for her to come back to me. Then she took my hand and led me to her bedroom.

Annie was afraid. I knew that was true. What she couldn't know was that I was, too. I wanted so much to be in her arms that I was willing to risk exposure and humiliation.

She turned on the light in her bedroom as we walked in. A Harley-Davidson gas tank hung from the ceiling. "You like bikes?" she asked me. I nodded. I walked over to the light switch and snapped it off. She stood awkwardly near her bed. I came up behind her and rested my hands on her shoulders. I lifted her hair with one hand and nipped the nape of her neck with my lips. I pressed my pelvis gently against her ass as I pulled her shoulders back so that my mouth could take more of her neck.

Annie turned and gently pulled me down on the bed. She trembled. "Are you afraid?" I asked.

"Fuck you," she answered with a twisted smile.

"You've been hurt before," I said to myself out loud.

"What woman hasn't?" she snapped.

I rolled over on my back and pulled her against my body. "I'd really like to make you feel good," I whispered. "If you'd trust me enough to show me what you want."

"What's your trip, mister?" she snorted. "You want to fuck or not?"

"We can if you want to," I said. "Or we can do other things. It's up to you."

Annie did a double take. "Whatdya mean it's up to me?"

"It's your body. What do you want? I mean, you can show me how you really want to be touched. Or you can act excited and hope I come—not too quick, but don't take too long—right?"

Annie shook her head and sat bolt upright. "You're scaring me," she said.

"Because I want you to really be there when I touch you?"

She nodded. "Yeah, exactly." I lay quietly.

"I don't know if I can," she said.

I sat up and took her in my arms. "Try," I whispered, and pulled her down on top of me. I rolled Annie over on her back as I kissed her, deep and long. I unbuttoned her blouse with slow, steady fingers and teased her breasts for a long time before I came near them with my fingertips. Then I brushed them, lightly, and felt her body shudder. I took each nipple in my mouth and played with it ever so gently. Somehow she told me with her body where to touch, how to touch, when to touch. As I rubbed the front of her jeans, I could feel her passion building, but she deserved the luxury of wanting it real bad.

Then she said something to me I knew took a lot of courage. "I've always wanted to come before I fuck." She turned her head away in shame.

I kissed the part of her throat she left exposed. "Anything you want."

She turned her head to look at me. She had tears in her eyes. "Anything?"

Together we began to undress her—my need, her urgency. I pulled off my chinos and my dress shirt. I was wearing only a white T-shirt and BVDs.

My hands ran up her thighs and down the inside crevices. I could feel her heat and wetness through her underwear. I began to work my body down her, using my lips and tongue to create new erogenous zones all over her rib cage and stomach. My fingers took hold of the elastic on her underwear and began to slide it down her thighs as her hands grabbed my ears firmly and stopped me.

I looked at her with a question on my face. "I'm just gettin' over my period," she said.

I shrugged. "So?"

Emotions played across Annie's face: disbelief, anger, relief, pleasure. Pleasure was the unmistakable emotion still on her face as I began to tease her thighs with my mouth. She gave in to her own desire and, in doing so, reached her orgasm with an almost relaxed trust.

I held her close to me as her breathing slowed. She ran her fingers through my hair, stroked my back. Her touch felt so good that tears welled up in my eyes and spilled down my cheeks. "What's wrong, darlin'?" she asked with concern. I shook my head and buried my face in her shoulder. For the moment her arms protected me from my own life.

My mouth was near her nipple. I felt Annie's breath

quicken. She tugged at my T-shirt. "Take it off," she insisted. I hesitated. It was dark in the room. I was on top of her, so she couldn't see the two lines across my chest that revealed it had been reshaped.

I took off my T-shirt. Annie ran her nails across my shoulders, down my back. I shivered with pleasure. Her nails pressed deeper into my flesh as she moved her pelvis against mine. She was relaxed with me, until the moment I was above her, ready to enter her. I stroked her thighs until she looked up at me. "It's for you, or not at all," I told her.

"I want you so bad," she whispered hoarsely. We both moaned softly as she said that. I pulled my dildo carefully out of my briefs in the dark, afraid of being discovered. What made me think this could work?

I rolled a condom onto my dildo. "I don't think I can have any more kids," she told me.

"I don't want to take any chances, and it's up to me, after all."

"Well, ain't that a switch." She laughed.

I pushed the head of my cock gently inside of her. She tensed her body; I waited. Then Annie relaxed and her hips began to move, pulling me into her. When I was deep inside of her, I lay still on top of her. Our bodies relaxed, fitting into each other. I didn't move until she did. I stroked her just a little slower than her motion demanded; her body demanded more.

I felt her orgasm building long before she came. As she began to come, her hands clawed at my back. Once she pulled my hair so hard I cried out with her. As her orgasm began to ebb, I followed it gently—circles in the broken surface of a pool of water. I searched with her for the next orgasm before the last one had subsided. Together we found it, and later a smaller one.

"Oh, Jesse." It sounded so pretty the way she sighed my name. Her fingertips slid down my back like warm raindrops.

I was still rock hard inside of her. We both realized it at once. "What's the matter, darlin', you stuck?"

"I can't come with a rubber on," I said. "Let me take it off and I'll pull out just before I come, I promise."

She turned her head away. "I've heard that one before."

"I promise. Trust me."

"Lord, have mercy, those are the four most dangerous words out of a man's mouth. Okay, sweetheart, you're lucky I don't think I can get pregnant again."

It's true I faked an ejaculation, but not my pleasure. Annie's body felt so good. She kissed me deep and slow, moved for me, gave me everything a woman can give to a lover, and I was excited. At the moment when it became unbearable for me to go on any longer I pulled out gently, ground my pelvis against the sheets, and cried out.

I lay facedown on the bed with my head resting on her belly. Her hands played with my hair. Her fingertips ran across my shoulders, arousing the surface of my skin. I wished I could just stay in that moment in time.

We lay together without speaking for a while. "I have to go to the bathroom," I said.

"Me, too." She laughed.

"Me first." Still facedown I tucked my dildo into my briefs. I turned away from her, slipped on my T-shirt, and headed to the bathroom in the darkness. I locked the door, pulled my bag out from behind the tub, and replaced my dildo with a sock in my briefs. I looked in the mirror as I splashed cold water on my face. Still me looking back at me.

There was a knock at the bathroom door. I unlocked it. Annie came into my arms and kissed me deeply. She put her hand gently between my thighs and squeezed the sock. "I got a lot of pleasure out of this tonight," she said. "It was like magic." My body tensed, and she withdrew her hand.

I stroked her hair. "All magic is illusion," I admitted.

The light was on when I returned to the bedroom. I clicked it off. Annie came back and sat down on the edge of the bed. "Hungry?" she asked me.

"Mmm." I pulled her back on top of me and kissed her until I realized I was making promises I couldn't keep. "I'm tired," I said, "but I want to hold you."

Annie came into my arms and nestled against my shoulder. "You are one strange man."

"Whatdya mean?"

"First of all, I never met a guy who wasn't afraid of a little bit of woman's blood. But you know what's the weirdest about you?"

Every muscle in my body got hard, except the sock. Annie laughed. "Relax, baby. I'm not complaining. What really blew me away is that you knew I had to take care of my kid and you didn't demand my attention till she went to bed. That, and the fact that even my ex-husband never did the dishes, and he's the one that dirtied most of them."

Annie shook her head. "You don't fuck like some other guys, either." I rolled over on my stomach protectively. She massaged my shoulders. "I mean, you take your time, you know. It's like you got a brain in your dick instead of a dick for a brain, you know?" We both laughed and rolled around the bed together.

I fell asleep, safe in her arms.

The first voice I awoke to was Kathy's. "Can I turn on the cartoons?"

Annie mumbled, "Go ahead." Shortly afterward she kissed me on the ear and got up to make breakfast. While Annie cooked pancakes, Kathy sat on my lap and told me everything she could think of about the Road Runner and Wile E. Coyote. Annie tried to hide her pleasure at watching us together. "She's usually scared of men," Annie said when Kathy left the room. "You're real good with her."

I noticed Annie's body language as she cooked. "Something on your mind?" I asked.

She turned and wiped her hands on her apron. "I know this is crazy to ask you."

"Go ahead."

"Well, my sister's getting married tomorrow, and, well, it's crazy, I mean it's too short notice and you didn't commit to nothing last night—"

"Yeah, sure."

Annie sat down in a kitchen chair next to mine. "You really don't mind?"

"I really don't mind, as long as you understand."

She pressed her fingertips against my lips. "My heart asks for more sometimes," she said, "but my head wants the same thing you do." I nodded.

Annie got up and walked to the stove. "There's one catch," I added. She didn't turn around, but her entire body clenched like a fist. "What?" she said over her shoulder.

"We have to go on my Harley. It's the only wheels I got."

Annie took off her apron, threw it in the sink, and came over and sat in my lap. She kissed my mouth so sweetly. "Nine o'clock," she said, "not a minute later."

I got near her place at eight-thirty actually. I turned off the engine a block away and rolled it in front of her house so I wouldn't wake the whole neighborhood. I sat on her porch, smoking a cigarette, until I heard her door open and Annie said, "You comin' in or not?"

She looked me up and down appreciatively. "You look real handsome, darlin'." My blush visibly delighted her. "I gotta finish gettin' dressed. I made coffee," she called out from her bedroom.

"I'll get it," I yelled back, "you want some?"

She came to the door of her bedroom, holding the back of her dress together. "Yeah." She smiled. "Help me zip my dress up first." She looked back at me over her shoulder as I did. I kissed the side of her face. Her hair was swept up and held in place with bobby pins. I kissed the base of her neck. "You keep that up and I'll never get ready, darlin'." She pulled away from me.

I made two cups of coffee and brought them to her bedroom door. The door was ajar, but I knocked on the doorframe. "Your coffee's out here."

When she came out moments later, I sucked in my breath and let it out slowly. She smoothed her dress. "How do I look?"

I sighed. "Like I died and went to heaven." She made a face and lifted her arms to wrap them around my neck, but I pulled back and handed her an orchid corsage I bought the night before.

She blinked back tears. Then she sounded angry. "Whatdya go and do that for?" she scolded. I smiled at the powerful woman who stood before me. Her face softened and she smiled back.

"Where's Kathy?" I asked her.

She scowled. "With Frances, from the restaurant. My ex-husband might be skulking around the wedding." I didn't understand, but I let it drop.

The wedding was a formal church affair. I'd never been to a wedding before. Everyone in the audience looked so teary-eyed and melted by the ceremony. Annie's sister honestly had to promise to obey this guy for the rest of her life before the priest would proclaim the two married. I thought it was kind of feudal.

The reception was held outdoors. There were tables and chairs set up all over the lawn. Drinks and food were served under a huge striped tent.

Annie introduced me to all her people who'd traveled up to Buffalo for the wedding. She stayed on my arm the whole time. I met Cousin Wilma. She flashed an evil smile. "How wonderful it was of you to agree to come with Annie today." Annie squeezed my arm like a tourniquet.

"It's my pleasure." I put my hand on Annie's hand, which was cutting off the circulation in my arm. Without taking my eyes off Annie's I told Wilma. "It isn't every day that a woman as strong and beautiful as Annie will give me the time of day." Wilma turned on her heel, and Annie chuckled into my shoulder.

"Get us a bottle of champagne," she said.

I did. "How many glasses, sir?" the bartender asked me.

"One." I picked up a small bottle of club soda. "Can I have this?" The bartender nodded.

"What's that for?" Annie wanted to know.

"Hell, somebody's got to drive us home." She kissed me so tenderly right then and there under the tent that not a man or a woman within eyesight didn't stare wistfully.

Annie and I found a shady place under a tree where we could watch all the goings-on. She kicked off her shoes. I put my suit jacket down for her to sit on. Annie shook her head. "Your momma sure taught her little boy some manners."

She gave me the lowdown on all her folks: who was a closet drunk, who beat or cheated on his wife, and who was giving it to the milkman.

"That fag," she said contemptuously. I was stunned at the hatred in her eyes. She was glaring at a man in his early fifties. His arm was around the shoulder of one of the many aunts who roamed this reception. "Who let that queer in here?" Annie hissed.

"Is he really gay?" I asked her.

"You bet. Probably fuckin' all the children in the family."

"Jeez, Annie." My blood ran cold. "How can you hate somebody just because of who they love?"

She looked at me with shock. "You like faggots?"

I shrugged. "We aren't all the same, Annie. So what?"

She shook her head and spat on the ground. "I wouldn't let a faggot near my daughter."

I thought before I spoke. "Annie, if anybody was gonna fuck with Kathy, it would probably be a straight guy, not a gay man."

"Yeah?" she yelled. Annie stood up and gripped the champagne bottle tightly at her side. "Well, I ain't lettin' no funny men around my daughter. I left my own husband 'cause I caught him molesting Kathy. I tried to kill the man with my bare hands. No fucking fags are coming near my girl, you understand?"

I did understand that this conversation could go no further. Annie kicked up some dirt and grass with her pumps and then sat down again. "Aw, shit, what're we wasting our time talkin' about queers for anyway?"

I couldn't wait till we left the reception. Annie rode with her arms around my neck and her face against my back. By the time we got to her home, both her shoes were gone and the exhaust pipe had burned a hole in the hem of her dress. "Pay it no mind," Annie said. She was drunk.

When we got to the porch, she threw her arms around me. "You comin' in, darlin'?"

"Naw," I said. "I gotta get ready for work in the morning."

She looked down at her stocking feet and back up to my face. "I ain't gonna see you again, am I?"

I looked down at my shoes. "I don't think so."

She nodded. "Why not?" It hurt my heart the way she asked it.

"I'm afraid I'd fall in love with you." It was partly true, but it sure didn't tell the whole story. It's one thing for the magician to reveal the art of illusion. It's another thing to tell a straight woman that the man she slept with is a woman. That's not what Annie agreed to get into. Sooner or later it was going to blow up. And after this afternoon, I had even more reason to fear the explosion.

"What's wrong with falling in love? What's the matter with you guys, anyway?" she slurred.

"I've been hurt, Annie. I need time."

"Shit, I thought you were different. You ain't any different from any other guy who stands up to pee."

"Well"—I shrugged—"maybe just a little different."

"You tell that woman who hurt you I'm gonna come after her and rip her to shreds. She spoiled it for the rest of us." Annie's smile faded. "Ain't no use us standing out here talkin', is it? You best be goin'."

I nodded. We looked at each other for a long moment. I took the keys from her hand and unlocked the front door. I kissed her lightly on the mouth.

"Hey, thanks for what you said to Wilma back there."

"I meant every word of it."

She looked me straight in the eye. "Thanks for everything, darlin'." I smiled and turned to go. She stood on the porch and watched me kick-start my bike. "Hey," she yelled over the roar of the engine.

"What?" I cupped my hand near my ear to hear.

"The wabbit."

"What?"

"Kathy's wabbit."

I nodded and strained to hear what she was repeating.

"Kathy's wabbit isn't a girl, it's a boy!"

None of the Above

Bernadette Lynn Bosky

I stood in front of the mirror, trying to decide whether to apply my body makeup now or when I arrived at the party. A breeze came in from the open window, cool on my moist skin. My bush was still wet from the shower, too; small droplets of water clung to the hairs, sparkling like small jewels. I couldn't bring that effect to the party with me, I thought, but—I reached for the edible glitter, as well as the nipple rouge and flavored labia gloss. Better to doll myself up now and be prepared. I'd heard that sometimes, at parties like this, you might not make it past the front hall before your clothes came off—often with more than a little help. Besides, why not apply the lotion and makeup while I have time to fully enjoy it?

I touched my breasts briefly in anticipation. The prospect of the party had already excited me, and my nipples hardened surprisingly quickly. As I finished drying myself, I relished the immaculate feeling of the soft cotton towel. Its touch was dry and clean, strangely intimate in places that few human lovers ever touched. Was I already preparing myself, thinking in terms of such radically different eroticism? The combination of excitement and mystery was almost staggering. By the time I set down the towel, my nipples were tingling, and my bush was beginning to moisten again.

"Business before pleasure," I told myself. First the glitter, to allow it time to set. I took down a small silver pot, then paused; finally I took down the metallic blue as well, to match my garter belt and camisole. I remembered shopping for them the day my invitation had arrived: they'd cost two weeks' salary, but I had no regrets. People who can't afford clothes like that just don't get invited to body-morph parties, let alone something as rare as this. It was fun to pretend that I was one of the salary-elite, even though I really wasn't.

I still wasn't sure how I got invited to Kikito's party, although I wasn't complaining. She knew me casually from volunteer hours at the medical co-op, but we hardly spoke. Apart from the obvious differences in social class, she seemed temperamentally quiet and withdrawn, so I didn't push it. I had no idea I'd made an impression until her card arrived, complete with foil-base holo-print and delivered by personal drone. When I saw what the invitation was for, I was even more impressed. And not a little scared, but most of all excited.

Well, I thought, if it's my body she wants, here it is—all of it, all ready for action. I scooped a dab of glitter with my fingertips. Then, slowly and smoothly, working from the armpits in and the cleavage out, I applied it; silver to highlight the large, pale globes of my breasts, blue to emphasize the valley between them. Just a hint of silver to show provocatively above the collar of my duster. The round, repetitive strokes were like a massage, not quite sexual but almost hypnotically sensuous. Good tits, I thought. I used to think they were my only good feature, but things had certainly changed in the past few decades. As the glitter set, it began to spread its delicious warmth through my skin.

Taking more silver glitter, I drew a dramatic horizontal slash across the full expanse of my belly, like the trail of a shooting star. Just a drop of blue, to highlight my navel, and I was finished. I imagined strangers stroking the soft pillars of my thighs or the hills of my hips and ass, resting on my round, cushiony belly and breasts. Here I was, all curves and dimples and tender white skin, and all of my flesh was wanted—even lusted for—at what was probably the sexiest party of the year.

How things change, I thought. Science could keep us young and healthy, no matter what our shape. But with the advent of AIDS and crack, being thin began to carry a far different message than it used to, and people like me reaped the benefits. Now there was the immunoshot, but crack had been superseded by whiz and glacier, and thinness was less likely to mean diet spas, more likely to mean your food-credit had run out. There was some talk about optimum bodyweight adjustment, but—like the talk of an oral-dose spermicide since the invention of the vas-valve—no one really cared anymore.

I rubbed the last of the gel off my fingers, knowing where I'd put those fingers next. I never was good at delaying gratification. The deep heat in my breasts and belly demanded an answering heat between my legs, and I trailed my fingers down to play teasingly in the curls there. I traced the rim of my dewy inner lips, imagining alien limbs touching me. The warm tingle of the hardening glitter gel heightened my awareness, but altered it—what living surfaces could rub against mine to excite me in the same way? As I fingered myself, I closed my eyes and thought of orifices opening and closing on my nipples—or my toes or ears. I rubbed my clitoris, wondering how sex would be if it could taste or hear, as well as feel. I thought about orgasming in colors or smells. I imagined the unimaginable, because that was what this party was all about. When I came, I screamed, and for a moment it sounded like someone else.

By the time I'd applied the rest of my makeup and slipped into my soon-to-be-discarded clothes, it was almost time to go. I'd decorated the soft bulge above my stockings with stik-on jewels, and I could both feel and hear them swish against my skirt as I walked. I pulled on my coat and hood, giving myself one last look in the subhall mirror. I'd probably overglitzed myself, revealing myself as the poor little submanagerial I am, but what the hey. I knew that nobody would be looking at me that intensely anyway. Not with the two Hiyo there.

It seemed like a dream, but there it was, in holofoil. Kikito had listed the two Hiyo as hosts, rather than guests of honor, which meant that they would be active participants in the party rather than observers. I knew some people who would kill to have sex with a Hiyo; gossip was that some people had, and that the Hiyo found it uproariously funny. Yet the nature of the Hiyo, as revealed in sex, was said to be tender, searching, patient, and literally empathic. No one could explain this contradiction. No one could explain anything about them. They were just infinitely, literally alien.

For a number of reasons, the Hiyo had been rumors long before they had become news. First contact may have come years before even the first tentative newsleak about an alien species on earth. Were the powers-that-lead-us trying to determine if contact was safe? Or, once the Hiyo had made their first immodest proposals, had the higher-ups not wanted to share a good thing? One story was that the first leak came from a jealous wife, but that was poppycock, since there's no reason that she couldn't have joined in, too. More likely, the Hiyo began to insist on more variety, and so the knowledge of their existence spread. Still, most people were too embarrassed to make the Hiyo bignews. Scientists blushed at the Hiyo's reactions to the most impersonal probes and analysis, and even afternoon talk-show hosts hesitated to ask how the Hiyo ate or washed or prepared for bed.

And here I was, going to a body-morph party at which the two "hosts" were Hiyo-ba and Hiyo-ka, the first two of their kind to land on our planet and mingle. I had no idea how Kikito rated. She was rich, but probably not that rich, and I knew she had never held office. Still, the address for the party was an estate in a governmental trans-urb—maybe her mother or father could pull in some favors. Most of all, I was still astonished that *I* rated. I was ex-urb, I was submanagerial, and I'd never had the slightest body-morphing done. On the other hand, I had lots of flesh and lots of desire to share it. Some people say that the Hiyo have a kind of sixth sense that reads sexual appetite or life energy, regardless of distance and without any direct contact—who knows? All we really knew about them was that we didn't know anything.

Again, I felt a fear that was really more anticipation. I thought about how rare it is for adults to experience something totally, radically new. I'd heard these parties described as losing your virginity all over again, but I knew it was even more than that, even more unimaginable.

The person who answered the door was clearly male, severely morphed toward some indeterminate species. His odor was powerful, and small rows of spikes strained up against the fabric of his satiny briefs. Ferret? Cat? His face was furred, but scales ran down his impressively broad back; his abdomen was large and sculptured. That much work couldn't have been done in fewer than three operations, and it must have been expensive. But from his deferential manner, it was clear that he hadn't paid to have it done. He ushered me inside, the perfect blend of hired help, status item, and conversation piece. I thought about those spikes on his penis and wondered if his tongue had been morphed as well. Maybe I'd get a chance to find out later, I thought. First, I'd look for Kikito. And the "hosts."

More guests were looking at me than I had expected, and all of the looks seemed to be approving. I, on the other hand, was trying not to gawk, while taking in as much of the wild parade as possible. First I focused on the surroundings: shockingly large rooms with an eclectic blend of high-state fixtures and expensively retro furnishings. One room had a four-wall ForRest-Seen, but was furnished in antique chrome and glass. The people, as I had expected, were even more impressive. After dozens of seemingly disinterested glimpses out of the corner of my eye—horned shoulders or magenta buttocks here, a flash of extended membranes there—I at least trusted myself to view my fellow partyers head-on.

It was one thing to see the self-shaped salary-elite in restaurants as I passed, or behind the darkened windows of purring vehicles, and another to be so close that my breath stirred the feathers and fronds on their cheeks or forehead. One person touched me with delicate, feminine hands, pulling my fingers down to a leathery flap in per abdomen; when I lifted the flap out of the way, a huge, deep purple cock reared up, larger than my forearm. "Too much for you," the person said, and laughed. It was half comment and half question; I just nodded and smiled. My new acquaintance smiled back and walked on, heading for a mouth-morphed woman I'd noticed earlier. Good choice, I thought, imagining the oral sex they'd have.

A few moments later I noticed another natural like myself. I have to admit that I was relieved, though also ashamed of my relief. Maybe I was more isolated, off in ex-urbia, than I had thought. I could overlook or accept small changes like Kikito's, but the morphing here left me overwhelmed and exhausted. I'd often looked down on holy-rollie preachers who ranted on about the un-naturalness of body-morphing, re-creating humans in the image of our own whims. Yet here I was, happy beyond words to see someone whose face and body even remotely resembled mine. And call me cynical, but my guess was that the desire and arousal I also felt didn't make me any different from the holy-rollies, either.

Finally, I realized that I'd been doing something I'd successfully avoided until then: staring. The fellow natural, a blond, golden-skinned woman about my height and size, didn't seem to mind. Her dress was surprisingly modest, yards and yards of a plain, heavy fabric, buttoned from navel height to right under her chin. But it was trimmed in what appeared to be real alligator leather, so I guess she expected to be gaped at. The licenses don't come cheap; and if she could bribe her way around the lack of a license, she was even more credit-heavy.

"Are you looking for someone?" she asked me.

"I'm looking for the hostess," I replied, and then stopped. The woman raised one eyebrow, showing that she'd noticed my mistake. I hoped she realized what my intention had been. "I met Kikito doing hours at the med co-op, and I don't know anyone else here," I said to clarify whom I'd meant. It was one thing to mistakenly refer to Kikito as the hostess, far worse if I'd used a gendered pronoun for the Hiyo.

"So *you're* the one she keeps talking about," the woman said, putting her arm around my shoulder and smiling at me. I smiled back, happy that she had whisked us past my clumsy opening. Her breath was very sweet and smelled slightly of violets. Probably the glands had been engineered, but it was hard to tell. "I'm Pie," she said, as if that ought to mean something to me. I was still assimilating the idea that Kikito talked about me—or that the quiet, elegant woman "kept talking" at all, as far as that goes.

"Y'know," the blonde said. "Pie. Kikito's my birth-sister. On our mother's side."

Kikito had, of course, never said anything to me about a sister. But the more I looked at Pie, the more resemblance I saw, despite the obvious differences. Kikito was taller, muscular, and almost slender, though still roundly female and huggable-looking. Still, she and Pie shared the same lush mouth and the same cleft chin. Pie's face would have been shaped very differently, but Kikito's air-gills—her only body-morphing, or at least the only one visible in public—gave her the same round look as Pie's natural contours. Mostly, I saw the similarity in their eyes. Kikito's were round and dark as her skin, while Pie's were oblique and ice green, but both sisters shared the same expression, at once wistful and playful.

"Does she really?" I said.

"Does who really what?" Pie replied, pulling me closer. I couldn't tell if she was kidding or not.

"Kikito," I said somewhat thickly. "Does she talk about me? To you I mean. I guess."

Pie cuddled against me until I could feel her flowery breath on my face. Her lips were a deep, almost bloody red, apparently without makeup-tattooed, maybe, or even engineered. I began to wonder just how "natural" she was, after all. On the other hand, she didn't seem to care that I wasn't morphed, and I found myself caring less and less that she might be. Under the voluminous dress, her round body felt solid yet giving, a comforting presence in my arms. How strange and wonderful it feels, I thought, to hold a body this much like my own.

"Oh, you're really my sister's type." Pie's voice grew even deeper and more musical; she half-whispered, as though sharing a secret. "We fight over lovers all the time.

"Would you let me see what you have under there?" she said, pulling my skirt up with one hand and reaching out to stroke my leg with the other. Before I knew it, her hand rested warmly on my lower thigh. The feel of it through my stocking reminded me of my earlier fantasies: an interface of flesh and not-quite-flesh, textures unnervingly strange and exquisitely erotic. Then her hand climbed past my stik-on jewels, and it was flesh on flesh for sure. Very much. Indeed.

Well, I thought, this is what I came here for. In a way, Pie was as strange to me as a morpher would be, though of course not over-the-edge like the Hiyo. In her case, the strangeness came from familiarity: I'd never made love to a woman whose size and shape were this close to mine. I felt as though I were holding my exact breast and belly, hips and thighs and ass. As though my image had stepped out of the mirror while I had my orgasm and was meeting me here so we could do it again.

"You first," I whispered into her ear, past her thicket of gloriously blond hair. I grazed her earlobe lightly with my teeth; in response, she moved closer.

I wanted to feel the texture of her skin, which I imagined would be much like mine: soft and smoothly dimpled, warm curves giving beneath my fingers. And most of all, I wanted to experience the protected triangle of her sex, to know if that was like mine, too. Because of the thick fabric of her dress and the wide band of strategically placed leather, I could feel her general shape quite well, but these details were kept mysterious. As she no doubt intended.

"Are you sure you're ready?" Pie asked. "You know I'd hate to have you spoil the surprise too early. . . ."

"No surprise to me," I said, nuzzling her neck. I opened the first two buttons of her dress, bending down to kiss her chest and tits—

—and stopped, my eyes inches from the field of blue bumps that pulsed, ever so slightly, with each beat of her heart.

"No surprise, oh?"

Pie didn't seem offended, although it must have been clear that her skin was as awful to me as it was awe inspiring. Maybe that's the reaction she wanted, or maybe she just didn't care. She smiled as I began to brush her skin lightly with my palm. Then she shuddered and arched her chest to my hand, taking in a sharp, deep breath. Clearly, her skin had been engineered for sensitivity as well as for exotic looks. The bumps were surprisngly soft—much like the skin I had expected, but textured in an intricate topography of hills and valleys.

I undid the next five buttons, and Pie's dress fell open to her navel. The bumps on her abdomen were much larger; from her waist down, they alternated with horizontal ridges, the same pale green as her eyes. I was amazed that I could have held her without knowing. But the thick fabric and full drape of the dress were clearly designed to make this possible.

Many people, I knew, would have found Pie's skin disgusting. On the other hand, many people would have been disgusted by her size and shape—*our* size and shape—only a few decades ago. My first reaction had been a matter of shock as much as anything else. An alien familiarity, familiar alienation—was this any more unnatural than age retardation, skin regeneration, or any of the dozens of procedures that were considered medical instead of morphing? And why was I here at this party, anyway?

"Oh, surprise, yes," I whispered, reaching back up to her exposed chest. I spread both of my hands out, cupping her flesh, massaging her skin with my thumbs.

She sighed and leaned toward me, increasing the pressure of my hands against the delicate tissue on her chest. I could feel her pulse. It reminded me of the warm, soft twitch of my own pussy, when I caress myself alone at night. Or maybe both reminded me of something else: the rhythm of an insect just out of the chrysalis, pumping its quivering wings in the sun. I thought of butterfly wings spread—as I sometimes spread my own labia to enjoy their velvety texture, as Pie's skin was spread before me, so naked and unashamed in the passion it was made for. As I stroked and held her, Pie's response was immediate. I could tell her pleasure from her breathing, the small sounds she made, and her movement under and into my hands. Her hips did not move, though mine began to, as I caught her excitement.

I bent down to kiss Pie's chest, no longer surprised at what I was doing. In addition to the salty taste I expected, her skin had a sweet, flowery flavor. Finally I placed it: the same violet tincture as her breath. I began licking Pie's skin. My tongue worked in broad, moist strokes across her breastbone, then tickled the plump curve where her neck and shoulders joined.

Pie moaned for me to continue—maybe words, and maybe not. Whichever, her meaning was clear. She slumped toward me, and I could feel her body going even softer in my arms. I studied her face: round and golden and yearning, as beautiful as any sight I had ever seen. Her eyes were closed, her face tight with bliss and a growing need for release. Rubbing her extraordinary chest against my own clothed softness, she tipped her head back and up, invitingly offering her mouth to mine.

We kissed deeply, matching our movements to each other's urges as though we could read minds. I knew that others at the party were probably watching, but I didn't care. If anything, it made the whole experience even sweeter.

Her lips were hotter than any I had ever experienced—engineered for sure, I thought with what was left of my logical mind. I felt enveloped and inflamed, nurtured and hungry. Soon, I shut my eyes, and my awareness narrowed down to one throbbing beat of her lips on mine, of her exquisitely embellished chest pressing against me, of my wet and hungry pussy.

As I was beginning to grow crazy for orgasm, it seemed that Pie was approaching hers. I was surprised, but pleased, especially for her: if you can come just from necking, I thought, more power to you. I rubbed and squeezed her nipples, which looked like alien, dark blue pebbles. That didn't do anything for Pie, though, and neither did stroking the paler, smoother surface of her breasts. She gently took my hand and replaced it on the hilly skin of her chest, without breaking our kiss. When she did pull her mouth away from mine, it was to whisper, more breathlessly than ever, "Lick me here again. Like you did. Please."

Pie's hands had worked their way up under my dress and were resting, tantalizingly, on my thigh and hip. There was a dancing light in her pale green eyes, and she smiled at me as I paused. It could hardly have been more clear: she knew what I wanted, but she wanted me to ask her, as she had asked me. She even played with my garter belt and panties, her fingers toying with the elastic and just barely avoiding contact with my pussy. Her own excitement grew more and more obvious. Finally, for one delicious moment, she touched the dewy outer lips; then her fingers withdrew again.

"Yes, please, touch me!" I called out, not caring who heard or what per reaction was.

"Yes!" she said, smiling. "And we'll finish together."

Immediately, as though it were one movement, she plunged her hand into my underpants, and I began lapping and kissing and sucking her exotically sculptured skin. No wonder she had steered my hand from her nipples, when each blood-hot nodule was like a nipple, or more. I ground my hips against hers; she wriggled her torso under the stimulus from my tongue and lips. I held her tightly as she played my pussy with a delicate yet expert touch. After teasing my labia, she began stroking my clitoris with her thumb—first gently, then more and more firmly. A deeper need had just begun to build in me when she satisfied it, plunging two fingers into my vagina. Riding her hand, I licked her flowery sweetness with more and more speed and enthusiasm.

It felt strange, yet somehow right—not cunnilingus, kissing, or nursing, but some combination of the three that was even more erotic. As I nuzzled and nipped, sucked and smooched, I could hear her whimpering into my ear.

"Suck me," she said.

And I did, sucking one node of her skin after another, always startling and satisfying her as I switched from place to place. Sometimes I used my tongue to tickle the valleys in between; usually, then, she would gasp, a soft, ragged sound that made a shudder run through my own body.

When her orgasm started, she shoved her two fingers completely into me, and I began to climax, too. I licked her throat, where the morphed skin faded into soft creaminess so much like mine; she moaned and shivered and almost screamed, working my pussy in the same rhythm as my mouth against her chest. I held her, my knees weak and my hips bucking uncontrollably. During my own release, I buried my face almost completely in her chest and shoulders, shouting my triumph into her hot, velvety skin. Afterward, she stood, panting and flushed. I clung to her, exhausted and energized. I was ecstatic and speechless, changed in some way I couldn't define.

"So, are you enjoying the party so far?" she said.

We both started laughing. For a while, I was afraid that I wouldn't stop. I had worried so much—about the strangeness of the party, about the status of the others who'd be there—and the sex had happened too quickly for my feelings to catch up. As we laughed, she put one arm around me in a friendly hug: in some ways, that was as satisfying, and as much of a release, as the sex had been.

"Imagine what could have happened if we'd actually taken our clothes off!" I managed to say, before hooting with laughter again.

Pie looked at me oddly for a moment, as if she were trying to answer a question. Then her smile returned. I noticed once more how much her mouth reminded me of Kikito's.

"Oh, I don't think that would have made much difference," she said. Her tone of voice, like the look she had given me a moment earlier, was mysterious. While still affectionate, Pie's voice conveyed some kind of distance, as well. This bothered me, especially after the closeness of our postfinish laughter.

"I guess not," I said, mostly to be saying something. I wanted to prolong the intimacy we had had, or reinstate it. Finally I cuddled closer against Pie and said, "Do you want me to feel you again? Anywhere else?"

Pie's look was again unreadable: more mischievous than before, but maybe a bit sad as well.

"Sure," she said.

I kissed her, happy to have her strange, familiar lips back on mine. I quickly grew aroused again; my whole body tingled, especially where her abundant flesh pressed up against me. We kissed deeply and strongly, Pie running her fingers through my hair and pulling me even closer to her. If she could finish like that from the skin of her torso, I thought—no matter how much morphed and sensitivity engineered—imagine what she'll do when I feel her *here*. As I reached down into her dress, it suddenly occurred to me that her genitals could be morphed as well. Before I could wonder, however, I knew.

First, I discovered that she wore no briefs, just as she had worn no upper foundation. Thrilled and made bold by the freedom that gave me, I immediately reached further to stroke her pubic hair. And got the second surprise of this encounter: nothing.

Between per legs, Pie was as smooth and anonymous as a dress-up doll. For a moment, I held per featureless groin, hopping to cover for my astonishment. I was embarrassed, too; I didn't know if the cause was Pie's real nature or my own mistaken ideas about per. It was too late to try to remember if I'd spoken the pronouns aloud at any time, too late to undo any of the interior assumptions I'd made so naively. Time only to wonder how I could cover, and where we could go from here.

And a small moment to marvel that I'd already made sex with a transgender body-morph. Without knowing it at the time.

"Do you think I should have my skin done down there too?" my body-morphed partner said. Pie was trying to be gentle, but I felt as if every arrogant, shameful thought in my head was open and clear to per. I said nothing, though I did lean my head on per shoulder.

"That's such a common place, though, isn't it?" Pie continued. "And I don't think I need it. Do you?"

I snuggled up to per ample body more closely, enjoying the comfort and human warmth I found there. Our stature and size were so deceptively similar, yet for me that had become overshadowed by how different we were—as different, I thought, as two humans could be. It was still tough for me to think of Pie as transgendered. I hugged her—no, *per*—full, yielding breasts and kissed per red lips. Then I gently traced the contours of per torso skin with my fingers and felt myself smile.

"No," I said. "I don't think you need anything more. Not at all."

We kissed again; I put my arm around Pie and felt per relax beside me. In a moment, Pie started buttoning per dress. I helped her and couldn't keep from noticing the cloth—even thicker, with more concealing bulk and stiffness, than I had guessed.

"Yeah, well, I thought you might be surprised. In my job, all my clothes have to keep it subtle. Can't disturb the little ex-urb naturals I work with, y'know?"

I'd assumed that Pie, like per sister, had known my status but hadn't cared. That remark left me both stung and curious: was it mere carelessness, or had my own shocked reaction hurt per feelings, and this was a small payback? I never had time to find out.

At that moment, Kikito came into the hallway. She put one hand on my shoulder, one on the shoulder of the person to whom she was birth-sister. As she kissed Pie on the cheek, Kikito's air-gills quivered slightly.

I'd always thought Kikito was beautiful; that night, she was splendid. She wore only makeup, body-sheen, a garter belt, and stockings—the last of which framed not only her beautiful ass, but also a small, furry tail. In front, her pubic triangle was shaved and powdered, but clearly nonmorphed and female. When she drew close, I could tell she smelled like honey. At first I wondered if that, like Pie's scent, was the product of bioengineering; finally, I realized that the scent came from the powder. Edible, no doubt. More than ever, I wondered why she had invited me here. But I cared less than ever, because I was completely ready for anything she might suggest.

"You wouldn't be stealing my invitee, would you now, sibling dear?" Kikito smiled at Pie and then, more reassuringly, at me.

"I told you we have the same taste in women," Pie said, to me but also clearly for per sister's benefit.

"Ummm." Kikito licked her lips. "Like that comedian on the 'Now Show' said—'I like my lovers the way I like my Coff-E-Cream. Rich, sweet, and full-bodied with fat.' "

The latter two, maybe, I thought. I may have reacted visibly to the casual assumption that everyone there was "rich," but no one seemed to notice.

There was some tension between Kikito and Pie,

obviously present but hard to figure out. It seemed like more than just a rivalry between co-sibs. Kikito looked at Pie at least as much, and as intensely, as she looked at me. Was it my imagination that Kikito's touch on Pie's shoulder was something other than sisterly? I wondered about Kikito's stance, and Pie's as well: close to each other but rigid, avoiding touch beyond the one contact point of Kikito's hand on Pie's shoulder, their breathing just a bit harder than usual. Overall, the effect was enough to make me wonder about Kikito's taste for round women. Maybe, I thought, Pie's shape and Kikito's preference in lovers had more to do with each other than either sibling would admit.

"I think she's had a good time," Pie said to Kikito. "A good time, and a few—surprises. Wouldn't you say so?"

I swallowed hard and then nodded. "Very surprising, but very pleasant," I said finally.

"Well," Kikito said to her sibling. "I'm sure you can find others to surprise." She looked Pie up and down and then turned to me.

"Let's walk," she said. "I'll get you a splash and a nibble, and then—" She patted my ass, swishing her own pert little tail as she did so. "And then, we'll get you out of those clothes—nice as they are—and introduce you to our hosts."

Kikito steered me to the refreshment stations, taking my arm in hers. The contrast was delicious: my arm pale, solid yet soft; hers brown and muscular. Her breasts swung as she walked. Their full weight, and the generous swell of her hips, complemented the athletic tautness of her limbs and abdomen. That was an unfashionable look, associated with time spent in selfish physical entertainment instead of helping others. But Kikito was the kind of person who didn't care what others thought, and I admired her independence. Anyway, I knew the stereotype was completely untrue in this case. Not only did she put in more hours at the med co-op than I did, Kikito was also known for her work in the animal wing of the bio-accidents depot, which she ran almost single-handedly.

Despite the release I had had earlier with Pie—and another at home, before I left—I found myself stimulated by Kikito's presence. She and I drew closer as we walked, until her breast brushed my arm with each step we took. The texture of her skin on mine made clear that her breast had been dusted with powder, too, and I found myself imagining the taste of it.

At first I took only brief glimpses of Kikito, glancing at her body and then back up to her face when she spoke. Soon, however, it became clear that she didn't mind me looking. In fact, it seemed to please her that I wanted to. I especially liked the look of her thighs, lean but thick enough with muscle. When the light caught her pubic lips from the right angle, the taste-powder sparkled, more subtly but at least as brightly as my own edible glitter. I was clearly outclassed; but to my surprise, I didn't feel on the defensive. Her smile was warm and reassuring. And I found myself imagining what it would be like to taste the honey-powder there, as well. "Pink punch, tea, or pop?" Kikito asked when we reached the drink station. "Pink punch is doused with E-rose," she said casually.

Once again, my shock must have shown on my face; Kikito giggled, then stifled it. Her brown eyes were warm, and I felt much more comfortable than I ever had with Pie. She knew I was an ex-urb, submanagerial rube. And it was no problem.

"No pink punch, I guess," she said. "The E-rose is really gold plate on the lily anyway, what with the Hiyo and all. Still, a little arousal and empathy never hurt anyone, did it?"

My look must have told her that I wasn't so sure, but she smiled dazzlingly at me, anyway, as she poured some pink punch for herself.

"Just tea for me. Assam, if you have it."

"Fine," she said, sipping her pink punch and smiling even more stunningly. "But if that's the way you feel, I'd better take a shower before we go down with each other."

I didn't know which was more astounding, the casual offer of sex or the idea that her powder was doused with E-rose. On second thought, I wondered if it was an offer of sex or merely a suppositional statement. At least she acknowledged the possibility of sex between us. For now, I thought, that's enough for me.

Kikito finished her punch and set down the cup, which was quickly whisked away by someone with a bland, gender-free face and green hair down to the hem of per skirt. Again, I had to marvel at the ostentation. I knew it might be just for this party, but I was still astonished to see this many body-morphed servants. And when they were doing jobs that could have been done by a simple, single-command mech—well, even for the salary-elite, that's showing off.

We walked past the nibbles and sweetmeats at the various food stations. I sipped my Assam, too distracted to eat anything. Kikito was usually a hearty eater, but I knew she wouldn't be consuming much tonight—not with the E-rose coursing through her system from within and without. She picked up a small form of marzipan and chewed at it thoughtfully.

"You know," she said, "we used to think that sex is the most basic human drive, but the Hiyo have shown us it's not."

I looked around, taking in the refreshment stations and the hallway beyond. In one corner of the room, two people were intertwined, forming a mound of multicolored feathers. I couldn't tell where one left off and the other began, and I wondered if they themselves knew. Closer to us, a gangly figure, over nine feet tall, bent down to stroke the back of someone morphed into a quadruped. In turn, she—the gender was very obvious from where I stood—was beckoning for a naked, rainbow-hued trio to leave the drink station and come join the fun. I thought about what I had just experienced with Pie. How right it had felt—not only natural but vitally important. And I knew, with an unshakable certainty, that at that very moment someone else was licking and sucking per skin, as I had been earlier. With or without gender, how could we do without sex?

Kikito studied my face, again reading my opinion there. I looked at her in return, feeling comfortable and unashamed. She set down the marzipan and continued in a slow, distant voice, overenunciating to keep her words from slurring.

"No, really. The drives for power and status are clearly more important. Think about it.

"What do people spend more time on? And how many people let their pay-work interfere with their sex lives? Do you know even one person whose sex life is so primary that it jeopardizes per job?" I started to speak and then stopped myself. I could quibble with that example, but on the whole I felt Kikito was right.

Kikito's round, dark eyes were soft and dreamy; she was clearly skimming high on the E-rose. She grinned and brushed an imaginary crumb of marzipan from her breast. My eyes followed her hand intently, and I felt my pussy clench in a brief, involuntary spasm. Her gaze locked on mine, still dreamy, and she laughed.

"Oh, I'm not saying sex isn't important. And more for some humans than others." She laid her hand gently on my arm. "That's why we're here tonight, after all."

I set down my empty teacup and moved toward her, into her embrace. Some of her powder clung to my dress, and I knew it was time to disrobe.

"But sex *is* the basic drive of the Hiyo," Kikito continued. "They think of it as often as we think of money, acceptance, and power all together. Their culture is based on it, as ours is based on domination of resources and each other. It's their security, their goal, their daily employment—" She held me close, looking intently at my face, yet focused beyond it as well. The light shone through her dark, thick hair like a halo.

"You'll see," she said, and kissed me.

I had to agree with Kikito's point about which human drives were more basic. And yet—and yet— For all my worries, and all of the signs of status-upping I'd seen here tonight, the facts were that I had still been invited, that I was here, and that I was probably as accepted as I wanted to be. Certainly as much as I needed to be. Nonetheless, Kikito's words had made me feel even more thrilled—and anxious—about meeting the Hiyo.

At that moment, however, all fears were drowned as I enjoyed the full experience of Kikito's kiss. Unlike Pie, Kikito's lips were cool, slippery with a fruity-tasting gloss: artificial, but made-up rather than engineered. Her mouth was as full as Pie's, though, and as inviting. We held each other when the kiss ended, as comfortable as though we had been partners for years.

"Let me get you ready," Kikito whispered to me, her mouth only inches away. Her breath was moist, tickling the depths and surfaces of my ear. Its brief, phantom caress stirred my pussy: still wet down there, I knew I was becoming wetter still.

Kikito began to undress me, as I had hoped and known she would. First she unfastened my duster, unhooking the collar and drawing her fingers down both sides of the new-zip. As its magnetic teeth unsealed and the duster parted, Kikito paused to take in the sight she had uncovered: the camisole, the glitter gel, and all the lush fullness of my body underneath. The duster's skirt opened and fell away, and Kikito grinned appreciatively. She ran her fingers lightly over my jeweled thighs, above the stockings; but I knew she was really looking at the irregular, dark spot on my briefs, a clear sign of my arousal. Then she helped me take off the rest of my duster, licking above the top of my camisole as she slid the blouse over my shoulders. When we kissed again,

I knew, I would taste the glitter gel—and perhaps my own skin—on her mouth and tongue.

More than just preplay to get me ready, the undressing was an act of sharing in itself. Skimming high on E-rose, Kikito was in turn playful, fierce, tender, and almost maudlin. She looked sad when she folded my duster and gave it to a waiting drone, but maybe that was just impatience at any delay. A moment later, she laughed gleefully as I pulled the camisole off over my head. And when she unsnapped my remaining underclothes, she clapped her hands like a little child. Soon I, like Kikito, had stripped down to a garter belt and stockings. We stood facing each other, holding hands. Enjoying simply looking and being looked at.

"Do you like-a my tail?" Kikito said, turning around. Looking over her shoulder, she wiggled and wagged at me. Her voice had a singsong rhythm, but was deeper and stronger than her usual voice.

"Yes," I replied, amazed to realize I was speaking the truth. "The perfect complement to your perfect, squeezable ass."

In fact, the first glimpse of her tail had shocked me less than her air-gills do even now. Small, furry, and curly, it seemed somehow friendly, like the tail of a young puppy. Its movement was obviously under Kikito's conscious control, as well: kept still and limp to hide under her clothing, but marvelously expressive now that she was showing it off. One part of my mind noted how much extra the will-linked neurological work must have cost, but the rest of me cared much more about how it would respond to my touch and how it would feel in my hand.

"Talk about *my* ass!" Kikito faced me and reached out her arms. "I've wanted to feel that tuchus of yours since you first wore those red pantaloons to the co-op."

I flushed, realizing how oblivious I had been for so long, and how much her feelings meant to me now. My own feelings were as strong as the lust I had felt for Pie, but different—and, I sensed, far more important to both of us.

"Did you ever wonder if I'd been morphed?"

Kikito laughed and made a dismissive gesture: none of this mattered nearly as much as most people thought.

"No," she said. "Umm—your clothes made it clear—and the way you looked at me—"

I knew what she was saying, and what she was avoiding saying. It didn't pay to ignore the human drives, whether status or sex; but there was no reason to take them too seriously, either. We were from different soc-worlds, but in other ways we were made for each other. Only the future would tell which was more important.

"Could we go somewhere?" I asked. I could feel my heart beating more quickly. And I wanted Kikito to hold me close enough for her to feel it, too.

Kikito paused, her head cocked. She seemed to be listening for something, but I had no idea what. All I could hear was the mixture of voices and noises—chitter-chat and carnality—that had filled the room since we entered. Maybe she was hearing something from the E-rose, I thought, or maybe her hearing had been engineered to go along with the tail. Then I noticed the small bump, just under her hairline. Of course! More proof of what a rube I was, not to think that she might have had an innercom implanted. Even some people in my ex-urb were starting to get those.

"Later," she said after a moment. Her voice was warm and inviting—a promise, not a put-off. She kissed me again, not as hard but even more passionately than before. Her mouth was still sweet with my glitter gel; for one instant, I felt as if I were swimming in the taste, everything else in the world obliterated. I wondered if the E-rose in her taste-powder was affecting me through the skin. Then I wondered if the transport I felt was due to Kikito alone. Finally, I decided it didn't matter.

"Now, I think it's time for you to meet our hosts."

As we walked through the mazelike hallways, Kikito made sure I knew the protocol. We'd be met by a human, an office-appointed diplomat and keeper for the Hiyo. Per presence was nonnegotiable. After the introductions, however, the person would almost certainly leave me alone with the Hiyo, if I knew what I was doing.

"Alone?" I asked. I was slowly realizing that Kikito wouldn't be there with me, either. The thought was disappointing, yet also thrilling.

Kikito patted my arm. "You'll do fine."

When I was young, I'd had an uncle who was a researcher in history for the info-feeds. Not a very impressive position, but it was salaried. He isn't around now: a few decades after I was born, he'd given up on age retardation. No one in the family could persuade him to change his mind, and finally he died. I certainly didn't understand it then, and I still don't. But I think it had something to do with his work with history, with the grasp it gave him of how things rise and fall and fade away.

That night, I thought of some of the research my uncle had told me about. The field was called "fairy tales," or maybe "folk tales." It was a literary genre, of a sort—stories people told each other, especially when they were premature. They'd been very popular for a while, he said. I think it made him sad that they weren't anymore, although it was hard to tell.

Whenever I was home alone at night, he would dial me up and tell me some of the stories. At first I listened mostly because it pleased him, and he was a nice person—scary as he grew wrinkly and fragile, but nice. The stories seemed very simple, and I couldn't see that there was much to them. But over time, I discovered that they stayed with me, somehow, more than stories that had seemed much more interesting at the time. I

would find myself thinking of little bits of the stories—
a character or event or setting—at odd times throughout
the day or night.

Long after my uncle was gone, I looked at the world
around me and thought: we have become like those
stories. The prince with the one swan-wing. The talking
audio-animo mirrors or doors or fountains. The fox-girl,
cat-woman, or goose-girl. And most of all, the poor,
marginal match-girls and bellboys, looking for the magic
that will turn them into trans-urb royalty.

As we embraced and Kikito turned to leave me, I
knew that I was about to face the highest royalty, the
strangest magic. Soon, the hallway was empty except
for me—although they had known not to stop us, I
wondered how many of the body-morphed partyers we
had passed were actually officials and guards. The door
was heavy, like those in my uncle's stories. I think it
may even have been real wood, though I hated to think
how much that would have cost. I knocked, then heard
a human voice answer from within.

I felt I had finally learned my lesson. No matter
who answered, I was ready to use *per* mentally and avoid
using any pronouns aloud, until I could check with Kikito. However, the person who opened the door was
clearly male, in a way that left nothing to the imagination. He was morphed, his natural male genitals surrounded by ruffles of orange flesh, the purpose of which
I could not begin to guess. By that point, though, I was
ready to take that in stride. It shocked me only slightly
more than his complete nakedness, which is to say not
much.

In the next moment, I noticed something odd about
his eyes. They looked natural, but their movement was
not, tracking things in short, staccato jerks. Then the
light hit them just right, and I saw a small glowing spot
in each. Each spot was too small to be tapetum, though
that had been my first guess, because the treatments

had become so popular lately. Of course, I thought. He still had the old cyborg-style eye-cams, instead of having switched over to full biological models like almost everyone else. I realized that had to mean he was old—decades older than I was, even older than the uncle I had just been thinking about. He looked just barely postmature, but that certainly meant nothing. Almost everyone did.

"Welcome," he said, and held out his hand to me. It was tattooed with elaborate swirls and three interlocking rings.

"The sign of my office, given to me by these two Hiyo." As he was answering my unasked question, he pointed to a ridge that bisected his scalp and parted his spiky, red hair down the middle. I had assumed the ridge was decorative, but again I had been wrong. All the info-feeds had announced that telepathic innercoms were possible, but I hadn't been sure whether they were in use yet or not. Certainly, I'd never imagined I'd meet anyone with one. Yet another first for this evening, I thought.

"I'm Tapano Gan," he said. "Please, call me Tappi." His voice was friendly, bubblesome yet calm. In fact, despite the body-morphing and the outdated cyborg-cam eyes, his main effect was reassuring but enthusiastic—like a best friend's older brother taking you to a pub-den, protective but ready to let you in on all the fun. He offered to disable what he called "the human-specific channel" of his telepathic receiver, so that he could no longer read my thoughts. With an inner sigh of relief, I told him I would prefer that.

"The main purpose of the device is to interface with the Hiyo," Tappi told me. His tone of voice, when he mentioned interfacing with the Hiyo, was strongly laden with emotions I could not interpret. Pride? Protectiveness? Arousal? Surely something personal and important. I realized that whether or not he participated directly in what the Hiyo did with others, it affected him; that he would be a part of what I experienced this evening, no matter what.

"They've asked that you shed the rest of your clothing. They prefer all humans naked."

That explained Tappi's nudity, I realized, and even the Hiyo's choice of a tattooed symbol rather than a badge or vest-patch. I also realized that he was in communication with them as we spoke—that the Hiyo were meeting me through his senses. Did they prefer his cyborg-cams to a more modern bio-fix? Did it give a picture more like their own senses? It was impossible to tell or even guess.

Tappi helped me out of my stockings and garter belt. His touch was friendly and helpful, neither intimate nor coolly distant. He did have some trouble undoing one garter, in which the polarity of the Snap-It threads had become misaligned. He chuckled and then looked up at me, smiling; I met the clear gaze of his baby blues, and I smiled, too. I wasn't aroused by him yet, but I decided that I did like him. And it would be very easy to desire him, in the right circumstances.

"Are you ready?" he asked, pointing to the door—short and wide, made out of shiny pink metal—at the other end of the room.

"As I'll ever be," I said. He smiled again and took my arm, escorting me to meet the Hiyo.

My first impression was the delicate smell that wafted out to meet me as Tappi opened the door. I've since talked to other people about their encounters with the Hiyo. Yes, the government discourages such talk, and supposedly it just isn't done. But like anything else associated with sex, people in the right situation will usually go ahead and do it anyway.

In these conversations, everyone I've talked to has mentioned that odor, and no one can describe it. Elusive yet strong, not the odor of flowers or food but somehow similar to both—one person I talked to called it "the olfactory equivalent of breakfast in bed, waking up on solstice morning, and a hot bath. All in one." I can't do any better than that.

"May I introduce our hosts," Tappi said, gently pulling me forward by our linked elbows.

"Hiyo-ba," he said, nodding to a frighteningly huge, elaborate, multilimbed creature filling one side of the room, "and Hiyo-ka," nodding to a smaller pile of flesh, dun-colored and amorphous, quivering in the middle of the other half of the room.

"They say they are very happy to meet you, and they wish you many fine orgasms this evening." Then Tappi switched from his official translator's voice and whispered, "It's okay. They wouldn't have picked you if you couldn't enjoy it. Go ahead."

The Hiyo had picked me? But I had no time to ponder that.

Even as Tappi spoke, I had felt all worry and anxiety leaving me. From small personal embarrassment to the deepest terror of the alien shapes, any fear was washed away within moments. Perhaps the odor from the Hiyo was chemically active, permeating and soothing my brain. Perhaps that change was the first foretaste of the deeper mental communion I had with them later. At the time, the effect was so deep that I didn't even wonder where or what it came from. I felt one stray bit of wonder and a hint of gratitude, and then nothing. I searched all the corners of my psyche and found only happiness. And the beginnings of sexual anticipation.

In describing the events that follow, I can't always tell you what information was told to me by Tappi and what came from my link with the Hiyo. For all I know, Tappi may have used his innercom again, to send me thoughts instead of reading them. This aspect of the Hiyo is hard to understand, yet vital: our minds, linked like the circles in Tappi's tattoo, became one field of play, a shared erogenous zone at least as important as any flesh or skin.

Many humans say they know the erotic importance of thought, but only a few tantra-technicians even approach living that awareness the way the Hiyo do. We shared physical touch and we shared thoughts, and all of it was sex. In the Hiyo language, Tappi later told me, there wasn't any vocabulary to make the distinction clear. "Of course," he said, "they have a term for thoughts *about* sex. But it isn't used very often."

At Tappi's suggestion, I sat down within touching distance of Hiyo-ba. Upon first seeing the two Hiyo, I had been most intimidated by Hiyo-ba: not only per size, but the feelings the alien generated. And as I seated myself on the floor, I still felt that I'd be more comfortable with Hiyo-ka. Perhaps, I thought, that reluctance was why Tappi wanted me to approach Hiyo-ba first. Later, I decided that there could have been other reasons as well.

I had known that the aliens' sexes were referred to as "push" and "pull." Apparently, sex with pull was much more in demand among humans, but generally— for anyone short of, say, state regent—sex with push was required as part of the deal. Hiyo-ba was clearly the push member of this couple.

Still, I could not be afraid of Hiyo-ba. And the more I studied per, the more attracted to per I became. Unlike the featurelessness of Hiyo-ka's surface, Hiyo-ba was an intricate knotwork of protuberances: short and long, tentacles and segmented limbs, coils that ended in claws or probes, and delicate-seeming sensory fronds of all kinds. Beyond all these beautiful extensions, per skin was dark and opalescent, with highlights like the sheen of oil on water.

How could I stand not to touch such beauty? My hunger to feel per body was like ordinary sexual desire, and yet unlike it. There was no pressure to hurry, but a complete assurance that nothing could ever be more

wonderful than what I was about to do. Fired by enthusiasm for the Hiyo, my imagination was strong
enough for me to feel phantom pressure on my fingers,
even before I had reached out.

When I did make contact, I felt a spark shoot
through my head, a ripping ecstasy like golden barbed
wire in my mind. And in the next moment, that mind
was no longer mine alone. I embraced Hiyo-ba totally
and felt my entire being suffused by that sharp, golden
electrical charge. A thrill rose from my painted toenails
to my scalp, and beyond.

My pussy was wet, almost itching. I felt exhilarated
and driven by unquenchable need. I didn't know if the
excitement was mine or Hiyo-ba's, and it didn't matter.
Later, as the link grew stronger, I could almost tell the
difference: per sex, I decided, was stronger, harsher,
more all-consuming. Later, I wondered if that was just
an area of my own sexuality that Hiyo-ba had helped
me experience for the first time. Probably it was both.

One of Hiyo-ba's grasping limbs—a beautiful spiral
tentacle, mottled lavender and dark crimson—took my
right hand and directed it to a stoma in per skin. The
hole was oval, surrounded by slack, pale lips that were
slightly sticky. As I gently stroked its delicate rim, the
stoma closed, then opened again, exhaling a small gust
of air. It felt good to my hand and smelled strongly of
the delicate, lovely odor that permeated the room. Was
the opening for breathing, eating, or excreting? Or
something else, something I could never even imagine?
I thought about the question at the time, but it would
be hard to convey how little it meant to me. I felt our
mutual need grow.

By that time, Hiyo-ba's desire was in me, deep and
hard—more than any flesh ever had been or could be.
I stroked the slick lips of per stoma and felt per desire
swell within. At one point I penetrated the opening,
hooking my finger briefly inside. That seemed to be too
much for Hiyo-ba, and I did not do it again.

Soon, I felt a shift, as clear yet as ephemeral as the awareness that precedes a partner's orgasm: yes, this is it, we're entering the next phase now. Hiyo-ba touched me with one hairy, segmented limb. It was a glancing touch, and yet I knew I had been hugged. The shining excitement I felt was joined by something more nurturing: a calm, like the rocking depths of the ocean. The touch was physically cold, like the skin of the stoma, and I shivered. But inside I felt a deep warmth join the scintillations and shocks.

Hiyo-ba's entire body trembled, a delicate wave from one end to the other. I felt myself being drawn to what seemed the center of per body: near the top, a bit off to one side. It was the only space bigger than my head that had no protuberances.

To reach it, I had to climb Hiyo-ba, actually ascending per like a small carnal hill. Each time I set my foot down at the root of one of per limbs and hoisted myself up by another, I felt our excitement grow. And with each part of per body I touched, my own responded differently. I was overheated and then more coolly relaxed, breathing hard and then gently. I felt arousal in every part of my body, sequentially: my breasts so heavy and nipples so hard they almost ached, then genital excitement so strong that I felt my own juices running down my leg. Even my fingers and toes clenched and unclenched; even my scalp flushed and tingled.

By the time I reached the top, my entire body hummed with lust. It seemed that our excitement must fill the whole room: I thought briefly of Tappi, but couldn't bring myself to look in his direction. I felt Hiyo-ba in each monad of my consciousness. I was displaced, or transformed. Hiyo-ba's pleasure filled the universe, so how could I have been anything other?

The climb was strenuous, and by the time I reached Hiyo-ba's finishing-spot I was breathless from exertion as well as from sex. But I could no more have paused for breath than I could pause for breath during orgasm.

Not that this was our orgasm, yet. I shivered at the knowledge of how much more intensity I was to experience.

Hiyo-ba did not have to guide my hand; by that time, per wishes were mine, on what seemed like a cellular level. I put my hand flat on per ultimate sensory zone and felt another explosion of delight and yearning. I could also feel the beginning quakes of my own physical orgasm, though that was much less important. Per skin was smooth and tender; I felt it not only under my hand, but up through my arm and into my heart. Suddenly, I could hear every sound in the room, from my own breathing to a rustle of Hiyo-ba's limbs in Tappi's direction. Each sound was like a caress on my skin, but also phantom through all of my flesh and beyond. I knew Hiyo-ba's physical release had begun, and I had to hurry.

I rubbed my relaxed hand, fully open, back and forth across Hiyo-ba. Our delight rose and climaxed, and we finished together.

For a moment, I felt like a child's inflatable toy that has been overfilled but cannot explode. Every speck of my tissue, every thought of my mind, was filled. I felt the universe turn red; I felt as though I were immersed in lead, slowly dispersing in a molten sea. I was infinite and powerful, yet with a dull, dark current. This pulsed through me in waves, each cresting just when I couldn't stand it anymore, yet wanted it to go on forever. My being rose and fell, a small silver cord like a tightrope through the abyss of energy that we had created together. Later, I wished I'd let go of even that.

My first awareness afterward was of a pressure in my head, just below a headache. My second feeling was sadness that I was again forced into the limitations of my individual self. I felt frenzied and elated, sleepy yet charged with energy. Moreover, although Hiyo-ba and I had clearly finished together, I felt charged rather than relaxed. The climax, powerful as it was, had come just short of release for me, as though one state of tension had been substituted for another.

Hiyo-ba, however, was obviously exhausted. Per skin grew cool under my hand. There was another shiver through per body, this one leaving a sense of satisfaction and quiet in its wake. As I climbed back down, I felt a series of affectionate farewells, like hugs or kisses from the inside out. I began to feel more stable, no longer in danger of bursting from the energies inside me. When I passed it, I stroked the stoma that Hiyo-ba had directed me to before. I felt a small, happy hiccup as I did—a last giggle of joy in our shared being-space, before we parted. I noticed I had a good taste in the back of my mouth, that my vision was sharper than it had been, and that my own skin smelled like the Hiyo-smell.

Tappi rose as I approached him. His flesh, like mine, was flushed and wet. I noticed that I had lost most of my glitter-gel, but we both shone with perspiration. I'm sure that he had enjoyed a sexual experience as well; but what kind, I don't know and wouldn't guess. Still, through the afterglow in the room, we came together intimately, like old lovers. Holding me, he stroked my arms as though he were discovering a new continent. As though he were holding human flesh for the first time.

"We chose well," I heard both through my ears and in my mind. The effect was harmonic, rather than confusing: counterpoint within one muse-box. I realized that Tappi's union with the Hiyo ran even deeper than what I'd experienced, or at least was more permanent. In fact, I wondered if, despite his genitals, Tappi was really a human male any longer. Or totally human at all. Could a person be spirit-morphed, human in shape but essentially alien in being?

I've often said that the strangeness of the Hiyo didn't matter. In this case, Tappi's alienness did matter. It made him even more desirable to me. I felt sympathy with his familiar humanity and a desire to encompass his otherness. I have to admit that I had had similar feelings, though weaker, with men in the past—separated as we were, in those cases, by the gulf of gender. I think part of me would always want to meet that otherness and get to know it, finding the strangeness within myself and the common ground I shared with the aliens. Maybe that's part of why I was invited to share sex with the Hiyo that evening, although I'll never know for sure.

Tappi held me, and before I knew it we were kissing. He certainly felt like a natural male: I could feel the light scratch of his beard stubble against my cheek. His kiss was more forceful than Kikito's and less varied than Pie's, but still attentive and responsive. I felt his morphed ruffles of tissue brush against me, tickling me below my navel but above the pubic hair. Soon, I felt his natural equipment stir as well.

"Ready for Hiyo-ka now?"

It was not really a question, but my face-wide smile was correctly taken as an answer.

From the very beginning, my experience with Hiyo-ka was less awesome, but every bit as wonderful. Per mate was aggressive, filling; Hiyo-ka was enveloping and soft, though every bit as strong and exquisite.

I approached Hiyo-ka quickly. Before I was arm-length from per, the alien was pulling me toward per mentally and reaching out for me physically. Yet it was one motion, into a shared being-space. I felt stirred-up inside, like the one time I'd tried popping whiz but without the jangly edge. I felt like an ice-skater, following my own gliding path up into the stars. But Hiyo-ka was my goal and path, both.

Hiyo-ka's amorphous body, I found, concealed an array of possibilities even more wonderful and varied than Hiyo-ba's. Per pseudopods could appear and disappear magically, flexing their luxurious, thick bulk and then smoothing back into Hiyo-ka's strong, rippling curves. No part of per was ever stationary, or even the same from one moment to another. The kaleidoscopic dance of per extensions was entrancing, transporting.

And I was in the middle of it. I needed to hold Hiyo-ka close, to feel per skin against every possible inch of mine. I knew that Hiyo-ka was glad: glad that I was happy, glad that I felt such skin delight, glad that I had such a generous expanse of skin to feel delight in. I experienced a hint of my own body as Hiyo-ka perceived it: too limited in both size and ability, but also warm and giving like per own.

In the best of human sex, I think, the partners are so close to unified that only a split second interposes itself between desire and fulfillment. Just a moment between the aching clitoris and the answering tongue; just a thought that some other touch might be better, before the change. With Hiyo-ka, there was no delay. In fact, there was no space between us, no gap to allow for the possibility of a delay. It was impossible to tell my wish from per action, my need from per response.

And so per extensions penetrated my every orifice, finding and answering my need within. Always just deep enough, just thick enough, just hard enough—I began to orgasm and did not stop. I sucked on Hiyo-ka, feeling my ass and pussy clench in alternate waves of ecstasy, bearing down harder and harder on Hiyo-ka's adaptable, intoxicating organs. Per touch was careful yet strong, probing and satisfying me. I felt per on my breasts and around my thighs, stroking my neck and lightly brushing my clitoris, stroking the shell of my ear and oozing between my toes. Hiyo-ka responded to longings I never knew I had, and it was per joy to do so.

Soon, I could no longer keep my eyes open. Stimulated throughout my skin and full in every orifice, I drifted in our tender, welcoming space. It felt comforting, yet mysteriously exciting. Like being tucked in between clean sheets, or a clear blue sky on the first day of summer vacation; like a familiar tune when you're in a foreign country. Hugged in our mutual being, I flew free. It was refreshing and happy-making, thrilling and ice-silver. Per presence was everything to me, yet nothing in itself. We made the gate and walked through it, simultaneously. And my orgasms continued to explode in and through me, shaking every corner of our being.

Hiyo-ka was receptive, yet somehow demanding. As the orgasms coursed through me more and more strongly, I felt my being widening, diffusing through the room. Hiyo-ka's merriment penetrated me, asking for more.

I sensed Hiyo-ka's satisfaction, as I had sensed Hiyo-ba's, but Hiyo-ka's was even more alien. Per nature was to respond to mine; it was like dancing with the figure in a mirror. Yet—completing the cycle—there was no separation between my orgasm and per bliss. It was not a cycle of my sexual responses stoking Hiyo-ka's inner fire, but rather a unity of shared delight. I don't know if Hiyo-ka felt anything that did not come from me. But the alien created fields of infinite potentiality, and I felt the exquisite necessity of expanding to fill and fulfill per.

Toward the end, I had lost all awareness of my body. Ultimately, it was too poor a conduit for everything a sex partner of the Hiyo thought and felt. With Hiyo-ka, however, my being didn't even try to contain itself, but stresslessly slipped beyond my physical self. I felt like a king, floating amid lush purple robes; like a goddess, sailing across the blue sky, holding the sun in the palm of my hand.

I do not know what happened when we actually finished. For a moment, my being penetrated everything, but could hold nothing—not even awareness of itself. In that moment I knew why sex with a pull-Hiyo was more desirable than anything on earth; but it was an awareness I could not bring back with me.

When I returned to consciousness, Hiyo-ka was shuddering. Deep, world-shaking quakes ran through per, not surface-trembling like Hiyo-ba but flesh waves, strong and solid, a meter high from crest to trough. I couldn't tell if Hiyo-ka was still finishing, or if this was an aftereffect. Tappi was stroking Hiyo-ka's skin and singing in a low, soft voice. It sounded like a lullaby, though it could have been a love song; I couldn't make out the words, if there were words. I was standing a meter or more away from Tappi and Hiyo-ka, completely unaware of how I had gotten there. Though teleportation had been proven impossible decades ago, I wouldn't have been surprised if Tappi had told me I'd disappeared from one place and reappeared in the other.

I felt refreshed, renewed from the inside out. Full of energy yet balanced and light, I was aware of every inch of my body, and the awareness was exquisite. I examined my flesh, half-surprised it didn't glow with life.

"Is this—sex?" I asked.

Tappi looked up, his eyes still hazy with love. In any other condition, I would have felt jealousy: I'm vacationing, I realized, and he lives there. As it was, I felt further connected to him by that insight. And sad, although I didn't know why at the time.

"As close as we come to it."

Then he stood up and walked toward me. He took his hand from Hiyo-ka only at the very last minute, stroking per almost wistfully as he did. Per body shuddered one last time and then rolled over, toward the corner and away from us. I wondered if Hiyo-ka was in postcoital sleep. Or whether the Hiyo slept at all.

"Or maybe it's something else," he continued, "something bigger, with sex only one part. Even Hiyo sex.

"My mother was a holy-rollie, and I after my first time with the Hiyo, I thought—*that* was what she'd been talking about. But I dunno. It didn't seem sexual for her."

"Your mother was a holy-rollie?" I chuckled, feeling the laughter in the muscles of my chest, in my throat and tongue and lips. It was exotic to speak with actual words. How odd and delicious, I thought, to be a mere human!

Tappi laughed, too.

"The Hiyo choose the strangest people, but no one they choose has ever turned them down."

This time, I did feel a pang of something like jealousy, though it was more like regret. How could I ever go back to human sex after that? And Tappi had it all the time, I thought. A combination of strangeness and sharing that body-morphers could only dream of achieving, no matter how many surgeries they had.

Then I realized that Tappi was crying. His eyes shuttled quickly from one side to the other; as he slowly batted his eyelids, fat tears streaked down his cheeks. He didn't cry as people usually do, and it was not just because of the cyborg-cams. But he was crying.

"I heard you earlier, you know." The tone of his voice, saying the word *heard*, made clear that the process hadn't necessarily involved sound.

"I think I *am* soul-morphed. And I don't know whether I'm glad or not."

I held him tightly, patting his back and then smoothing his spiky red hair back over the ridge bisecting his scalp. At first there was nothing sexual in it, just one human being reaching out to comfort another.

But Tappi and I had just been through intense sex together, although we had never touched. Neither friends nor lovers, we were somehow both, and more. He cried and I held him, feeling his emotions with the limited, vulnerable empathy that is all we humans have. Did he really feel what I imagined he did? I realized that we'd never really know, but that this was good enough. In fact, that desperate guessing seemed somehow more wonderful than any alien certainty.

Soon he looked at me and grinned, one tear nudged off his cheek by the smile. I caught his tear as it fell and brought my salty finger up to his lips, for him to kiss.

He continued to cry for a moment, his grin behind the tears like the sun shining through an afternoon shower. I kissed his nose.

"You're human," I said. "You don't lose what you have because you get more." As I said it, I realized how right that was. And how much it applied to me as well. "Of course you're different. Who isn't?"

Tappi kissed my nose, and then my mouth. Our arms were wrapped around each other; I pressed my body to his more tightly. He grabbed my ass in his broad hands, pulling me even closer. I still felt that profound awareness of my own body, and now it extended to my awareness of him. I felt him gently sigh into my chest as he bent to kiss my breasts. His groin brushed my leg, and I felt his flesh stir against me.

Suddenly, I realized that his penis had not been erect at any time during the Hiyo-sex. Only with me. I'm sure he'd had orgasms, as I had. But it had not been human sex, and he had not been excited in ordinary human ways. I wondered how long it had been— Every joy was unique, I realized. Nothing was a substitute for anything else.

As he sucked my nipple, Tappi reached his hand up and into my pussy, delicately probing between my engorged labia. He smiled when his fingers entered wet heat. I could see that he was ready, too: his cock stood up proudly, the head blushing a deep red. His morphed ruffles were also swollen, especially between his genitals and navel. They were thicker and had darkened to a rich pumpkin color.

"You're so beautiful!" he cried. I could hear his fingers pumping in and out of my vagina, a slobbery sound that made me even hotter. Why not? In that moment, I accepted my own sex in a way I never had before, reveling in its clumsy, natural, wet humanity.

I sank to my knees, eye-level with his cock. His balls hung down loosely, and I cupped them in my hands. I licked the scrotum, enjoying the contrast between the silky skin and wiry copper curls. He clasped his hands tightly to my shoulders and moaned, tipping his pelvis forward and bracing his legs. I stroked him, happy to feel the twin nodules of vas-valve surgery. And amused that this was the first time I'd had to think of contraception all evening.

Careful not to bring him to orgasm, I licked and sucked his cock and balls. First I sucked the glans alone, then I took his shaft deep into my throat. As he drew back, I massaged his dick with my firm, rounded lips, laving the glans with broad strokes of my tongue. He began to thrust in and out of my mouth, though gently and with firm control. When he pulled the shaft out, I was delighted by how it gleamed, wet with my saliva. I felt my own excitement rise with his, and I thought about the difference between that and the psychic interpenetration I had just experienced. About how our skin separated, yet joined us. As I licked his scrotum again, one delicate pearl of juice rose to the tip of his penis. I caught it as it fell and stood up to offer it to him: a lascivious echo of his earlier tear.

"I want you in me now," I said. He smiled and led me to a couch, flanking the pink metal door we had entered through. I glanced at the Hiyo, who seemed silent and unmoving.

I knelt on the couch, my torso braced against the back and my broad ass pointed invitingly toward Tappi. In one instant I felt his hands on my hips—in the next, his prick probing against my labia—and then he was in. I bucked back against him. He stroked forward even more forcefully.

I wish I could have told him how wonderful it was. More than ever, I felt both separated and joined by our flesh. His thick prick was a welcome presence, filling me inside but leaving my deeper being whole and untouched, as the Hiyo had not. Yet the greater awareness of a separate self, I realized, also meant having more to voluntarily share.

The sex was warm, funny, companionable. I felt as though we were fully partners, in every important sense. He tweaked my nipples, and we both laughed. His pelvis slapped firmly against my round, lush ass; I imagined I could feel his rough, red pelt rubbing my pale skin. His morphed skin teased my labia and caressed my hind-cheeks. I shook my ass from side to side and he moaned appreciatively.

I leaned back further, bracing myself between Tappi and the couch, the fabric rough on my flushed skin. As my own heat took me from inside, all I could do was whimper. The tempo of my sounds matched his thrusts, speeding up as they did. Joy pulsed through me, screaming for release.

We finished together. Just as my tension broke into orgasm, I heard him yell and felt his pulsing gush. I felt the sheath of my vagina flex and grasp, milking his cock deep within me. Before I had stopped, he was leaning forward, peppering my neck and back with spontaneous, happy smooches. It was a few moments before we both could stand.

By that time, I had become fully aware of something I'd not quite noticed before: the Hiyo-smell was rising in the room, already overpowering and growing even stronger. Tappi looked over his shoulder at the still-quiet forms, then back at me.

"I think it's time for the next introduction."

I wondered if the Hiyo had just finished their equivalent of a refractory period, or if the sex between Tappi and me had awakened them. Later, it occurred to me that they might have allowed us our time together, then decided we'd had enough.

Tappi escorted me through the pink metal door and to the wooden one, hugging and patting me and smiling reassuringly. I didn't know if I'd ever see him again, although I knew we'd be friends and lovers if it did happen. I had shared with him through the Hiyo and as a human, skin to skin. In each case, he'd given me something that I hadn't had before. We'd touched each other in pleasure, and in the heart.

As he ushered me through the door, he thanked me. Uncertain what to say, I hugged him again, then kissed him good-bye. As he closed the door behind me, I saw that he was crying again.

Before I could turn around, I felt a pair of slender, strong arms grabbing me from behind and heard Kikito's voice.

"So what's doing, kitty-pet? Didn't you love it?"

She, too, was now totally naked, except for a glowing pink party Streem-R draped over her tail. Her tail wagged, and the plastic strip waved back and forth in the breeze. Her hair was damp, and her skin shone. I wondered what she'd been up to. But my guess was that I'd find out.

I gazed at her dark, happy face, trying to figure out how I could ever put my feelings into words. After a moment I gave up, and we just hugged and kissed.

Kikito started down the hallway, tugging at my hand to pull me along. She moved quickly, bouncing on the balls of her feet, taking long strides; I ran to keep up with her.

"The party's winding down," she called back to me, "but I'm sure I can find you something to eat. And someone to eat it off of." Her eyes no longer had the telltale dreaminess of E-rose, but there was magic in them nonetheless.

"Don't worry. All the sweet-powder is *long gone* by now. There was this guy with a morphed tongue, see—"

I put on a burst of speed and caught up with Kikito. When I plucked the Streem-R from her tail, I discovered the fur was even softer than I had imagined.

• • •

By the time Kikito and I walked hand in hand to the front door, only a few people were left in the front rooms and hallways. One person, body-morphed with scaly armor, was asleep in the foyer, curled up like a pangolin or armadillo. Five, who appeared to be naturals, slept together in the main hall, in one comfortable, indeterminate pile. By the refreshment stations, two people licked pink punch from each other's breasts; I couldn't be sure what gender they were, though all five breasts involved were twice the size of mine. Pie was nowhere to be seen, but of course the house had many rooms I hadn't been in. No doubt she was somewhere enjoying herself.

I accepted my clothes from the same body-morph who had greeted me—now exhausted, fur matted and scales sticky with pink punch. Apparently others had explored the spikes visible through his briefs, though I hadn't had time to. Well, maybe next time, I thought.

It felt odd to be dressed again. Like that princess in my uncle's stories, putting on her finery at the stroke of midnight. But instead of a coach pulled by six white thunderbirds, I'd be taken home by limousine. The same limo that Kikito had promised to send for me in a week. She'd apologetically explained that she wouldn't have another party until next month, but— I'd hugged her and honestly said I'd be even more glad to have her alone.

As we kissed good-night, Kikito fastened something to the collar of my duster. She'd taken it from a basket by the front door, which I'd noticed as I came in: it was filled with message-badges that said NONE OF THE ABOVE. At the time, I'd dismissed it as more politi-prop from the Committee to Unelect the President. Thinking about it again, I wasn't so sure. About the same time that option was added to the ballot, it had to be added to the census question about gender, as well. Perhaps a finite range of choices would always be too limiting. Even for us naturals.

"Remember, kitty-pet," Kikito whispered in my ear, "no one else could be like you, no matter how much they tried. Don't think you have to change." She kissed my cheek. "Or stay the same."

Of course I'm different, I thought. Who isn't?

I was already looking forward to next week.

The Waking State

Gerry Pearlberg

She had a reputation. Even now, when I say her name, people tell me how terrified or obsessed, repulsed or fascinated, they were by her. Everyone knew about her back then, everyone but me. When we danced that night, she was lewd. I wasn't sure I liked the way she touched or talked to me. It wasn't disrespectful, just sleazy.

Her dormitory cubicle was like a little church, a shrine to perversion. She caught me scanning the titles on her shelf: all sex books. Some I recognized by a kind of sexual osmosis. Others were new to me, like a neat row of distant, wriggling mirages capable of doing damage, but also holding promise.

We showered together down the hall, and when we returned to her room, she told me she'd be right back. "Check out the books," she said, "and see if anything strikes your fancy." Her brief disappearance was calculated. It gave me time to absorb the implications of being in this room, wrapped in her towel, reading her well-worn copy of the *Leatherman's Safety Guide*.

When she returned, she showed me her black velvet "bag of tricks," explaining the purpose of each exotic or mundane item it contained. As she spoke, my mind began ticking like a logic clock. Fantasy was one thing, but what did I really know about this person, anyway? I had work on Monday. Dinner with Mom on Tuesday. Who I was and what I was doing here did not seem to reconcile, yet I was transfixed. She must have known she did not need to push. We climbed to the top bunk of her double-decker bed and had vanilla sex. I came hard just feeling her fingers gliding on me and thinking about that velvet bag lying like a wishing well on the floor below us.

Early the next morning, we lay in bed together, chatting before she left for class. She told me about her lovers, women in Boston and New York who'd asked her to tie their hands above their heads, make them panic with longing, and eventually, if they were lucky, to fuck them, let them fuck themselves, make them fuck her. "I admire bottoms," she said wistfully, "I really wish I could trust someone enough to let them do things to me." I rubbed the thorny crown of her new crew cut, her warm and vulnerable head like a bird's nest in my hand, and wondered what it would be like to take control of someone that way, to set up the field of their fantasy, plant its seeds, nourish its crops, and finally plow through its maze of delicate but deeply set roots, nerve endings of desire.

"I want you again," she said, breaking in on these

new thoughts, "but not like last night. Can you meet me back here at lunchtime?"

I arrived promptly at noon. This time, fear competed with anticipation. I could claim no excuses for being there: it was, after all, the middle of the day, and there was no loud music, no bar atmosphere, and no beer to create a ready context for this visit. My erotic intentions were undiluted. I was there in the full bloom of the Waking State.

She was wearing a black leather jacket. I wore a chain necklace with delicate multicolored metallic links. Anywhere else, it would have seemed innocuous, even cutesy. Here, it was loaded. She noticed it instantly, fingering it in a knowing way. We started necking. The smell of her jacket was a fetish cologne. I ran my fingers along its snaps, buckles, and loops. This simple paraphernalia created an ambivalent, insistent friction between my body and brain.

After a few minutes, she stiffened and, taking my wrists in her hands, planted my arms at my sides. "I'm famished," she whispered, staring me down, "but for what, present company excluded?" She bit her lip in mock concentration, running her fingers lightly up and down my forearms. "A hero would suit the occasion, don't you think?" she said at last, her eyes twinkling. "Go and get me a hero, a hero with everything on it."

I asked if I could wear her jacket, feeling able to leave only with this part of her, a part of this. I wanted her skin on me when I exited her domain to fulfill her wish. I would wear it like a visceral embodiment of her command. She obliged me, lifting the heavy coat around my shoulders, kissing my throat and the base of my skull. I ran my hands along her bare arms and white cotton T-shirt. She seemed so fresh and naked this way. When I leaned into her, she sent me out with a caustic smile.

I felt conspicuously queer and overtly aroused walking down the sunny New England street to the sub shop across the square. I glanced in store windows, catching quick reflections of myself. It was like seeing another person there, someone familiar, but not quite known. In the glass I witnessed the physical embodiment of a deeply planted wish, a tulip bulb blooming in the dark. My heart was a bright penny twitching at the bottom of a fast-moving stream. I wondered if anyone on this all-American street could read the hidden meaning of the jacket and this errand, or whether they perceived the reconstruction of mundane experience that these things implied.

I wore the jacket while she ate her hero hungrily, tearing off pieces of bread and meat and cheese and feeding them to me as if I were a tender creature of metal and hide sidling against her for sustenance. I, too, felt hunger, but mine bit well below the belt. I wanted more than meat from her hands; I longed for her blood on my lips, her fingers in my mouth, her knee between my legs, unlikely things in unexpected places bringing pleasurable discomfort and reassuring dissonance. Watching her eat, wearing her leather skin, the experience of waiting became a sexual entity all its own.

Eventually, she pushed the hero aside, pulled me slowly toward her, and kissed me again, erotically aloof. Once more, she touched the chain around my neck, coolly signaling that the games had officially begun. We deep-kissed, and when my tongue found its way into her mouth, she held it firmly between her teeth. Till it almost hurt. Till it hurt a little. Till it really hurt. She looked me in the eye while doing this, till I began to hum, to moan, resonating like a tiny bee hanging on an orchid's blazing crimson cliff. Her hand went down my pants and began stroking my clit; all the while she restrained my aching tongue in the prison of her white-hot teeth. Throbbing hard, my mouth became a second vortex of sensation, shimmering against a perfect moment of intimacy, stillness, and possession. A sudden orgasm bit through me like a steel-jawed eel. She held my tongue till the pounding subsided, then released, generating a second dose of sharp decompression. I slumped against her, exhausted. Running my teeth lightly over my tender tongue, I pressed a long string of bright aftershocks through my blasting cunt.

I was late for my ride back to the city. She watched me collect myself. She watched me pee. She took her jacket back. We exchanged telephone numbers, smiles, and a long kiss in the doorway. She plucked gently at my collar before I turned to leave. Genius of the small, irrevocable gesture.

A few weeks later, she called me at work. I told her I'd bought myself a motorcycle jacket. She sounded flattered when she congratulated me and advised me on its proper care and treatment. She mentioned a special cream that would soften the leather. "You'll appreciate the way it tastes when I make you lick it off *my* jacket," she said, inducing my first long-distance blush.

She was coming to town for the weekend. Did I want to get together? She could bring her bag of tricks. Two sides of an alarm clock went off inside me, tiny hammers rapidly banging opposing bells. One was desire, a flash flood between my legs. This I had expected. The other was fear. Fear of her, fear of the feelings she aroused in me, and fear of her intrusion upon my "real" life. Her offer was an earthquake, dislodging the bridges between awake and asleep, good sex and bad. My inner fault line tore open before me, violently dividing my body's terrain from that of reason, intellect, and self-restraint. It cut right through the Waking State, which I'd called home, and which had somehow accommodated within its generous borders both the instinct toward and the terror of the sexual end of the world where mythical beasts take mysterious forms, churning whole oceans to fire. I bit my lip and chose my ground. My apartment had such thin walls. My mother would die if she ever knew. My roommates would never let me live it down. Besides, the things she did were well beyond illegal in the Waking State to which I pledged ambivalent allegiance when I told her, "No."

A Tooth for Every Child

Abigail Thomas

Louise, who is pushing down the tall grasses near the land of menopause, accepts an invitation from Mona, who is not that far behind. Mona could use the sight of Louise. "I need a drinking companion," she says. Louise can hear the twins wailing in the background.

"We don't drink anymore," Louise reminds her.

"But we can talk about it, can't we? Remember pink gins?"

"That wasn't us, Mona, pink gins. That was our grandmothers."

"Don't quibble. Just get off the bus at Concord. I'll pick you up."

"I'll come Friday. Thursday I've got my teeth."

The only man in Louise's life right now is her Chinese dentist. Her entire sex life consists of his warm fingers in her mouth, against her cheek. She thinks of them as ten slender separate animals, so dexterous is he. She is undergoing root canal, paying the coward's price for years of neglect. Every Thursday she settles herself in his chair and he sets up what he calls the rubber dam. Eyes closed, Louise imagines a tent stretched from tree to tree. Under this canopy he sets to work chipping and drilling, installing a system of levees and drains. He stuffs tendrils of gutta-percha in the hollowed-out roots of her teeth and sets them on fire, reminding Louise of the decimation of the tropical rain forests. She imagines bright green parrots flying squawking out of her mouth, lizards running up the fingers of her dentist. Loves may come and loves may go, but dental work goes on forever, thinks Louise.

"You owe me nine thousand dollars," says Dr. Chan.

"We're having a lot of work done," says Mona apologetically as they pull off the country road and onto the rough dirt path that leads to the house Mona and Tony have built overlooking the lake.

"Aren't you embarrassed to be so successful?" asks Louise.

"It's not me, Louise. Blame Tony. All I've been recently is fertile. Wait till you see little Joe. He is anxious to see you."

Mona and Louise have been friends for thirty years. Louise had her babies first, four of them; she has been married twice, divorced twice. Her children have all grown up and gone except the baby, who at seventeen is in Italy this summer. Mona's first child, Joe, is five years old. She has twins, Ernie and Sue, eleven months. Louise wishes she had had her children later, when she knew better; Mona wishes she had done it when she was young. The two women are comfortable together, and Louise is planning to spend a week, playing with kids, sunning herself on the porch, reading.

Tony is off supervising the tennis court ("The tennis court?" Louise has repeated, incredulous), and Mona and she and little Joe are in the kitchen, Joe nestled in Louise's lap. Joe is learning about where babies come from. Mona is horrified to discover he thinks babies and peepee come from the same place, and Louise has taken it upon herself to explain about the three holes. A hole for peepee, a hole for poopoo, and the babyhole. "The babyhole is just for babies," Louise explains, proud of her succinctness. She had told her own children, years ago, that she had made them all by herself, out of a special kit. "What is the babyhole used for when there aren't any babies?" asks little Joe, not unreasonably. Louise looks mournfully at Mona. "Well, not really much of anything," she says, "in a bad year." Mona bursts out laughing and the two women cackle until their noses turn pink.

"The place is crawling with workmen," says Mona later. "You always wanted a guy who worked with his hands, remember? And the roofer is really quite choice. Fifty-three. Good hands."

"Do you talk like this in front of Tony?" asks Louise.

But it is the boy who catches Louise's eye first. Standing beside the path leading to the lake, he is bent over a snapping turtle the size of a Thanksgiving turkey. Louise doesn't know which to look at first, the long brown back of the boy or the spiky ridged shell of the turtle. So she stands there in the middle of the road looking from one to the other. Then the boy straightens up and turns toward Louise. "Oh my God," is what she says. She hopes he will think she is talking about the turtle.

"Ever seen one this big?" he asks, nudging the shell with the toe of one work-booted foot, and hitching his belt slightly so the hammer hangs down his left hip. His upper body is bare, his shoulders smooth and deeply muscled. His eyes and hair are almost black, and he has a red bandanna tied around his head. He is smiling at her.

"Not for a long time." Louise notices the turtle's head come poking out of its shell. "Careful," she warns him, "he might bite you." She is a mother, first and foremost.

"Nah, he wouldn't dare. I'm so mean I have to sleep with one eye open so I don't kick myself in the ass." He laughs, finding himself vastly entertaining. His teeth are remarkably white and there is a fine powdering of sawdust on his right cheekbone that she would like to brush off. "Don't you come too close, is all," he says to her. "This baby take you in his mouth, no telling when he'd turn you loose." He grins at Louise, who is oddly flustered. She feels fourteen years old. The boy shows no sign of boredom, of turning away from her, no sign of having anything better to do than to stand there and talk to her. She looks around to see who it is he is really talking to. Some young girl somewhere he is trying to impress.

"You up here for the whole summer?" he is asking her now. She shakes her head. "Friend of Mrs. Townshend's?" She nods. "Nice lady," the boy says, "very nice lady." He pauses. "So how long are you staying?"

"Just a week," she says. "I'm from New York."

"Figured that," he says, pulling a crumpled pack of Marlboros out of the back pocket of his jeans. "Smoke?" He offers her one.

"No, I quit. Three packs a day I used to do." Louise

is bragging. She watches him cup his hands around the cigarette he is lighting, shake out the match and flick it in the dirt.

"No, I mean do you *smoke*," he says, making the quick sucking sounds of a joint.

"Oh, do I smoke. No," she says firmly. "I hate to smoke. I get paranoid."

He cocks his head to one side, "No kidding," he says. "Not me. Hey, know what I call 'paranoia'? Heightened awareness," and he cracks himself up again. He takes another drag and says after a moment's hesitation, "Would you like to see the countryside around here? I can take you for a drive later. That's my truck," he says proudly, pointing to a black Ford pickup parked a little down the road. It has a bumper sticker that reads TOO CUTE TO STAY HOME.

In one of those moments Louise is famous for, when she decides to do something without thinking, "Yes," she says, "sure. Thank you very much." And then regrets it. "Well," she says, "see you," and hurries into her cabin where she goes directly to the bathroom and peers at herself in the mirror.

"What was he talking to?" she asks out loud.

"So when is he picking you up?" Mona asks. The twins are having lunch in their high chairs.

"I don't know," says Louise. "I ran away. I'm not going."

"Of course you're going," says Mona, cutting up a hot dog for the twins. "You're doing it for me. If you don't, we'll both get old. Now go sit out there on that porch and wait for him to tell you what time."

"I can't. I feel like an enormous piece of bait," says Louse. "I feel like a ridiculous elderly baby bird."

"Out," says Mona firmly. "I'm going to ask Bridget to clean in here and you have to be outside in the sun," she says, spooning mashed potato into Ernie's little mouth.

Louise sits tilted back in her chair. She has Auden facedown in her lap, her own face is turned toward the sun. Her legs and feet are bare against the railing of the deck. The house is built on a wooded hill above a lake, and through the trees Louise can see water glittering in the sun. She has been remembering the first time a boy opened her clothes. It was 1957 or '58; she and Tommy Morell were leaning against the scaffolding of what was to become the Loeb Student Center in Washington Square. She was wearing a new blue coat from the now long-defunct DePinna; it was freezing cold and they were standing out of the wind, kissing. She can remember today the taste of his mouth: decay and wintergreen. Every time somebody walked past, she would hide her face against his shoulder. And then she felt his hands on the front of her coat, the sensation taking a moment to travel through the many layers of her clothes, like light from a star, and his fingers were working at the buttons, the many small, difficult buttons of this coat, and she was not pushing his hands away. Louise sighs. Amazing what else she has forgotten, but this scrap of memory is as real as yesterday. This morning.

Louise is deep in daydream when hammering begins under the porch, startling her. As she sits in her thin cotton dress, the hammering directly beneath feels particularly intimate. She hears murmuring of men's voices, and the next thing she knows the boy has swung himself up over the railing, defying God knows what laws of physics, and is hunkering down next to her on the porch.

"So I'll pick you up at seven-thirty? I need to go home and get a shower first. Okay?"

"Well, sure," she says. "That's fine. Sure."

"See you later," and he grins and bounds back off the deck. His head reappears a moment later. "I'm Donny. You're . . . ?"

"Louise."

"Just wear what you have on," advises Mona, after Louise has changed her clothes three times. "That nice dress that buttons down the front."

"You don't think I look as if I'm trying to look like Little Bo-Peep?"

"Louise, that's the last thing I'd say you looked like. You look fine. Really good, in fact. No wonder he asked you."

"Mona, what are we going to talk about? What am I going to say to this boy? I'm forty-fucking-six years old. I certainly can't talk about my kids. They're probably older than he is."

"I don't think you're going to be doing a whole lot of talking," says Mona "I don't think talking is Donny's specialty."

Donny comes to the door to pick her up just like a real date. He is wearing a shirt tonight, which has the odd effect of making him seem even younger. Louise feels unbearably awkward when he says hello to Mona, calls Tony "sir." Louise can't get out of there fast enough. "Take my sweater, Louise," calls Mona. "It's outside there on the rocker."

Donny opens the door of the truck and closes it behind her when she is safely inside. Then he runs around and hops up on the driver's side. "Do you have any idea how old I am?" asks Louise when they are both sitting in the truck. She feels she should get this over with right away.

"Well, I know you're older than me." Donny turns to look at her. "I figure you're twenty-eight or so." Twenty-eight or so? Dear God. Twenty-eight or so?

"Oh," says Louise. "How old are you?"

"I'll be twenty-one next month."

"You're twenty," says Louise, closing her eyes briefly. "You're twenty years old."

"Yeah, but I'll be twenty-one next month," he repeats, and turns the key in the ignition and the truck starts to vibrate pleasantly, reminding Louise, not surprisingly, of an enormously powerful animal just barely held in check. "Ready?" he asks.

She is looking at how loosely his hand rests on the stick shift. She nods, watching his hand tighten on the stick, the muscles in his arm bulging slightly as he puts the truck in first and they begin lurching down the steep path that leads to the highway.

"Wahoo!" he yells, thrusting his upper body half out the window, then he ducks back in and grins at Louse. "Couldn't help it," he says sheepishly. "I just feel good." She smiles at him.

Louise is now completely at ease. As soon as the truck started moving, she felt something inside her click into place. She knows exactly who she is and what she is doing. She is a blond-headed woman in the front seat of a moving vehicle, she is nobody's mother, nobody's former wife, nobody's anything. Louise is a girl again.

A mile down the highway Donny fishes around under his seat and comes up with a Sucrets box, which he hands her. "Can you light me up the joint? Matches on the dash." Louise opens the box and picks the joint up. It is lying next to loose grass and on top of a bunch of rolling papers. Louise hasn't smoked a joint in a long time. The last time she did, she became convinced that she was about to become dinner: about to be minced, put in a cream sauce, and run under the broiler. She was at a party being given by her then-new husband's old friends.

"I don't really smoke," she begins, and then, "Oh, what the hell," she says, shrugging, and lights the joint. "Maybe I've changed," she says, talking mostly to herself.

"Maybe the company has changed," says Donny, and she can't imagine what he thinks he means by that, but they are passing the joint back and forth and Louise is beginning to feel pretty good. Something lovely is happening deep in her throat, some awareness of throatness she has never experienced before. "God, I've got such an interesting *throat*," she says, and Donny laughs.

"You're getting high," he says.

"I am?" Louise sits up straight.

"You okay? Feeling okay?"

"I think I feel good," she says, taking stock. "Yes," she announces rather formally, "I feel really quite good." Donny slows down and takes a right turn into what he calls a sandpit. It is a parking area off the road, behind a kind of berm. "Let's roll another," he says, proceeding to do so. Louise watches fascinated; she has always loved watching people use their hands. When he licks the paper to seal the cigarette, she sees his tongue is pink. This kid's tongue is actually pink, oh, Lordy Lordy, thinks Louise.

"Why don't you have a girlfriend?" she wants to know.

"I had a girlfriend. She moved out three months ago. She left me a note saying she was going to California." Donny snaps the Sucrets box shut now and looks for the matches.

"Oh. Crummy. Were you sad?"

"For a while. Thing that made it easier was she took my damn stereo. Hard to be sad and pissed at the same time. But yeah, we had some good times. Bummed me out she couldn't tell me to my face she was going."

"She probably wouldn't have been able to leave, then."

"Yeah. That's what she said in her note." He offers her the new joint to light but she shakes her head.

"What was her name?"

"Robin. But anybody asks me now how's Robin, know what I say? Robin who, I say. Robin who?" Donny laughs and then turns his head to look out the window. "Company," he says, as a red Toyota pulls in. "Let's go somewhere a little less public. Want to see the lake?"

"Sure," says Louise, "anything." What a nice state New Hampshire is to provide lakes and sandpits for its citizens to park in, Louise is thinking. They head off and stop along the way to see the school Donny was kicked out of. It is a plain, one-story brick building that Louise thinks privately looks pretty depressing, but Donny is driving around it slowly, almost lovingly. "You had a good time here?" she asks him.

"Yep. I had a good time here."

"How come they kicked you out?"

"Oh, this and that. I was a hothead then, I guess. I'm a lot calmer now, though you might not believe it. Straightening myself out. Full-time job in itself." He laughs. "Full-time job in itself."

"I like hotheaded," says Louise. "I always did."

Donny, who has been circling the school building, pulls over to the far end of the lot and parks under a tree. He turns the engine off and they look at each other in the fading light of the summer evening; a little moon starts to show between the trees, a streetlight blinks on thirty feet away. He reaches quite frankly for her, or perhaps she reaches for him, but his hands are on her dress, the front of her dress at the buttons, and his dark head is against her neck, his breath everywhere. Her hands are in his hair, under his shirt, feeling the tight muscles of his belly above his belt. Fumbling. Then they are kissing, and because his window does not close completely, the truck fills with mosquitoes and they are kissing and slapping and slapping and cursing and laughing and kissing and kissing and kissing. Donny drags a blanket out from behind his seat and they stumble out of the truck and onto the grass and Louise is lying down under a million or so stars. "I wanted to fuck you the first time I saw you, to tell you the truth," Donny is whispering as he lowers his body down on hers.

They sleep in the truck that night, parked near the lake that seems to be everywhere. Or rather, Donny sleeps, his head in Louise's lap. Louise is awake all night, watching the woods drain of moonlight and fill up again slowly with a misty brightness that seems to rise from the ground. Donny's body is arranged somehow around the gearshift, his head and shoulders resting on Louise. He sleeps like a baby. She looks at his closed eyes, dark lashes, his straight black brows. His skin is beautiful, like silk. Dear God, how came this beautiful wild child to be asleep in my lap, thinks Louise. At six, she jiggles his shoulder. "Time to wake up," she says. "We've been gone all night."

"What if I refuse to take you back?" he asks sleepily. "Suppose I just decide to keep you?"

Mona is up, of course, when Louise gets in. The twins are out with Bridget; little Joe and Tony are down by the lake doing something with boats. "Don't let Tony see you," says Mona. "I told him you got in late last night. You know Tony." Tony has never approved of Louise, not since she asked him if she could upend herself in his laundry hamper. "For the pheromones," she had explained. "It's been so long since the last good kiss." Louise had read somewhere that women who lived without the company of men were apt to age more quickly.

"Why can't she just ride the subway at rush hour?" Tony had asked irritably. "Plenty of nice hair tonic and body sweat in there. Why does it have to be my laundry?"

"Come on, Tony, it's just your gym socks. Be a sport," Mona had said.

"So?" says Mona now, pouring two cups of coffee. "Or don't I really want to know?"

"I'll say one word," says Louise, "to satisfy your

morbid curiosity because I know it's on your mind. Hung."

"Comme zee horse?" Mona is leaning forward.

"Comme zee horse."

"Ahhhh."

"And you know what else? I like him, I actually like him. He's working so hard to grow up. His girlfriend left him and he had to move back with his parents because he couldn't afford the rent by himself. He works his ass off. I like him."

"Yeah? Well, great, but don't start taking this seriously."

"He's picking me up again tonight. You know what? Staying up all night makes me feel young again, isn't that weird? I haven't been this tired since I was young."

"Go lie down. I'll wake you up at lunch."

"Mona? I loved not talking about my kids. It was like being twenty myself, you know? It was like not having a tail I had to fit everywhere. I'm never going to tell anyone about my kids again."

"Louise, you're delirious. Go upstairs and lie down."

"Good night."

"Louise?" calls Mona as Louise disappears up the stairs. "You're being careful? I'm not talking about babies, you know what I'm talking about."

Louise's head appears around the corner. "Mona," she says, "what could be safer than a twenty-year-old carpenter from New Hampshire?"

Two days later Donny takes off work. "I've got vacation time coming," he says. "I'm taking you four-wheeling. That is if you want to drive around with me for a few days."

Mona is worried. "I hope you're not taking this seriously," she keeps saying. "I know how you can get, Louise, and I don't want you to get involved with a twenty-year-old boy who lives with his parents."

"Come on, Mona, I haven't had this much fun in my whole life," says Louise. "I'm twenty years old myself this week. The last time I was twenty I had two children and an ex-husband in the making."

Mona's expression relaxes. "All right, but I don't want to hear a word of complaint out of you for eighteen months, and I hope you have plenty of raw meat for the trip."

Louise feels like a summer house this kid has broken into, pushing his way through doors that haven't been opened in years, snapping up blinds, windows, pulling dustcovers off furniture, shaking rugs, curtains, bounding on the beds. A fine, honorable old house, and he appreciates the way it has been made, the way it has lasted, the strength of its structure, noble old dimensions. It has been a long time since Louise was put to such good use.

"What's the longest you've ever gone without making love?" she asks him. He thinks for a second.

"Fifteen years," he answers.

She loves his raw energy, and the lavish way he squanders it on pointless undertakings, impossible feats, such as driving the truck directly up the steep wooded side of a mountain whenever he thinks he spies faint tracks. (Louise sees only dense woods.) He screeches the truck to a stop, leaps down to lock the front wheels, jumps back inside to do something sexy to the gears, pausing to kiss Louise for five minutes, and then he coaxes, bullies, cajoles the truck off the road and into the trees. Louise loves it. She loves everything about him by now. She loves the muscles in his shoulders, the veins in his forearms. "I like how you touch me," he whispers. She wants him to explain everything he knows, the difference between a dug and an artesian well, how to build a ladder, hang a door, put a roof on. "You're really interested?" he asks her. "You really want to know?" She nods. "The plumb line is God," he begins gravely.

Louise is as close to carefree as she has ever been. There is nothing behind her, her past is not part of this trip, and nothing in front but a dashboard full of music and the open road. They like the same music, sing the same songs. Stevie Ray Vaughan, The Georgia Satellites, Tom Petty and the Heartbreakers. "Break Down" is their favorite song and they blast it all week, yelling it out the windows, singing it to each other in the truck: "Break down, go ahead and give it to me," and then they collapse laughing, this forty-six-year-old woman and this twenty-year-old boy who are having the time of their lives. They rent a room in a motel when they get tired of fighting off the mosquitoes. Louise uses her Visa card, expecting the long arm of the law to grab her any minute by the collar, bring her to her senses. Donny is bent over the register saying, "You want an address?" and Louise hears the manager saying, "Oh, just put anything," with a knowing snicker. For just a second, she feels gawky, naked. How many good years does she have left, she wonders, before she appears pathetic? Right now she can still get away with it, but fifty approaches, the hill she will one day be over is looming in the distance. So when the manager shows them the room and it contains two double-decker beds, one cot, and a king-size four-poster, Louise rubs her hands together largely for his benefit and says, "Good. We can really use the room."

They order Chinese takeout that night from an improbable place down the road, and Louise bites into something hard in her mooshoo pork. Spitting it into her hand, she sees it is a human tooth. She hurries into the bathroom and locks the door. "You all right in there?" asks Donny, knocking. It is Louise's tooth, her temporary cap, and she rinses it off and jams it back in her mouth praying to God it will stay. "Donny," she says, coming out of the bathroom, "I've got to tell you how old I am. Guess what, I'm forty-six." He doesn't seem particularly interested. "I'm forty-six, did you hear me?"

"Yeah?" He is lying down on the big bed, his hands behind his head. "So?"

"And what's more I have four kids and three of them are older than you and I have two grandchildren on top of that." Louise seems out of breath all of a sudden. He just looks at her.

"Come here," he says. She goes there. He grabs her hand. "I guess that makes me some kind of motherfucker," he says with a lazy grin, pulling her down on the bed. "Stick with me, I won't let you get old," he says into her hair. "But I am old," she wants to moan, "I already am old."

"Why are a woman's breasts always softest in the evening?" he wants to know, pulling her toward him.

Louise is awake all night. "You can't kiss all the time," a friend of hers once said, by way of explaining her having picked up a few words of Italian one summer. "You can't kiss all the time." Louise thinks she knows this, she knows it is time to go back to the grown-ups, back to New York, her office. Back to real life. This isn't real life, this relationship relies too heavily on rock 'n' roll and the open road. Real life is not this dream come true, it is long winter nights with nothing to talk about. You can't kiss all the time. "I'll build you a house," Donny said yesterday. "Stay. I'll build you a house."

He knows before she tells him that she is going home. He is quiet all morning, sullen even. "What's the matter?" she asks, but he shakes off her hand.

"You're leaving."

"But I'm coming back. I'm coming back for your birthday."

"But you're leaving, right?"

She nods.

"Well, I'm bummed."

She tells him about the office, the mail, her apartment, bills unpaid, her daughter coming home from Europe soon.

"What do you want for your birthday?" she asks him.

"You."

"You've got me. What else?"

"More of you."

"You've got me. What else?"

"Am I asking too much?"

Back in New York, Louise is lonelier than she expected to be. New York is gritty, dirty, sad. Her apartment is so empty, quiet. Louise is of an age now when most of the men in her life are former lovers who fly in from nowhere for a couple of days every six years or so; they sit on her chairs, eat at her table, sleep in her bed, and when they leave, they leave a kind of half-life behind, an absence so palpable it is almost a presence. The furniture rebukes Louise on these occasions. "So where'd he go?" asks the white sofa, the pink chair. The bed. But Donny has never been here, so she has to conjure up his memory out of whole cloth, so to speak, and she misses him more than she thought she would.

In fact, she talks of little else. She is as apt to pull pictures of Donny out of her wallet as of her grandsons. "You're in luck," she might have said a month ago. "I have fifty-three new pictures of my grandsons." Now she takes seven photographs out of her wallet, they are all of Donny, and she lays them out on the table like a row of solitaire. "So," she says to anyone who will listen. "You know that poem by Auden? 'Lay your sleeping head, my love'?" Her friends are respectful, for the most part silent. They let her play it out.

"Do we sleep with the young to stay young ourselves or just to lie down next to all that beauty?" Louise wants to know. Mona is irritated. They are together in Riverside Park with the kids. Joe is in the sandbox, Mona and Louise are pushing the twins in the little swings. "Neither," says Mona. "How should I know?" she snaps. Then more gently, "To lie down next to all that beauty."

"I knew it," says Louise, hopping. "I knew it!"

"I'm worried about you," says Mona. "I mean I hope you're not being faithful to him or anything."

Louise bursts out laughing. "Come on, Mona. Who am I going to go out with? The dry cleaner?"

"I'm just concerned you might get hurt. You let your emotions get involved."

"Well, of course I let my emotions get involved. What the hell is the point if you don't let your emotions get involved? But it's not like going out for ice cream and coming home and saying, 'Gee, I wish I hadn't had that ice cream.' I liked the kid. I loved the kid, if you want to know."

"Just what I was afraid of. And I certainly don't think you should go back up there for his birthday. Enough is enough."

"I promised him I'd go. I promised him."

But Louise has not heard from Donny, and though she has left messages with his mother (an exquisitely humiliating experience) he has not returned her calls. The night before she is supposed to get on the bus, she finally gets him on the phone. She does not want to keep her end of the bargain and wind up sitting on a suitcase in the parking lot at Concord waiting for Godot. It is a bad connection and she can barely hear him, and she has to keep repeating "What?" into the telephone like an old woman with an ear trumpet.

"Are we still on for tomorrow?" she shouts, although she already knows the answer.

"Things have changed around here," Donny says. His voice sounds so foreign, so young.

260

"So do you still want me to come up tomorrow?" Louise is amazed at how painful this is.

"I guess now is not a good time," he says, but she can barely hear him.

"What?"

"No," he says. "Not this time."

"Well, happy birthday to you," she says, hanging up the phone.

"Would you mind removing your lipstick," says Dr. Chan, handing Louise a tissue. He always makes this request, but Louise wears it to his office just the same. She likes to look her best for the dentist. Dr. Chan wears his hair cut short except for three very long, very skinny braids, and Louise has always been too shy to inquire as to their significance.

"Today we put in your permanent tooth," says Dr. Chan, setting out his instruments, mixing his little pots of cement.

"That's good," says Louise, "because this one fell out over the summer and I had to put it back myself. 'A tooth for every child,' " she adds, but Dr. Chan does not ask after her meaning.

She settles back in her chair. The land of menopause stretches out behind her closed lids as Dr. Chan easily removes the temporary cap. It seems to be a quiet place, resembling a kind of savanna. There are mountains in the distance. There doesn't appear to be much activity beyond a certain amount of flank-nuzzling, as far as Louise can tell. But who knows? She has heard some odd cries at night, down by the waterhole.

Contributor Biographies

Marianna Beck lives in Chicago where she co-publishes *Libido*, a magazine she started six years ago with Jack Hafferkamp. She has one very cool son, several pets, and her favorite palindrome is . . . Satan, oscillate my metallic sonatas.

Bernadette Lynn Bosky is a writer and teacher who has approached topics from renaissance alchemy to Stephen King. She also writes about size acceptance and body image. She lives in the suburbs of New

York City with her two spouses, Arthur Hlavaty and Kevin Maroney.

Mark Butler has written plays and comedy revues that have been produced on many New York City stages, including "Rubbervision," "Naked Mannequins," and "Escalator to Hell." His unfinished autobiography is tentatively titled "Hooching and Smooching."

Pat Califia is an influential lesbian author whose books include *The Melting Point, Macho Sluts, The Advocate Adviser*, and *Doc and Fluff*. She lives in San Francisco.

M. Christian is a firm believer that persistence will persevere: after many years of trying, he sold his first story, "InterCore," which was then accepted by this collection. He also believes sex sells.

Leslie Feinberg is a long-time socialist activist and author of *Stone Butch Blues*. That novel has won the 1994 American Library Association award for best lesbian and gay literature and a Lambda Literary Award. Feinberg is currently adapting the novel into a screenplay and is working on a picture history of transgender and a new novel entitled *Drag King Dreams*.

Sigfried Gold is a feminist computer programmer living in Chicago. His stories have been published in *Blue Light Red Light* and in *Frighten the Horses*.

Linda Hooper is the author of many stories, essays, newspaper articles, inciteful letters to the editor, and a book of poetry, *Prepositions*. Her work has appeared in *SexMagick: Women Conjuring Erotic Fantasy* and *Worlds of Women: Sapphic SF Erotica*. She promotes lesbian culture in Santa Cruz County, California.

Michael Lowenthal's writing has appeared in the anthologies *Men on Men 5: Best New Gay Fiction*, *Flesh and the Word 2* and *3*, and *Sister and Brother*, as well as in periodicals including *The Advocate*, *Lambda Book Report*, *The James White Review*, and *The Boston Phoenix*. He has a standing agreement with his mother whereby she congratulates him when his smut is published, but does not have to read it.

Debra Martens supplements her fiction income by writing book reviews and essays, editing, and teaching writing workshops, in both Montreal and Ottawa. Her short stories have been published in various journals, and in anthologies such as *Celebrating Canadian Women* and *Baker's Dozen: Stories by Women*. She has recently completed a novel.

J. Maynard is a regular person in a big city with a boring job. J. Maynard also edits two periodicals—*Beet*, which is like a literary quarterly, only interesting, and *Pink Pages*, which is mostly merciless whining about sex and sex issues, with occasional hot erotica.

Chris Offutt was born and raised in the Appalachian region of West Kentucky. He is the author of *Kentucky Straight*, a collection of short stories, and *The Same River Twice*, a memoir. His work has received a literary award from the American Academy of Arts and Letters, an NEA grant, and a James Michener grant. His stories are widely anthologized.

Gerry Pearlberg's work has appeared in *The Portable Lower East Side*, *Global City Review*, and *Sisters and*

Brothers: Lesbians and Gay Men Write About Each Other, edited by Joan Nestle and John Preston. She is currently editing an anthology of lesbian love poetry due from St. Martin's Press in 1995.

Bart Plantenga is a New York resident, born in Amsterdam. He is author of *Confessions of a Beer Mystic* (a novel of beer and light), *Womanizer*, and published most recently by Semiotext(e)-Autonomedia, *Wiggling Wishbone: Stories of Pata-Sexual Speculation* and a co-edited collection entitled the *Unbearables Anthology*. His work has been published in *Yellow Silk*, *Bikini Girl*, *Paramour*, *Pink Pages*, and *Carolina Quarterly*.

John Preston was one of the most prolific pioneers and leaders in gay erotica. He published over thirty-five books. Among them are the acclaimed *Flesh and the Word* series, *I Once Had a Master*, *Mr. Benson*, *A Member of the Family*, and *Hometowns*. He passed away in Portland, Maine, in May 1994.

Carol Queen is a San Francisco writer and sex activist. "Sweating Profusely in Mérida" is a true tale of vacation adventure. Queen's work has appeared in *Best American Erotica 1993*, *Madonnarama*, *Dagger*, *Herotica II*, *Doing It For Daddy*, *Leatherwomen*, *Bi Any Other Name*, and other anthologies. Her work is regularly published in the polymorphous 'zine scene.

Donald Rawley is the author of three books of poetry, *Malibu Stories* (1991), *Mecca* (1991), and *Steaming* (1993). His poetry and short stories have appeared in *Buzz*, *Yellow Silk*, *Rain City Review*, *Mindscapes*, and *The Olympia Review*. His collection of short stories is entitled *Slow Dance on the Fault Line*.

Abigail Thomas's first collection of short stories, *Getting Over Tom*, was published this spring by Algonquin Books of Chapel Hill. She is also author of the children's books, *Lily*, *Pearl Paints*, and *Wake Up Wilson Street*, all published by Henry Holt.

Anne Tourney lives in the San Francisco Bay Area. "Full Metal Corset" is her first published story.

Danielle Willis was kicked out of Barnard in 1986 and has since worked as a nanny, poodle groomer, stripper, and dominatrix. Her play, *The Methedrine Dollhouse*, was produced at Exit Theatre in 1989. "Elegy for Andy Gibb" is from her third book, *Dogs in Lingerie*.

Reader's Directory

Many of the stories in *Best American Erotica 1994* were first published in the following magazines, journals, and 'zines, which regularly include or emphasize erotic literature.

Beet
Pink Pages
Just like literary quarterlies, but interesting. Published by Joe Maynard at 372 5th Avenue, Brooklyn, NY 11215. Three copies at $7, single copies, $2.

Frighten the Horses

A document of the sexual revolution. Mark Pritchard and Cris Gutierrez, co-editors. Published quarterly at 41 Sutter St. #1108, San Francisco, CA 94104. Subscriptions are $18 for four issues.

Future Sex

Editor, Lily Burana. Published quarterly by Kundalini Publishing, Inc., 1095 Market Street, Suite 809, San Francisco, CA 94103. Subscription rates are four issues for $18.

Lavender Reader

News and reviews for Santa Cruz County's gay and lesbian community. Jo Kenny and Scott Brookie, editors. Published quarterly at P.O. Box 7293, Santa Cruz, CA 95061. Subscriptions are $12 per year.

Libido

The journal of sex and sensibility. Marianna Beck and Jack Hafferkamp, editors/publishers. Published quarterly at P.O. Box 146721, Chicago, IL 60614. Subscriptions are $26 per year.

Paramour

Literary and artistic erotica. Publisher/editor, Amelia Copeland. Published quarterly at P.O. Box 949, Cambridge, MA 02140-0008. Single copies are $4.95; subscriptions are $18/year.

Yellow Silk

Publisher/editor, Lily Pond. Published quarterly at P.O. Box 6374, Albany, CA 94706. Subscriptions are $30 for one year, $56 for two years and $78 for three years.

Credits

About the Editor

SUSIE BRIGHT is the author and editor of numerous books and articles about sexual politics and erotic expression. She lives in San Francisco with her four-year-old daughter, Aretha.